NO SON OF MINE

C.L. SWATMAN

Boldwood

First published in Great Britain in 2024 by Boldwood Books Ltd.

Copyright © C.L. Swatman, 2024

Cover Design by Head Design Ltd

Cover Photography: Shutterstock and iStock

Every effort has been made to obtain the necessary permissions with reference to copyright material, both illustrative and quoted. We apologise for any omissions in this respect and will be pleased to make the appropriate acknowledgements in any future edition.

A CIP catalogue record for this book is available from the British Library.

Paperback ISBN 978-1-83603-211-3

Large Print ISBN 978-1-83603-212-0

Hardback ISBN 978-1-83603-210-6

Ebook ISBN 978-1-83603-213-7

Kindle ISBN 978-1-83603-214-4

Audio CD ISBN 978-1-83603-205-2

MP3 CD ISBN 978-1-83603-206-9

Digital audio download ISBN 978-1-83603-209-0

Boldwood Books Ltd
23 Bowerdean Street
London SW6 3TN
www.boldwoodbooks.com

For Jilly, Nicki and Lisa. For the laughs, encouragement and Prosecco.

PROLOGUE

The arrogant smirk was all it took for the red mist to descend. I barrelled into his chest as hard as I could. As we collided, I raised my fist. But before I could smash it down onto his face, a blinding pain ripped through my shoulder.

He'd twisted my arm behind my back.

'Who sent you?' he hissed, his spittle spraying my cheek.

'No one,' I managed against the agonising roar of tearing muscles.

He pulled tighter. More pain shot through me.

A scream, visceral, raw, came from deep inside me. I tried to push him away but he was much stronger than me. His other hand snaked round my throat. Panic flared. I couldn't breathe. He was going to kill me.

Summoning all my remaining strength I reached behind me with my free arm. Struck something solid. Folded my fingers round it, lungs burning, vision blurring.

Then from somewhere I found one last surge of fury and swung my arm.

CRACK.

A beat of silence.

Air rushed back into my lungs, the pain in my arm dulled. Dazed, I turned round.

Watched as his body fell in slow motion and he hit the floor with another crack.

Silence followed. Total, smothering silence.

I stood still, paralysed. Chest burning.

I inched forward. Leaned over the figure lying prone on the hearth.

A marionette with his strings cut.

I held my breath, listened for breathing.

Nothing.

I leaned closer again. That's when I saw the blood. Oozing thickly from his head like a river of mud. It pooled round his face, seeped into the floorboards.

Time stood still.
And then reality hit me.
He was dead.
And I had killed him.

1

Alex was beginning to think her son might be evil.

Evil was a strong word, but it was one she'd been thinking about a lot since her previously well-behaved fifteen-year-old son Milo started getting into trouble. And not just for little things either, like forgetting his homework or arguing with teachers. Serious trouble.

Bullying.

Fighting.

Stealing.

Lying.

Calls from school and the police. Meetings with the headteacher followed by threats of suspension. But nothing had made a difference.

When she spooled her mind back over the last few months it was hard to work out when it all began. Was it when Alex had excitedly told him he was going to be a big brother, or was it a few weeks later when, heart-broken, she'd had to tell him she'd lost the baby? Or could she trace it to way back before that, to when Milo's pathetic excuse for a father had upped and left and never bothered with his son again?

Or maybe it was simply genetics. Alex had spent much of her childhood watching her father beat the crap out of her mum; listening to him begging for for-giveness, promising he'd never do it again; her mum forgiving him, and then it starting all over again. Surely some of the blame for Milo's behaviour could be placed at her father's door.

Her husband Patrick – Milo's stepdad – thought she worried too much. 'He's basically a good kid, he'll sort himself out,' he said.

She hoped he was right but there was no escaping the fact that Alex was Milo's mother, and she blamed herself.

Today, she was being hauled into school to speak to Milo's headteacher about a possible suspension. There had been no single inciting incident, more an accumulation of events, as though the teachers had simply run out of ideas on how to handle him.

She couldn't blame them. Because so had she.

'Everything okay, love?' Patrick made Alex jump as he entered the room. She forced a smile as he wrapped his arms around her, resting his chin on the top of her head. Patrick, always so solid, so dependable. Milo might not be his son by blood, but he'd been more of a father to Milo since he was three years old than Milo's own father had ever been.

He peeled away and looked down at her, his dark eyes wide. 'Are you sure you don't want me to come with you to face the wrath of Mrs Kingston?'

She shook her head. 'No, it's fine. You need to work.'

'I can take time off. One of the joys of being your own boss.' He smiled.

Part of her wanted to accept his offer, to tell him she needed him there. She had always needed him, whenever things had got tough. But she'd felt herself withdraw from Patrick recently when the situation with Milo had become tricky. Was it because she knew he felt resentful about the rift Milo's behaviour had opened up in their previously solid marriage? Or was it because she was acutely aware that this was her problem, not Patrick's, and he'd been left feeling sidelined?

'Honestly, I'm fine on my own,' Alex said, trying to

ignore the look of disappointment in his eyes as he made himself a cup of coffee in silence.

'Let me know how it goes then,' he said. She stood a moment longer after he left the room, the knot of tension in her belly tightening at the thought of dealing with this on her own. Then she grabbed her keys and bag and left before she could change her mind and ask for Patrick's help after all.

* * *

The door slammed shut and footsteps pounded up the stairs, followed by the bang of Milo's bedroom door. Alex slumped onto the bottom stair and hung her head between her knees. Her heart felt like a bruise as her tears mingled with the raindrops from her still-wet coat and pooled onto the wooden floor.

That was where Patrick found her a few minutes later. He didn't say a word, just squeezed himself beside her and waited. Eventually, she looked up at him.

'I take it that didn't go very well?' he said, his voice gentle.

Alex rested her head on his shoulder and stared at a point on the floor.

'You could say that.'

'Want to talk about it?'

She stayed silent a moment longer, letting the air settle. Upstairs, all was quiet, Milo probably already plugged into his gaming headphones.

'Well, he hasn't been suspended.'

'That's good news. Isn't it?'

'I guess.'

Patrick's shoulder rose and fell beneath her cheek. 'He's on a final warning.' She let out a long, stuttering breath and looked up at him. 'Patrick, he threatened to hit a teacher. And he pushed a year seven boy over in the playground. I—' She lowered her voice to a whisper. 'What have I done wrong?'

'Oh, Ally, you haven't done anything wrong,' he said, snaking his arm around her shoulders. 'You know that.'

She shook her head. 'Do I though? Nothing seems to work, not even the threat of suspension. It's as if he's just stopped caring about anything.'

Patrick was quiet for a moment, considering. 'You know how I feel about this.'

'But—'

'No, let me speak, Ally.' He rubbed his face. 'I know you believe the way Milo behaves is your fault – that it's in his genes, or some nonsense like that. I just wish you'd listen to me when I tell you that you're wrong. Milo is not evil. He's just a kid who's trying to find his place in the world. Who wants to be seen. And that has absolutely nothing to do with you, or me, and even less to do with his useless, absent father.'

'But that's just it,' Alex said. 'I think you're right that it's not because of Robert. To be quite honest I'm not sure Milo gives a damn about his father – why would he when he's got you? That's why I can't understand why he's still got this awful, evil streak.'

'Milo isn't evil.'

Alex sighed. 'No, I know he isn't really. I just don't know what to do.'

Patrick pulled her to him again and stroked her arm. 'Just be there for him, love, the same way you always are.'

'But what should I do about the trouble he's in this time? It can't go unpunished, surely?'

'Of course not. Take his Xbox away or ground him or something. The most important thing for you right now though – for both of us – is to listen to him if he needs us. We're his family.'

'You're right.' She hauled herself to her feet. 'I'll go and talk to him.'

'Good idea. Just go gently, yeah?'

She nodded. 'I will.'

* * *

Milo didn't answer when Alex tapped on his door, so she pushed it open and peered inside. He lay flat on his back on his bed, staring up at the ceiling, headphones plugged into his ears. The tinny drum beat was audible from several feet away.

'Milo?'

He snapped his head round and tugged an earphone out. 'What?'

'Can we talk?'

He let out a huge huff and looked away. 'If you want.'

Alex perched on the edge of his bed, trying to ignore the debris of dirty pants, scrunched-up T-shirts and empty crisp packets littering the floor. Milo continued to stare at the ceiling.

She took a deep breath. 'Will you look at me, love?'

His eyes slid in her direction. They were so dark, just like hers, but the emptiness in them shocked her. He'd aways been meticulous about his appearance but now his dark blonde hair was in desperate need of a cut, the fringe almost covering his eyes, and a smatter of spots marched across his chin. She longed to wrap her arms around him and never let him go but knew it wouldn't be welcome. She swallowed.

'What's going on, sweetheart?'

A shrug.

'I want to help you.'

Nothing.

'Milo, you were almost suspended from school. Don't think you can get away with ignoring me.'

'I fucking hate that place.'

'Milo!' Her voice came out louder than she intended.

'Forget it.' He turned his back, a full stop to the conversation before it had even got started. Dammit. Why couldn't she just stay calm?

She stood on shaking legs. 'We'll talk about this later.'

But he'd already stuck his headphones back in, so she left, blinking back tears of frustration.

* * *

Dinner was cooking and Alex needed five minutes to herself. She sat at the kitchen table and scrolled through X, Facebook, Instagram. She checked the weather, flicked to a news site. The usual stories about the government imploding, prices rising, the war in Ukraine. It was all so depressing.

She was about to click away when a short story in

the sidebar caught her eye. Or rather, the photo accompanying the story did.

She held her breath and tapped on the link, already imagining the worst. Then, as the page loaded and she began to read, the blood rushed from her head.

SON ACCUSED OF FATHER'S MURDER

The trial of a Hertfordshire man accused of murdering his 53-year-old father at their family home will begin on 20 March at St Albans Crown Court.

Samuel Jones, 23, was charged with killing Scott Jones after a fight at the family home on 25 January last year. Scott Jones suffered fatal head injuries following the altercation and died at the scene. His son Samuel was later arrested and charged with his murder.

Samuel Jones entered a not guilty plea and was remanded in custody at Pentonville prison in north London.

She dropped the phone onto the table as though it was about to burn her. Her head span and her tongue felt dry in her mouth.

This couldn't be happening.

But the story still glowed at her traitorously from the screen, searing itself onto her brain so there was absolutely no denying it: Samuel, the man accused of murdering his own father in cold blood, was her son.

2

Murder.

Samuel's face still glared at Alex from her phone screen. Even if she hadn't recognised the name of Samuel's adoptive father, she would have known immediately that this man was her son – because he was the spitting image of his brother.

Half-brother.

She picked her phone up again with shaking hands and typed Samuel's name into Google. There were dozens of entries from national and local news sites. Alex clicked on one at random. There wasn't much more information than she already had so she clicked on another, and another, hungry for details. Despite the seriousness of the allegation, it didn't seem like a huge story yet, and the only other shreds of information she could glean were that Samuel had been found by his mother – adoptive mother – Yvonne, by his father's dead body. He was covered in blood. Scott's head had been bashed with a blunt instrument that hadn't been found. Yvonne had been the one to call the police.

Alex dropped her phone onto the table again and paced across the room. She felt light-headed so she leaned against the worktop to steady herself and took some long, deep breaths.

An urge overtook her then, to do something she hadn't done for years.

She crept up the stairs and into hers and Patrick's bedroom, pulled the dressing table stool over to the wardrobe, then hauled the boxes down from the top.

Grabbing the small box at the very back, she stepped down and placed it on the bed. She swiped away the dust then prised it open, listening for footsteps, but the bass of Patrick's voice still rumbled through the ceiling from his office upstairs. She was safe for now.

She tipped the contents onto the duvet. It wasn't much. A couple of photos, a plastic hospital bracelet, a teddy bear, almost brand new. She picked up one of the photos, faded now, the colours muted. The scrappy face of a newborn peered out at her, a shock of corkscrew blonde curls. But it was the eyes that took her breath away. They always had. Eyes just like Milo's.

She put the photo down and picked up the bracelet, then twisted it so the writing faced her and ran her thumb over the words.

Samuel Bailey.

Her Samuel.

Except not her Samuel any more. Not since he was a few days old.

Alex had only been seventeen when she gave birth, and poor Samuel hadn't come from a place of love. A one-night stand after leaving home at sixteen to live in a series of squats and cheap bedsits, and a late pregnancy test meant she'd had to go through with it. Seventeen-year-old Alex had been young and naïve, unsure about this invader into her life. So when her father had insisted the boy would be better off if he was unofficially 'adopted' by acquaintances of his who'd had trouble having a baby of their own, she'd agreed.

She regretted it the moment she cradled Samuel's tiny body, overwhelmed by the strength of her feelings for him. When Samuel had been taken away, Alex had lain in bed with the teddy bear clutched to her chest, sobbing her heart out, consoling herself that at least he'd gone to a better life. As the pain began to fade with time, she bundled everything up and put it in this box, only bringing it out when she felt sad and needed to remember her boy. And most of the time, she succeeded in convincing herself that he didn't exist.

But not now.

Twenty-three years later, that tiny baby boy had crashed back into her life in the worst way imaginable: as a murder suspect.

If only she had someone she could talk to about it. But there was no one.

Alex had never told Patrick about Samuel. She'd wanted to, so many times, but Patrick already struggled with the fact that he didn't have a child of his own. His parents were relentless bullies who worshipped the ground his older and more successful brother walked on while criticising anything and everything Patrick did – particularly his overbearing mother. Not being a father was her biggest and most brutal stick with which to beat her youngest child.

So how could Alex have admitted she had another child that had nothing to do with him, and risk making him feel like even more of a failure?

If telling Patrick at the beginning had been difficult, years of failed rounds of IVF (*'Have you* still *not got Alex pregnant, Patrick?'*) had made it impossible.

It would have broken his heart.

She hadn't told her best friend Caitlin either, choosing to keep the whole thing parcelled away where it couldn't hurt her. A decision she was now regretting.

A noise from the attic made Alex jump. The scrape of a chair across wooden floors, the squeak of a door. Heart hammering, she stuffed everything back into the box and shoved it back in its hiding place. There were footsteps on the stairs and she hurried out onto the landing almost crashing into Patrick.

'Oh, you're there,' he said, smiling. 'I thought you were making dinner.'

'I was—' she stopped, flustered. A pain shot across her temple.

Patrick lowered his head to look at her. 'Hey, are you okay? You look really pale.'

She nodded. 'I'm fine. Just tired.' She gave him a weak smile. 'I need to go and check on the casserole.'

'Okay. I'm done for the day. I'll give you a hand.'

As they served up dinner for the three of them, Alex tried to put all thoughts of Samuel out of her mind. But it was impossible, the newspaper story slipping back into her mind, taunting her.

Her son had been charged with murder.

Her other son was so prone to violent outbursts he'd been reprimanded by the police and threatened with suspension from school.

And there was only one person connecting them.

Alex.

3

'You look terrible.'

Alex's best friend and business partner Caitlin hovered in the doorway of their office.

'Thanks a lot.' Alex attempted a weak smile. A band of pain pressed heavy across her temple.

Caitlin walked into the room, plonked a takeaway cup of coffee on Alex's desk, then sat facing her, elbows on the desk, chin in hands. 'What's happened?'

Alex took a sip of scalding coffee, almost burning her tongue. 'Nothing. Why, do I really look that bad?'

Caitlin peered more closely at her. Nodded. 'You look like you've been crying.' She sat back. 'Come on, you can tell me.'

Alex removed the lid from her cup and blew,

watching the surface of the murky brown liquid ripple. What could she tell her? She'd known Caitlin for the best part of twelve years, since they'd bonded at the school gates, two sobbing, snotty messes watching as their babies trudged happily into the playground, destined to become best friends forever – Alex's Milo, and Caitlin's Archie.

'I guess that's that then,' Caitlin had said, rubbing her nose the way, Alex now knew, she always did when she was worried or upset about something.

'Yeah.' Alex's voice had cracked.

'I've spent the last few years waiting for this day to come so I could get my life back, and now all I want to do is run across that playground and drag him back home with me.'

'Me too.'

Caitlin had laughed. 'What the fuck is *wrong* with us?' She stuck her hand out. 'I'm Caitlin by the way. I think if our boys are going to be friends, we should be too, don't you?'

And that was that. Since that day they'd shared everything about their lives, from failed IVF attempts and overbearing mothers-in-law (Alex) to caring for ailing parents and kids going off the rails (Caitlin).

Then five years ago they'd set up their nursery together and become business partners as well as best friends. Alex couldn't think of anyone she'd want to work with more. Everything about their friendship worked.

And yet even Caitlin didn't know Alex's darkest secret, the thing no one except Alex and her parents knew: about Samuel. Alex wasn't sure why she had never told her. Shame, perhaps? Or was it simply that she found it easier to pretend it had never happened?

Whatever the reason, she was currently regretting that decision deeply.

'It's Milo,' Alex said, returning to their usual topic of conversation.

'Oh, Ally.' Caitlin tipped coffee down her throat. 'What's he done this time?'

Alex flinched. 'The usual. More trouble at school. He nearly got suspended.' She rubbed her hand over her face. 'I honestly don't know what to do.'

Caitlin rubbed her nose and hooked her ankle across her knee. 'Have you spoken to him?'

Alex shook her head. 'I tried to last night and again this morning, but I messed it up. As usual.' She puffed out her cheeks. 'I just don't seem to be able to talk to him any more without it instantly turning into a row.' She looked up at her best friend. 'I'm scared it's all gone too far.'

A frown creased Caitlin's forehead. 'What do you mean?'

'You know. What if his behaviour has got so out of control there's no going back? What if he ends up really hurting someone? Going to prison?'

Caitlin watched her for a moment, her face unreadable.

'What's brought this on all of a sudden?'

Alex shrugged. What could she tell her? *'Oh, I've got another son you know nothing about and he's in prison, so I'm worried it's all my fault'?* Even thinking about saying those words out loud made Alex feel sick.

'I don't know. He just seems to be getting worse, Cait.'

Caitlin watched her over her coffee cup, her dark eyes narrowed.

'Remember what you told me?'

Alex looked up. 'When?'

Caitlin shuffled in her seat. 'Back when Archie was playing up.'

Playing up. That was one way of putting it, Alex thought. She shook her head.

Caitlin paused a moment, closed her eyes. 'You told me that no one is born bad and that his behaviour would just be a phase.' She shrugged. 'And you were right.'

Alex thought back to that time four years ago, when Caitlin, who didn't have a partner to support her, had been at the end of her tether with Archie. Similar to Milo now, Archie had been getting into fights, stealing, losing his temper out of the blue. Things had got pretty serious, with one parent even threatening to take out a restraining order against Archie.

In the end, they discovered that Archie's behaviour had been triggered by a group of boys at school teasing him about his dad being in prison, even though Caitlin had never told her son anything about his father Mick ('No good will come of him knowing anything about that piece of shit,' Caitlin always said). Alex could remember clearly how stressful it had been – but also how she had been absolutely convinced Archie would come through it.

So why did this feel different?

'Archie was only eleven then,' she said. 'Milo's fifteen.'

'So?' Caitlin placed her coffee cup on the table and leaned forward. 'He's still a kid, Alex. He's got you and Patrick to support him. And me and Arch.' She placed her hand on Alex's arm, her fingers cold against Alex's clammy skin.

Alex nodded. She felt the burn of tears behind her

eyes and was overcome with a rush of love for this woman who was always there for her, no matter what.

'Thanks, Cait,' she whispered, her voice scratchy.

They sat for a moment, utterly still. Then Caitlin pulled away and swiped her coffee cup from the desk. 'Do you want me to talk to him, see if I can get anything out of him? You never know, he might be more willing to open up to his Aunty Caitlin.'

Part of Alex wanted to say no, to tell Caitlin that she was perfectly capable of dealing with her own son. But she knew that was just pig-headedness – because she clearly wasn't.

'Would you mind?'

'Course not. I'll come round later if you like. Maybe Archie can give me some intel before I get there too.'

'Thank you.'

'Alex, you know I'd do anything for that boy. I'd do anything for *you*.' Caitlin fixed Alex with a stare. 'Why don't you take the rest of the day off? We've got a quiet one anyway, there's no point in you being here in this state.'

The children's nursery business they ran together had gone from strength to strength in the last couple of years. It had been a long, hard slog and lots of long hours, but it was finally even more of a success than they'd ever dreamed of, with three nurseries in three local towns, and a team of more-than-capable staff running them. It meant they could be much more hands-off than they used to be. But Alex still didn't like leaving Caitlin in the lurch.

'No, I'll stay for a bit, but I might leave early if you don't mind,' she said. 'Patrick's home with Milo and I don't like to leave them for too long when Milo's being like this.'

'No worries.' Caitlin stood and moved round to her own desk. 'In the meantime, I'd better get on with some work.'

Caitlin's desk was at right angles to Alex's which meant they couldn't see each other's screens. Although Alex had told Caitlin she was going to stay and do some work before she went home, what she actually wanted to do was a bit more research into Samuel.

Once she was sure Caitlin was completely engrossed in what she was doing, Alex pulled up a search engine and typed in Samuel's name, as well as his father, Scott's name. There wasn't much to read, no more than the few scant articles she'd read the previous day. But as she scrolled further down the page she noticed both of their names being mentioned from time to time in other articles. Scott had been arrested three years ago for possession with intent to supply, a couple of charges of GBH and a handful of other drug-related offences. There was also a small article about him being charged with fraud, something to do with a building firm he ran. She wondered briefly if it could be the same person who had ripped Caitlin off last year, who had taken a whacking great deposit then never finished. Surely that would be too much of a coincidence?

She kept reading. Samuel had also been charged with GBH after a fight in a nightclub, and on another occasion been done for theft.

Her stomach rolled over. All she could think about was Milo, who had gone from a sweet, funny, boisterous little boy to an aggressive, angry young man in just a few short months: a young man she sometimes felt nervous being around. Was this how Samuel had started – fights in the playground, threats to punch teachers, increasingly aggressive behaviour? She could see how it could so easily escalate from that to something as serious as – what, murder? Manslaughter? She flicked back to the original article and read it again. There was barely any detail, but there was one thing that stood out now. Samuel was pleading not guilty. What did that mean?

Had it been inevitable that this was going to happen from the moment he'd been born – a product of faulty genes, just like her father, always quick with his temper and his fists? – or was it a result of his up-bringing which, from the small amount she could glean, hadn't been a bed of roses?

And even more importantly, was Milo on the same path as his half-brother, or could he be helped before it was all too late?

It had been nagging away at her since yesterday, but now she made a split-second decision.

Heart thudding, she called up the name of the prison where Samuel was on remand and found an email address. Then, checking once more that Caitlin wasn't about to come and look over her shoulder, she emailed to ask how to get visiting rights.

There were some questions she needed to ask her son.

4

The metal gates of Pentonville prison rose above Alex's head, and she tried to ignore the tangle of barbed wire fencing that topped the high-rise walls. This was a day of firsts – her first time visiting a prison, her first time meeting the son she hadn't seen since he was a tiny baby – and her first time telling a huge lie to Patrick about where she was spending the day. Nausea swirled in her belly and her heart hammered an erratic rhythm.

She walked towards the imposing entrance on Bambi legs. She'd been in turmoil all morning about what to wear – there was no dress code for visiting a prison. She'd also been unsure about what to bring, or whether she was even allowed to bring anything at all.

She'd told the authorities at the prison that she was a writer, researching a book about people who kill family members. They probably didn't believe her – it would only take a simple internet search to discover her non-existent credentials – but they didn't seem to care all that much either. By some miracle, Samuel had agreed to add her to his visitor list too.

It had all happened so fast that, just a few days after sending through the request, she'd been surprised that her visit had been granted.

As she waited to go through security, she avoided looking at anyone. The other people here were no doubt visiting sons, husbands, uncles, brothers, friends in this men-only prison. They were probably used to this, unfazed by it. She was one of them now, the relative of someone incarcerated behind these walls. She felt her heart skitter in her chest.

She took a couple of deep breaths and reminded herself why she was doing this. It was for Milo, nothing more. If she could find out the truth about what had led Samuel to this place, she might have some idea how to help Milo, to stop him ending up here too.

Keep telling yourself that, Alex.

She emptied her pockets, placed her belongings on a tray, was patted down and scanned with a metal detector; a guard led her into the visitors' room, a buzz of voices, sharp clangs against metal, scrapes of chairs. Her eyes darted from table to table; would Samuel already be here, waiting for her? She hated the idea that he would have time to study her before she was ready. What if she gave the game away before she'd even started?

But no. She was led to an empty table where she almost fell into the cheap plastic chair, her palms sweating.

Not daring to look up, she arranged her notebook and pen on the table, then opened the notebook and wrote the date at the top. The letters were wobbly, and she gave her hand a shake, tried to make it work properly.

This was never going to work. She shouldn't be here.

Then the door opened and a man entered, and all the breath left Alex's body.

It was him.

Her Samuel.

As he walked towards her she took in his appearance. He was wearing a grey regulation prison tracksuit and black plimsolls, but there was still something hard about him, as though his smooth corners had been rubbed away, exposing the roughened edges below. His hair was shaved close to his head, two zig-zag lines running down the left-hand side just above his ear. Although he was only twenty-three, he looked older, as though he'd seen more in his short life than he should have.

He stopped in front of Alex's table. She stood, almost knocking her chair over. She gripped the edge of the table to steady herself.

'No touching,' the guard barked.

Samuel sat, folded his arms. Alex sat too.

She didn't know what to say. It was as though her insides had been scooped out.

This was her son. Her boy.

It was a lifetime ago, and just a heartbeat.

She'd tried not to think too much about how she'd feel when she saw him for the first time. Whether there would be an instant bond or a spark of love. Whether she'd feel revulsion or hatred or, worse, indifference.

She had her answer now. Her maternal instinct to protect him was there, washing over her like a tsunami. An overwhelming need to protect this man who was, really, no more than a stranger.

'All right?' Samuel's voice was a low rumble. Alex looked up and almost gasped. *His eyes.* The shape of his nose.

He was so like Milo it took her breath away.

'Hi,' she said, the word a squeak. She cleared her throat.

He studied her and she squirmed beneath his intense scrutiny. The silence stretched.

'I'm Ally.' Alex had no idea whether Samuel had ever been told about her, so had decided to use the shortened version of her name to be on the safe side. She fiddled with her pen as she waited for him to reply.

'Thank you so much for agreeing to talk to me,' she continued when it became clear he wasn't going to say anything. She breathed in deeply and clicked her pen open.

'You're writing a book?'

'What?'

He tilted his head at her notebook.

'Oh, right. Yes.'

Pull yourself together Alex. 'Yes, I'm writing a book about patricide and—'

'But I didn't.'

She stopped, held her breath as Samuel leaned forward and rested his elbows on the table. All his movements were slow, considered, as though he had all the time in the world. His gaze fixed on her, laser-like. 'I didn't know what that word meant when they told me about ya.' He shrugged. 'So I looked it up. It means killing your own dad, right?'

'That's right.'

He held her gaze a moment longer. 'But I didn't. Kill 'im, I mean.'

A beat. A thump in her temple. Her knuckles round the pen turned white.

'Right. Yes. I know.' She stabbed the paper with the nib of her pen. 'That's why I thought you would be good to interview for this, I guess. Because you're being accused of something you haven't done. I...' she trailed off, lost under his stare.

The hands of the cheap plastic clock above the door ticked on. Beside them, a woman let out a screeching cackle.

Samuel looked away. 'It's fine. Don't matter anyway, everyone here reckons I did it. Ask me what you want, I ain't got fuck all to lose.'

She glanced down at her notebook where she'd scribbled a few questions. They all seemed ridiculous now. She turned the page and took a deep breath.

'You say you didn't do it.'

'I didn't. Don't mean I'm not glad he's dead though.'

She flinched and tried to imagine Milo speaking like that about anyone. Patrick's parents were disapproving enough of Milo, especially at the moment. They'd have a field day if they knew about Samuel.

'Right. Can you tell me why? I mean, I assume you didn't have a good relationship with your father.'

He let out a bitter laugh, so cold she felt it in her bones. 'That's an understatement.'

'And why was that, would you say?' She really wasn't very good at this. She hoped he wouldn't notice.

'Because he was a bastard.'

Alex thought back to some of the stories she'd read about the trouble both Samuel and Scott Jones had been in. 'What—' She cleared her throat. *Focus*, Alex. She lifted her chin. 'I know you've been in trouble with the law before.'

'Yeah.' He sounded suspicious. She had to tread carefully.

'Was that because of your father?'

He frowned. 'What d'ya mean?'

'He was a drug dealer, wasn't he?'

'Among other things, yeah. Liked ripping off old ladies by pretending to fix their roofs then doing a runner with their money an' all.'

She thought about Caitlin and felt a flare of anger.

'And did he get you involved in any of his business?'

'Nah. I've never been interested in nothing he

does. Steer well clear of all that.' He rested his chin on his hand. His gaze was intense and Alex shivered. 'I didn't kill him, but don't mean I don't wish I had.'

She didn't know what to say to that so she waited to see if he would continue. After a couple of beats, he sat back and let out a puff of air.

'Listen, I don't know what you need for your – you know, your book thing.' He waved his hand dismissively. 'Did I kill my father – no. Am I sad he's dead – no. Do I know who did kill him – again no. But none of this helps you. So what is it you want from me?'

She froze, certain he'd seen through her, already spotted she was a fraud. He was clearly clever, maybe had learned through necessity to spot a liar a mile off. She stood, the legs of the chair screeching against the hard tiled floor. 'I'm sorry, I shouldn't have come.'

From the corner of her eye, she saw a guard move towards them.

'Everything all right?' he said, giving Samuel a hard stare.

And that's when she saw Samuel. Really saw him. He was just a little boy, sitting in a man's prison, lost, and scared. Whether she believed he'd killed his father or not, she could see he didn't belong here. She wished she could take him away, give him the life he should have had. Give him the chance to start again.

'Yes, sorry. We just... It's fine.' She sat back down and turned back to Samuel, who was watching her with interest. As the guard nodded and moved away, he pointed at the pad that still sat on the table between them.

'Shall I just tell you a bit about me dad then?' Samuel said.

'That would be great, thank you.'

He was silent for so long she began to wonder if he'd changed his mind. But when he eventually looked up at her she could see the pain in his eyes.

'He weren't always bad. When I was little – I mean, like, proper little, four, five – he used to take me to kick a ball around, to the park, push me on the swings. We had fun, you know?' He crossed his arms. A tattoo on his lower arm peeked out from the bottom of his prison top. 'He took me fishing once. I was about nine. A whole weekend together, just me and him. He'd even bought me my own fishing rod, and we sat on the riverbank and talked like we'd never talked before – or since.' He stared at the tabletop. 'When things were good, I thought I must've imagined the rest of it. It felt kind of nice. Normal.'

Alex scribbled a few notes in her notebook and waited for him to continue.

'The trouble was he was such a fucking charmer to

everyone else.' He laughed bitterly. 'Yeah, a right bloody charmer. But he ground me mum down, til there was nothing left of the mum I knew.' Something flitted across his face that she couldn't quite read. 'I think that's why she thinks I killed him, to be fair. Cos she wouldn't blame me if I had. Because she's glad he's dead too.'

'Is she?' Alex's voice was a whisper.

He shrugged. 'Actually, I ain't got a clue. Probably not. She does think I did it, but she *does* blame me, even if she hated him, in the end. Cos she loved him too. Fuck knows why.'

He slumped in his chair as if all the energy had drained out of his body. He couldn't have been more different from the confident, slightly cocky man who'd approached the table just fifteen minutes earlier. If this was the effect just thinking about his father had on Samuel, would it be any wonder if he *had* killed him? Alex wanted to move round to the other side of the table and wrap her arms around him. She gripped the edges of her chair to keep herself in place.

'Tell me about the trouble you've been in.'

He ran his hand across his chin. 'It's never been nothing really bad. Not like murder, anyway.' He crossed his arms, defensive. 'Fighting, stealing bikes, scooters, things from outside houses, that kind of thing. Fights in nightclubs. I beat someone up once because I was drunk and he looked at me the wrong way.' He gave a bitter laugh. 'I'm hardly a fucking criminal mastermind. I was just angry.'

'Angry?'

'Furious. Pissed off. Fuming. Raging. Whatever.' He rubbed his hand over his head. 'I hated my dad, had no respect for my mum, and could see my life going exactly nowhere. I ain't no psychiatrist but you don't need to be to work out I was trying to get them to notice me.' He shrugged.

A wave of – what? Love? Pain? *Guilt?* – surged through Alex. She'd always hoped she was giving her son away to have a better life, the way her father had promised; to get him away from poverty and life with a single mum, and have the chance to be happy, to make something of himself. Instead, she'd given him over to a life of misery.

'I'm sorry,' she said, the words woefully inadequate.

Around them, the hum of voices was interspersed with the occasional shout, followed by a shuffle of feet and the clatter of metal against metal. Everything about this place was so hard, so cold, and Alex wondered how anyone ever slept – or whether that was the point. Was it designed to make you go mad?

Slowly, the sounds around them began to change and she realised visiting time was coming to an end. She looked down at her notepad where she'd written a few short sentences, hardly anything. Her stomach rolled over. She wasn't exactly sure what she'd hoped to achieve when she came here today, but she knew she hadn't resolved anything in her mind at all.

Samuel stood. He towered over her, and suddenly her stomach was in knots about leaving here and never seeing him again.

'Can I come again?' she blurted.

'Really? I didn't give you much.'

'I just think your story could be really interesting. For the book.'

He studied her for a moment and she felt as though he could see right into her soul, see all the secrets and lies hidden there. Then he looked away and gave a small nod. 'It's not as if I have anyone else coming to see us. You might as well.'

Then he walked away and a small part of her cracked in two all over again.

5

Alex was still shaking as she walked away from the prison towards Caledonian Road Tube station.

She played over and over what Samuel had told her about his father. While Scott hadn't been physically violent the way her father had been, could a lifetime of being told you're no good, of being made to feel as though there was something wrong with you, have the same effect as watching someone beat the living daylights out of a person you loved?

Or could Samuel's criminal streak just be blamed on genes? Her father was bad, Samuel was bad, and now, it seemed, Milo was going that way too.

She descended into the station, and when she sat down on the train and caught sight of her reflection in the window she got a shock. She looked frantic, wild. What was wrong with her? This wasn't her. She was strong, unflappable. She didn't just lose control of herself at random times.

She had to compose herself, she couldn't let Patrick see her like this. She took some deep breaths and slowly felt her shoulders dropping, her jaw unclenching. By the time the train pulled into their station and she'd walked the short walk home she was calmer, her heart rate back to normal, her pulse slowed.

She let herself into the house, stood in the hallway and took in the silence. She hated to admit it but when Milo was at school the silence of the house felt less tense, less prickly – less like a pressure cooker about to blow than it did when he was here. She could breathe freely, at least temporarily.

What sort of mother was she, to be glad her son wasn't anywhere near her?

'Alex, is that you?' Patrick's voice floated down from the attic and a few seconds later there was a thump of footsteps and he appeared at the top of the stairs. He was in scruffy tracksuit bottoms with a smart shirt on his top half.

'Been in a meeting?' she said, smiling as he made his way down.

'Can you tell?' he grinned, peering down at his half-dressed state. He leaned in to kiss her, but as he pulled away he frowned. 'What's wrong?'

'Nothing, why?'

He squinted, then stood up again, still studying her intently. 'You look like you've been crying.'

'Do I?'

He sighed. 'Have you been worrying about Milo again?'

Milo. Of *course* she'd be upset about him. She always was.

'Yeah, a bit.'

'Why didn't you tell me?'

'There's nothing to tell.'

'I know you think he's your problem to sort out, but we're in this together. You know we are.'

Alex nodded. 'I do know that. I'm not trying to shut you out, I promise. But I also know how busy you are and I don't like to worry you.'

A look flitted across Patrick's face and disappeared just as quickly. 'So has something else happened?'

'No, just the usual. Really,' she added when he looked dubious.

He studied her a moment longer, then turned and walked towards the kitchen. She followed him.

'Good, because I wanted to talk to you about something.'

'Oh?' She tried not to panic. Had he found out where she'd been today? Had Caitlin said something about her not being at work? That was the problem with lies – the more you told the more you got caught in their ever-tightening web.

He stopped and turned round. 'Let me make you a cup of tea first.'

Alex lowered herself into a chair at the table and waited while Patrick fussed around boiling the kettle, finding teabags, getting milk from the fridge. She wanted to tell him to hurry, up, just get on with it and tell her what he wanted to talk about, but she knew Patrick, and could tell this was something he needed to build up to. She held her tongue, her heart hammering.

Finally, he placed a steaming mug in front of her and sat down.

'Thank you.'

He didn't reply. His hands were clenched in front of him so tightly his knuckles were almost white. She noticed he was doing that rapid-blinking thing he did when he was anxious. She waited.

'I want to try IVF again.'

Her body turned cold. 'I'm sorry, what?'

Patrick blinked at her again. 'You heard me.' His hands clenched even tighter. 'I think we should try for a baby one more time.'

'But we can't afford it.' Her pulse thumped at her temple. It wasn't what she'd been expecting at all, and it seemed completely unreal to be having a conversation about this when her mind was in so much turmoil. But of course Patrick knew nothing about any of that. Because she hadn't told him.

'You keep saying that.' His voice dripped with accusation.

'Because it's true, Patrick. We decimated our savings last time, you know that.'

He had the grace to nod. 'I know. And I know it was hard when you lost the baby last year. But the doctors said there was no reason for it, and that means it's unlikely to happen again. Plus I've got loads of work on at the moment so can afford to put some aside. Your business has taken off in the last few years. Even if we have to borrow some, we can easily afford to pay it back and—' he stopped, threw his hands in the air. 'I don't want to give up on having my own child. Not yet. I can't.'

The pain in his voice broke her. She knew how much it had always meant to him to have a baby of his own, to carry on the 'Harding gene' – the one his parents associated with greatness. Despite Alex's reluctance to pander to their misguided view of the world, she knew it meant a lot to Patrick too, and she'd always promised she'd do everything she could to make it come true for him. Plus he'd always been such a brilliant stepdad to Milo. How could she deny him the chance to be a father himself?

And yet how could she even think about this right now?

'I don't know if I want another baby.'

The silence that followed was deafening. Patrick's face turned grey, his body stiff as though he was turning to stone.

'Ever?'

She shook her head.

Then, without saying another word, Patrick simply got up, walked out of the room, and marched back up the stairs to his office.

Even though she knew the conversation wasn't over by a long shot, she only felt relief.

6

'You're going out again?' Caitlin's voice cut right through Alex.

'Sorry, I just – family stuff.'

Caitlin studied her and for a moment looked as though she was going to say something else, but then thought better of it.

'We'll have our meeting tomorrow then, shall we?'

Oh God, she'd forgotten they were meant to be having a meeting about opening a new nursery. It had been arranged for ages.

'I'm so sorry, Cait. Do you mind?'

She peered at her over the top of her glasses. 'Do I have any choice?' Alex felt as though she was being told off by a disappointed teacher.

Caitlin held her gaze a second longer, then turned away and flicked on the radio. Alex was relieved that the music filled the awkward silence. Despite appearances, she wasn't really doing any work. Her mind was too full of everything else that was going on. Milo, Patrick – and Samuel.

Samuel had approved another visit, but with visiting times limited she was forced to go during work hours – which was why she was letting Caitlin down so spectacularly today.

Alex wasn't even sure what she was trying to achieve any more. It wasn't as though she'd got any answers last time. But all she knew was that Samuel's trial was only three weeks away and she needed to see him before then, to see if she could find a way to redirect Milo onto a different, less destructive path before it was too late.

Suddenly she was aware that Caitlin had stopped typing and was sitting, grey-faced, her fingers hovering above the keyboard. She was staring at the radio and hadn't noticed Alex watching her.

'Are you all right?'

Caitlin didn't seem to hear her, just continued staring. Alex tuned into the news report – and her whole body turned to stone.

'...and the trial of a Hertfordshire man accused of

murdering his father will begin at St Albans Crown Court on 18 March. Twenty-three-year-old Samuel Jones has been accused of killing his father Scott Jones after police found him by his father's battered body in September last year—'

The words stopped abruptly. Caitlin had switched the radio off, and for a few seconds neither woman spoke. Then:

'Why were—'

'Did you hear—'

They both stopped. Alex spoke again first. 'Why were you looking like that?'

Caitlin rubbed her finger across her nose and sniffed. 'That guy,' she said slowly. 'The one who was killed.'

'What about him?'

'He—' she hesitated again.

'Caitlin? Did you know him?' *Surely not?*

'He – he was that builder that ripped me off.'

Alex stared at her, stunned. 'What? Are you sure?'

'Pretty sure. Scott Jones. His fucking name's etched in my memory. I can't imagine there'd be more than one of them round here.' She wrinkled her nose. 'I told you this at the time, don't you remember?'

'No,' Alex said. Her mind was a tangle of wires,

connections firing all over the place. It had briefly crossed her mind that there might be some connection but she'd never actually believed it might be true that Scott Jones – Samuel's *father* – was the man who had taken her best friend's life savings. 'Fuck,' she managed.

'Fuck indeed.' Caitlin pursed her lips. 'Jesus, I mean, I hated the man for what he did to us. It nearly broke poor Archie when he found out we might have to sell the house, but I never wished him dead. Although I suppose it is one less piece of thieving scum to worry about.' She peered at Alex. 'Ally, are you all right? You've gone really pale.'

'What? Yes, I'm fine.' Alex stood abruptly, her chair almost toppling behind her. 'I just need to go to the loo.'

She left the room before Caitlin had a chance to say anything further and hurried to the toilet where she locked herself in a cubicle and slumped on the loo seat.

Good God, could things get any worse?

Her head was spinning out of control and she took some deep breaths and tried to get her thoughts in order.

Scott Jones was Samuel's adoptive father.

Scott Jones was the builder who took Caitlin's money and left her with nothing.

Samuel had been accused of killing him but insisted he was innocent.

So if Samuel didn't kill Scott – who did?

As she tried to untangle the knotted threads of this story, something niggled at the back of her mind. Then slowly, a memory began to emerge. It was of Milo and Archie, in the back of her car sometime last year. She hadn't really been listening, her mind on the road, but her attention had been caught by something Archie said, and she'd glanced in the rearview mirror.

'What did you just say, Arch?' she said.

'Nothing.' He looked away, his gaze sliding over to Milo.

'I thought you said you wished you could kill someone.'

She waited a beat.

'I didn't mean it.'

'Who were you talking about?'

Archie looked as if he wasn't going to answer. Then Milo said: 'That bloke who stole all his mum's money.'

'He's a bastard,' Archie exploded. 'Mum says we might have to move because she can't afford the house any more. I just wish I could somehow make him give it back.'

Alex had wanted to tell him off, but he sounded so young, so worried, that she didn't have the heart. Besides, she couldn't really blame him. People like that bloody builder deserved everything they got coming to them.

'He'll get his comeuppance, Archie, don't worry. People like him always do.'

Archie hadn't said anything else, and she'd forgotten about that conversation until now. But now it swirled in her mind and she couldn't seem to shake one question. *Could* Archie, in some misguided attempt to get back at Scott, have had something to do with his death? She shook her head.

Don't be ridiculous, Alex. He was fifteen. Just a kid. An angry one, but a kid.

She needed to get a grip.

She waited while someone came into the cubicle next to hers, then left, washed their hands and the door clicked shut behind them. When she was sure the coast was clear she let herself out and peered at her face in the tiny mirror above the sink. Grey circles were smudged under her eyes and her skin was waxy. Her eyes were wild and rimmed with red. She splashed water on her face and patted it dry, then went back to the office, hoping she looked vaguely normal.

Caitlin glanced up as she entered and gave her a smile.

'You okay?'

'Yeah, sorry. Just not sleeping well. I feel a bit jittery.' That was the understatement of the century.

Caitlin nodded and looked back at her screen. Alex sat back down and let the words blur in front of her.

'I don't know what's going on with you at the moment but when you need to talk, you know where I am.' Caitlin's voice was low, and she wasn't looking at her. Alex felt the silence expand and retract.

'Thanks, Cait.'

The conversation was over. For now.

* * *

This time the prison felt less intimidating. Perhaps Alex was already becoming used to it. She was searched, her bag was locked away and by the time she entered the visiting room, Samuel was already at the table waiting for her. He looked up as she approached and Alex thought she saw a wisp of a smile cross his face.

She sat down, placing her notebook and pen in front of her.

'Thanks for seeing me again.'

Samuel shrugged. 'Fuck all else to do round here.'

She glanced down at the table. She was on edge, worried she was about to slip up, say something to blow her cover. But there was no way Samuel could know who she was, was there? She wasn't even sure Samuel knew he was adopted.

Not that it mattered. She wasn't here to be his mum. She was here for information, to help Milo.

She took a deep breath. 'So.'

'So,' he repeated.

Alex tried to block out the yells and the arguments and the hard metal clangs, the menacing spectre of the prison guards pressing from all sides, and pretend this was just a friendly chat.

'Tell me more about your father,' she said.

Samuel watched her from beneath a lowered brow. She felt like she was being inspected under a microscope and the look was so like Milo it took her breath away. Then Samuel spoke and the likeness was gone.

'I've already told you. He was a bastard.'

She nodded. 'You said that. And I know he belittled you.' She shuffled in her seat, trying to work out how to phrase her next question. 'I'm trying to work out if you got into trouble because he made you that way.'

He watched her again, his lips curled into a smirk.

'Or what? You want to know if I was born bad?'

Alex didn't dare speak. Samuel leaned forward and her pulse thumped in her temple. She squeezed her pen between her fingers.

'What makes you think that, Ally?' He put an emphasis on her name. Was he playing with her?

She needed to reassert herself. She pressed her pen hard into the paper and looked him right in the eye. 'As I said before, my book is about people who kill their fathers. But I also want to look at the link between nature, and how much of a part that plays in someone's character, and nurture. How much a person's upbringing shapes them.'

'Yeah, course. Your book.' He nodded and held her gaze, a challenge. What did he see when he looked at her? A harmless woman approaching middle age, or a threat? 'What do you think? Do *you* think people are born bad?'

She wouldn't be drawn in. 'I'd prefer to hear what you think. It's what I'm here for and I don't have all the time in the world.'

A beat of silence, then, 'Fair enough. I'll tell you about my shitty childhood, then you can make up your own mind if that's what made me end up here. Deal?'

'Yes. Thank you.'

He nodded and stared at a point just behind her right shoulder. His eyes darted back and forth then settled on something. Alex was desperate to hear what he was about to say, but at the same time, she wasn't sure she wanted to know the details of the life he'd had – because whatever bad things had happened to him were her fault.

'I was adopted. Did you know that?'

She shook her head, her heart in her throat.

'Well, anyway. It don't matter, but it don't make it easy to know whether I was born bad neither, cos I don't know who my real family were or what they're like.' His gaze was so intense Alex had to look away, the heat rising in her cheeks. 'So all I can tell you about is the things that have happened in my life that might have made a difference.' He shrugged. 'I ain't got a clue either way.'

He puffed out his cheeks.

'D'ya know how I found out I was adopted?'

He waited for an answer even though she obviously wasn't going to have one. She shook her head, and Samuel gave a smile that didn't reach his eyes.

'That was a good one, that. One of the cunt's best.'

Alex flinched at the word. Told herself to get over it. This was his story, told his way. She leaned closer.

'I was eight and Mum and Dad had friends round. They was drinking, laughing, shouting. I couldn't sleep so I came downstairs. Dad told me to go back to bed. Mum told 'im not to be so mean – she was drunk an' all, or she would never have dared speak to him like that – and he told me I was a little fucking brat. Everyone was shocked, but no one said nothing. They never did. But I didn't want to go upstairs so I pushed his drink over. Beer went everywhere, all over the table, the floor.' He picked at his thumbnail until it started bleeding.

'That's when he said it. He told his friends he was sorry about his son but I was adopted, and he wished you could send them back for being faulty. Everyone laughed at that.' He gave a bitter laugh. 'My father the fucking comedian. But I weren't laughing. I felt like I'd fallen through a trapdoor or summat.' He finally looked up again. The look in his eyes was pure pain and Alex could imagine the agony of the little boy hearing those words for the very first time.

'I'm so sorry,' she said. 'No one deserves to be treated like that.'

He shrugged. 'Couldn't give a monkeys now. But you asked what made me hate my father and I guess you could say that was the beginning of it.' He laughed again. 'It went downhill from there.'

Her heart turned to stone. All those promises her own father had made about her son going to a couple he knew who had been trying to have a baby for years, who could give him a better life than she ever could, a penniless teenage mum. And in the end, it had nearly broken him.

She glanced up at the plastic clock above the door. Fifteen minutes left. All she wanted was to take her little boy by the hand and lead him away from this place. But she needed to focus.

'Can you tell me what happened the night your father died?'

He looked up at her, his eyes flint.

'He weren't my father. Not at the end.'

She nodded but didn't say anything.

'I'd been living in a squat for a bit,' he said eventually. 'Anything was better than being near that man. I hated going round when he was there. But I was skint and needed food and a bit of cash to tide me over. I was gonna ask Mum for some.

'I let myself in the back door. It was freezing. I turned the light on but the house was quiet. I took me coat off, filled the kettle, had a piss.' Stared at his hands again, his nails torn and ragged. 'I must've been in the kitchen for five, six minutes tops, then I went into the hall and was heading for the stairs when—' He stopped. 'I saw summat. Dad's body, in the front room. I ran in, and he was just, like, lying there.'

She watched him as he remembered it, relived the horror of finding his father dead. He seemed oddly detached. Eventually he shook his head.

'His head was caved in, and there was blood all round it. He weren't moving and he was sort of grey. I didn't know what to do. I just sat there for ages.' He ran his thumbnail along the edge of the table and once again Alex saw the little boy behind the facade. The vulnerable little boy who had been bullied by his father, and yet who had been so desperate for his approval his entire life.

'What happened next?' Five minutes left. She held her breath.

'I was in shock, you know. I might not have liked him but he was me dad. You don't expect to see him, face down on the floor, in a fucking sea of blood, do you? I think I said something, shouted, but Mum wasn't in. I can't—' his voice cracked. 'I can't remember what happened next. I think I felt like I needed to do summat, help him. Save him? I dunno. The next thing I remember I was being led to a police car with fucking handcuffs on. I was covered in blood, it was everywhere. And I was like *what's going on, where are you taking me* but they wouldn't tell me nothing. Now I'm here.' He held his hands out, palms up. 'First class suite at the fuckin Ritz.'

'You don't remember anything else?'

He shook his head. 'They reckon I was kneeling by his side when Mum found me. Fuck knows why I'd do that. I can't—' he rubs his face. 'I must've lost it. I've never lost time like that before, except when I've been off me face.'

'But you're sure you didn't do it? You didn't kill him?'

He leaned forward and her body tensed. 'What with? Police reckon he'd been smacked over the head with one of them stupid football trophies he had, the ones all lined up on the shelf that he was so fucking proud of.' He shrugged. 'But they never found it. Weren't even sure one was actually missing, cos the only person who could have told them for definite was dead.' He gave a mirthless laugh. 'But they still reckon they've got all this evidence that proves I'm guilty. Motive. Opportunity. Fingerprints. Of course my fucking fingerprints were there, I used to live there. I'd just made a cup of fucking tea for Christ's sake.' He stopped, breathless. 'There's one thing they don't know though, and that's me.' He jabbed his thumb into his chest. 'I'd never kill anyone. I ain't got it in me.'

He was full of indignation. Because he was innocent, or to cover his guilt? Alex still couldn't be sure, although she knew what she wanted it to be.

She had one more question.

'Who do you think did do it?'

He shrugged. 'It could have been any of the druggies who hung round our place. They were always threatening each other. Or one of the poor fuckers he conned over the years, the ones with half a fucking house left and no money to finish it cos he'd buggered off with their cash.' Alex's mind flicked to Caitlin and Archie. How many other people had Scott ripped off over the years – people who really would want to exact revenge?

'But the police can't prove nothing, and they found me there, next to his body, literally with blood on me hands.' He shrugged. 'So it's a shoo-in. Means they don't have to do any work, don't it?'

'I'm so so—'

'Time's up!' a voice thundered through the room

before she could finish her sentence, and she jumped. There was barely time to gather her things before a guard was by her elbow, steering her away from the table.

'Thank you, Samuel,' she said over her shoulder. 'Good luck with the trial.'

He gave a smile. But as she walked away she was left with one overriding feeling: she believed him.

7

The call came as Alex walked through the door. No one ever rang the landline and she almost ignored it. But at the last minute, something made her snatch up the phone and she wedged the receiver under her chin as she slipped off her boots.

'Is that Mrs Harding?'

'Yes.'

'This is PC White from Watford police station.'

She stood bolt upright, suddenly completely alert.

'What's happened?'

He cleared his throat. 'I'm afraid your son has been arrested for fighting in the street this afternoon. We have him in custody now and need you to come down to the station.'

'Samuel?' The words were out of her mouth before she could censor them, her mind full of the meeting she'd just had.

'No, Mrs Harding. Your son, Milo.'

'Oh God. Yes. Sorry.' She swallowed. 'I'll be straight there.'

She slammed the phone down, put her boots back on, and picked up her bag. She was almost out of the door when she heard her name being called. She turned to see Patrick heading down the stairs.

'Everything all right?'

'It's Milo.'

'What's he done now?'

Her hackles raised at his assumption, even though it was a perfectly reasonable one – and true.

'He's been arrested for fighting.'

'Shit. Where is he?' He was right in front of her now and she could see the stubble on his chin, the concerned crease in his forehead. All of it made her so inexplicably mad, as though this was his fault.

'He's at the police station. I need to go and get him.'

'I'll come with you.'

'No!'

He froze halfway to reaching for his coat. 'Seriously? You want to do this on your own?'

She nodded. 'I have to. He's—' She stopped as Patrick nodded in slow recognition.

'He's *your* son. Right?'

'I wasn't—'

'Yes, you were. That's exactly what you were going to say.' His voice was steely. 'Never mind all the years I've given to bringing him up, treating him like my own.' He nodded. 'He's *your* son. I'm *very* sorry.'

'I didn't mean it like that.'

But he was already turning away. She couldn't bear that she'd hurt him so much. He was right. All the times he'd taken Milo to the park to feed the ducks when Alex was tired, or working, or just needed a break. The times he'd taught him to swim, gently holding Milo's little belly in the water while each week he progressed further and further across the pool; or patiently taught him to read, repeating the *Gruffalo* over and over again until he'd wanted to throw the book out of the window, or sat through his often tedious piano concerts. Patrick *had* brought Milo up like his own, been there for him through everything. What was wrong with her? She was about to tell him she was sorry, that she did need him, when:

'You know what, maybe it's for the best that you don't want a baby with me if it turns out to be like this one.'

Before his words had even sunk in, Patrick had walked back up the stairs and left her, alone.

before the words had even sunk in, Juliet had walked back up the stairs and left her alone.

8

Alex was glad when Samuel agreed to one more visit before the trial. She had no idea what he made of her being there but she found she didn't much care. She was desperate to get to know him better – and perhaps, she conceded, she even wanted to punish herself by hearing more about the life he had endured as a result of her abandonment.

'You know, I used to be an amazing pianist,' Samuel said out of the blue just after they sat down.

'Really?' Alex had played piano since she was a child and Milo had loved playing until recently too.

'Don't sound so surprised, I ain't completely useless.'

'No. Sorry, I didn't mean—' She gave herself a mental slap. 'Go on.'

He shrugged. 'Not much to tell. I used to play at school. It weren't cool, but I loved being good at summat my dad knew nothing about.' He threaded his fingers together and held her gaze. 'Course when me music teacher told him about it, he took that away from us an'all.'

'Why, what did he do?'

'What he always did. Said piano was for sissies and I weren't playing it no more. No arguments.'

'But didn't you keep playing at school?'

He shook his head. 'Nah. If he'd've found out he'd of gone mental.'

Her heart broke at all the things Samuel had missed out on because of the family he'd been brought up in. How different would his life have been if he'd stayed with her? Would he still have gone off the rails, ended up here?

'I'm so sorry,' she said. Woefully inadequate.

He shrugged. 'Don't matter. Mum got it worse than me. He once tried to sell our house without even telling her. People turned up to look round, everything. He tried to pretend he'd told her all about it, that she was useless, should get her brain sorted.' He tapped his finger to the side of his head.

'But that was just 'im. He loved making people feel stupid, especially me and Mum. I think he got some sort of kick out of it.' He shrugged. 'So there you go. He was a total arsehole and I won't miss him at all.' He looked round him. 'Just wish I weren't stuck in this place.'

They sat in silence for a while, letting the sounds of the prison wash over them. As Samuel's words sunk in, Alex knew these were exactly the sorts of details the prosecution would have a field day with. A boy who'd spent his life being bullied by his father suddenly snaps in a fit of anger. It wouldn't be the first time, and it certainly wouldn't be the last. In fact, the jury would probably lap it up. Because let's face it, if even she could see how that could happen, what chance did Samuel have of convincing people who didn't know him?

9

Milo was sulking in his room, but at least Alex knew where he was. No parenting awards for her.

Patrick was sulking too. He pretended he wasn't, but since Milo's arrest and the things he'd said, he'd been chilly with her, spending more time than usual in his office and going for long bike rides in all weather. Alex found herself feeling increasingly glad when he was out of the house because then at least she felt less on edge.

Maybe it's for the best you don't want a baby with me if it turns out to be like this one.

She'd chewed those words over in her mind endlessly. Patrick had never said anything like it to her before, or about Milo. Had her refusal to agree to another round of IVF been the thing that had broken him?

It wasn't just her home life that was falling apart though. She'd been off the boil at work too, and Caitlin had noticed.

'Look, Alex, I love you, but if you're just going to moon around getting in the way maybe you should take some time off and I'll get someone to cover for you for a few weeks,' she'd said yesterday.

'There's no need, honestly. I'm fine,' Alex insisted. They couldn't really afford the extra expense of paying someone else.

Caitlin looked as though she didn't believe her but said no more. She wasn't stupid. They knew each other almost as well as they knew themselves and it was only a matter of time before Caitlin would demand answers.

The trouble was, Alex didn't know how or what to tell her.

Although she believed Samuel when he said he didn't kill his father, there was still a seed that whispered *what if he did?* What if she did carry some faulty gene, and her children were destined to inherit it, to become prone to violent outbursts, the same way her father had been? If that were true, then Milo was doomed too.

The need to find answers, to work out how to help Milo, was becoming overwhelming. The trouble was, now she'd met Samuel – that face she hadn't seen for so many years – she couldn't stop thinking about him.

She thought about how lonely he looked sitting in the prison. How young, how broken. How could she abandon him now?

Which was why she had decided to go to the Crown Court to follow his trial.

It wasn't a decision she'd taken lightly. She knew the risks. This was a high-profile case and she'd more than likely come face to face with some of Scott's family. Not to mention the fact that she should be focusing all of her attention on Milo right now.

But as far as she could see, it *wasn't* a choice. It was simply something she had to do. She needed to be there, in the courtroom, to see Samuel's reactions to the things that were said about him, to hear him tell the jurors what had happened in his own words. It was the only way she was ever going to be certain in her own mind whether he was guilty or not, no matter the verdict.

* * *

Alex took the train, and the minute she arrived outside the imposing glass and brick building of St Albans Crown Court she was convinced she'd made a terrible mistake. Even from several metres away, she could see the journalists crowded round the entrance, cameras swinging from shoulders, microphones in hand. She'd known it was a big case but she'd under-estimated quite how big. She quickened her pace and kept her head down as she approached, praying no one would notice her or shove a microphone in her face.

She hurried inside the building, her heart ham-mering. What the hell was she doing? Was she go-ing mad?

She waited to get through security, checked the board, then made her way to courtroom two where Samuel's trial was being held. The small main en-trance was cramped and she had to shoulder her way through the press of bodies. She didn't dare look up, uncertain how many of these people were there for Samuel, or who might know him. What if they won-dered who this strange woman was?

She reached Court Two and entered the public gallery. She was early, so there were only a couple of other people here – a man and a woman huddled near the entrance, and another young man at the front with a notebook who she assumed was a journalist. None of them looked up as she entered so she kept her head down and made her way to the far corner.

She took the chance to take in her surroundings before anyone else arrived. She'd never been inside a courtroom before and the space was smaller than she'd imagined, with plain walls, wooden benches for the jury straight ahead, a raised platform for the judge to her right and, to her left, a section behind glass which she assumed was for the defendant. It was less grand than she'd anticipated, but that didn't make it any less intimidating.

Over the next ten minutes, the benches in the public gallery started filling up, but still nobody looked in her direction.

At ten o'clock on the dot, a shuffling at the side of the courtroom caught her attention.

'Silence in court, please stand.'

Everyone stood as the judge entered. She spoke briefly to the jury, then took her place as everyone else sat back down.

Then the door at the far end of the courtroom opened and Samuel came out, accompanied by a man at least a decade older than him who she could only assume was his lawyer. Samuel looked smart in a dark blue suit, his blonde hair slightly grown out. He looked younger than he had in prison and her heart squeezed. She glanced at his lawyer. Despite all the talking they'd done they hadn't really spoken about his defence, and she hoped this man would do his best for her son.

She watched as Samuel took his place behind the glass partition. She heard whispers behind her, and a shout, followed quickly by a shush. Samuel didn't turn, didn't flinch, just kept his gaze either straight ahead or towards his lawyer.

Next, the jury was called in, and filed into the two rows of seats opposite her. Alex wondered what their stories were: the well-dressed woman with the expensive suit; the skinny guy with the man-bun; the rotund middle-aged woman who looked like she could do with a good haircut. All these people with their own stories, their own problems – would they really see Samuel and understand what Scott had put him through, or would they simply see a hardened criminal capable of murdering his own father in cold blood?

The barrister for the prosecution stood to give an opening speech. The excitement in the air was palpable. Alex leaned forward.

Over the next ten minutes, the court heard how police had been called by Samuel's mother, Yvonne, who had arrived home to find Samuel huddled over his father's body, which lay on the floor by the fireplace in the living room, just as Samuel had described.

'You will hear witnesses tell you that Scott Jones was struck over the head with a blunt object. That he fell, hitting his head against the edge of the stone fireplace surround as he did so,' the lawyer explained. Alex studied the jurors' faces as they heard the details of what happened that day for the first time. One man near the back shook his head, while another looked confused and wrote something down on a notebook in front of him.

'You will hear from the coroner, who confirmed that the fatal blow that ended Scott Jones's life occurred when his head smashed against the fireplace, and that he was killed almost instantly. You will also hear that, although no weapon was found at the scene, neither had there been any sign that anyone else apart from Samuel Jones had been in the house. The only other fingerprints were those of Mrs Jones. No signs of forced entry. Nothing whatsoever that pointed to anyone else having been there at all. Which leads us to believe that there can also be absolutely no doubt that it was Samuel Jones who killed Scott Jones.'

Alex stared at Samuel. He didn't look at anyone, or make any movement. How did he feel about these terrible things being said about him? How would she feel if it were her?

It was time to start bringing out the witnesses.

Samuel's mother, Yvonne, was the prosecution's first witness to take the stand. She was a tiny, birdlike woman, with pale blonde hair that frizzed out around her head and twiglet wrists poking out of her too-big clearly borrowed suit jacket. Beside Alex, a couple of spaces away on the bench, a woman with badly dyed blonde hair said *go on, girl* slightly too loudly. She noticed Alex looking at her and scowled. Alex looked away and felt a heat flood her body.

From the stand, Yvonne glanced round the courtroom nervously, swaying from side to side as she was sworn in. She didn't once look at Samuel. She was questioned about the day Scott had died – about what she'd found when she got back to the house, and how long she had taken to call the police.

'And what was the relationship like between your husband Scott and your son, Samuel?' the prosecutor asked.

Yvonne lifted her chin and pushed her shoulders back. 'Scott loved that boy. Always had, from when he was a nipper. Doted on him, he did.'

Alex studied Samuel's face for a reaction to Yvonne's words which, if Samuel were to be believed, were nothing but a pack of lies. But he remained impassive.

'But he was an ungrateful sod, Sammy. Was always getting into trouble, fighting, being rude, staying out all hours, then he had the cheek to blame 'is dad for 'is behaviour.' She licked her lips, lizard-like. 'But none of it were Scott's fault. He did everything he could for that boy and he got it all thrown back in 'is face.'

Alex thought about the stories Samuel had told her about the way Scott had treated his mother and all she could see in front of her was a broken woman, battered by years of being undermined. Would the jurors see the same, or would they take Yvonne's word as gospel?

Next came the crux of their argument. The prosecution's killer blow, and the main reason for calling Yvonne onto the stand.

'The police say that no murder weapon was found at the scene,' the barrister said.

'That's right.' She frowned and it made her look at least ten years older, the lines deeper than they should be on a fifty-something-year-old woman. 'But if you ask me the police didn't look hard enough.'

'And yet you believe you know why that is?'

'Yeah. Yes.' She stuck her chin out defiantly. 'I

reckon Sam smacked him with one of Scott's football trophies. The police didn't so much as look at 'em.'

'Objection!' Samuel's barrister was on his feet. 'This is nothing more than conjecture. There has been no suggestion of this before now. Certainly as defence we have not been made aware of this claim, or any evidence to back it up.'

'Sustained,' the judge said. 'Mrs Jones, I would remind you that you should only testify what you know to be true. Now is not the time to throw unsubstantiated theories around.' But Yvonne seemed determined to keep talking, her reedy voice rising above the hum of dissent rippling round the courtroom.

'Cos they reckon it was a blunt thing, what someone smacked him with, don't they, the police. And there was loads of them trophies on that shelf. It would've been easy for 'im to have grabbed one and clonked him over the head with it, wouldn't it?'

'Mrs Jones, that's quite enough.' The judge raised her voice and Samuel's mother fell silent at last. 'If you say anything further you will be charged with contempt of court and taken to the cells.' Yvonne's face flushed and she raised her chin in defiance. The judge turned to address the jury. 'You will disregard this witness's comments about a football trophy.'

The judge called for a short adjournment, and as

everyone filed out of the courtroom, Alex felt her heart race. Huddled in the waiting area outside the courtroom, she wondered what everyone else made of what had just happened. If what Yvonne had said was true and the police had been remiss in looking for a murder weapon, what did it mean for Samuel? Would it put him in a better position in the eyes of the jury – or a weaker one?

They didn't have to wait long to find out because a few minutes later everyone was called back in, and the trial restarted.

This time it was the turn of Samuel's defence barrister to question Yvonne. She looked less sure of herself now, like a small child who'd been chastised, and Alex wondered what had happened during the short break away.

'Mrs Jones, before the adjournment you made certain allegations about the night in question. You have made the very serious allegation that the police did not – and I use your words here – "look hard enough".'

'Yes.'

'Surely you're not suggesting that the police overlooked some vital evidence?'

'They wouldn't have seen it if it was gone, would they? If he took it from the house?'

'You believe your son took the weapon from the house?'

'Yes. Yes, I do.'

'So, a trophy is missing from your home? One you could describe to this court and to the police?'

Yvonne's eyes flicked round the courtroom. She looked bewildered. The woman had lost her husband and her son all in one go. No wonder she was all over the place. Despite herself, Alex's heart flared in sympathy. 'Well, he must've done. But they all look the same don't they?'

'Was there one missing, Mrs Jones?'

'I think so, yeah.'

'You think so. But you couldn't say for sure?'

Yvonne's eyes darted back and forth again and a red patch crept up her neck. She wrung her hands in front of her. 'Well, no. Scott had loads of them trophies, didn't he, he was always so good at football. But it definitely looked like there weren't as many there when I looked later. That's why I didn't tell the police before, cos I didn't notice straight away.' Her voice was getting faster, more reedy with every word.

'I see.' The barrister cleared his throat. 'And yet despite the fact that not only was no alleged weapon found anywhere near or on your son's person, that you can't be sure there was definitely a trophy missing, and even if there had been, they were on an easily accessible shelf that most people would have been able to reach, you still believe with absolute certainty that it was Samuel who dealt the fatal blow that killed your husband?'

'Well, yeah, course. He was there, weren't he, covered in his dad's blood. Who else could it've been?'

Her reply hung there for a moment, suspended in the dust motes of the courtroom. Then, 'Thank you, Mrs Jones. No further questions.'

As Yvonne was led away, there were more mutterings. Alex studied Samuel's barrister's face. Had that gone the way he'd hoped? Was he worried?

Over the course of the day, the court heard from several other witnesses, who all tried to paint a picture of Samuel as a violent, out-of-control thug who'd held a grudge against his father.

They heard how Samuel had sent a text message to a friend after one argument saying he could kill his dad, that he wished he was dead.

'It's fair to say it's just a figure of speech,' Samuel's lawyer argued.

A neighbour reported how they heard shouting on the day of the murder – 'We often did but this seemed particularly aggressive' – and then a distant aunt of Samuel's took the stand, who told everyone she loved

Samuel, but she knew he didn't like Scott because Scott was always so cruel to poor old Samuel, and she wouldn't blame him if he had snapped. Samuel's face drained of colour, but his lawyer seemed less perturbed.

None of the descriptions of Samuel sounded anything like the man Alex had got to know over the last few weeks and, by the time the day came to a close earlier than expected, she was no closer to getting a sense of how this was going to go than she had been before they'd started.

10

Alex had planned to go straight home after leaving the court, but when she switched on her phone there were several irate messages from Caitlin.

> What time are you coming in?

> Are you on your way? We've got the new franchisee coming in half an hour.

> Well thanks for that, I looked really professional. AGAIN. I take it you're leaving all the decisions to me now then?

> FFS Alex where are you?

A, is everything okay?

Please let me know you're OK. Am really worried about you now. X

Guilt washed over her. She'd sent Caitlin a text that morning to tell her something had come up and that she'd be in after lunch. Such a cowardly thing to do rather than ring her but she couldn't face Caitlin's questions or her anger. Alex had planned to be in for the meeting but, once she was at the court, she couldn't have left even if she'd wanted to. She checked her watch. It was still early, not quite three.

She tapped out a message and sent it, then switched off her phone before Caitlin could reply.

I'm fine. Am on my way in. Sorry. X

Then she got on the train and headed into the office to face the music.

* * *

Caitlin's face was a mask when Alex walked in. She glanced up, looked like she was about to say something, then closed her mouth and continued typing.

Alex knew she was in serious trouble, and it sat in her belly like a stone.

Alex pulled her chair over and sat down right next to Caitlin so she couldn't ignore her. Eventually Caitlin let out a long sigh.

'Alex.'

'I'm so sorry.'

Caitlin gave an infinitesimal nod.

'I know I let you know down. I'm—' She broke off, a sob choking her words unexpectedly. Caitlin's eyes flicked towards her and immediately softened.

'Hey.' Caitlin reached out and tipped Alex's chin up so she was forced to look at her. 'I'm cross with you but I don't want to make you cry.'

Alex shook her head, tears dripping onto her lap. 'It's not you.'

'Then what is it?' Caitlin said. 'Talk to me, Ally. This can't go on.'

Alex sniffed and wiped her cheeks with her sleeve.

'I've made such a mess of everything.' She looked down at her lap, not wanting to see the look of disapproval on her friend's face.

'Oh, darling, come here.' Caitlin pulled her in for an awkward hug and for the first time in days, Alex felt some of the tension drain from her body. When Caitlin leaned away she took Alex's hands.

'Will you tell me what's going on? I'm worried about you.'

'Can we go somewhere?'

'Pub?'

Alex nodded.

While Caitlin bought a bottle of Merlot at the bar, Alex found a small table tucked away at the back. She shrugged off her coat just as Caitlin plonked the bottle and two glasses down on the table.

'Right, come on. Talk to me. You've been acting strangely for weeks, and you keep disappearing. I know there's something going on that you're not telling me.' She glugged red wine into the glasses almost to the top and pushed one across the smudgy table. Alex took a long gulp, then placed the glass back down and spoke before she could change her mind.

'I have a son.'

A beat. Then, 'I assume from the way you said that we're not talking about Milo here?'

Alex raised her eyes to meet Caitlin's. She shook her head.

'When I was seventeen, I had a baby. I gave him away and as far as I knew he'd gone to a good family.'

Alex ran her finger round the rim of her glass. 'I've never told anyone about him.'

Caitlin's eyes widened. 'Not even Patrick?'

'No.'

'Oh.'

Alex took a deep, steadying breath. 'The thing is, he... My son, Samuel... He's been accused of murder.'

To her credit, Caitlin didn't look shocked and for a split second Alex wondered whether she'd already known. But she couldn't possibly have done.

'I found out a few weeks ago when I read about it in the paper, and that was the first time I'd thought about him for years.' She shook her head. 'That's a lie. I think about him all the time, the baby that he was the last time I saw him. But I hadn't seen his face since then.'

Caitlin was watching Alex intently. Suddenly, Caitlin's eyes widened and her face paled.

'Oh my God, we're talking about Scott Jones, aren't we?'

Alex nodded.

'The boy who killed him, *that's* your son?'

'Yes. Except, well, he says he didn't do it.'

Caitlin picked her glass up and drained half of it. When she'd finished she sat back and folded her arms across her chest.

'The thing is I've been going to visit him in prison. And today I was at his trial at the Crown Court.'

'Right. And Patrick doesn't know any of this either?'

'No one does.'

Caitlin puffed out her cheeks. 'Fuck, Ally. This is massive.' She shook her head. 'I can't believe you've kept this from me all this time.'

Alex felt tears burning her eyes again and she blinked them back. Her hands were shaking as she picked up her glass and Caitlin noticed.

'No wonder you're a nervous bloody wreck.' Caitlin leaned forward. 'Would it help to talk about it?'

'I think so.'

So Alex told Caitlin, from the beginning: about falling pregnant at seventeen, about how her father had convinced her that her baby would be better off being brought up by friends of his, and how she'd agreed because she was so scared of him, of bringing a baby into the world where he existed.

'I called him Samuel, and I regretted the adoption from the moment I handed him over, but it was too late. By the time I met Patrick, I was struggling on my own and I already had Milo. I didn't want Patrick to think I had any more baggage. And then it just got too late to tell him. Things had gone too far.'

'What about me?'

Alex let out a long sigh. 'It's become a habit not to

tell people now. It's easier to keep it a secret from everyone.'

Caitlin topped up their glasses. 'So, what was it like seeing him again?'

Alex squeezed her eyes shut and tried to take herself back to that moment.

'Terrifying. I didn't know what to expect, and the first time I saw him I—' She paused, tried to work out the right word. 'I felt something for him. I can't describe it. Not love, not quite. But an attachment. But—' She stopped.

'What is it, Alex?'

This was the bit Alex beat herself up about the most. 'I'd judged him, Cait. Because of the way he looked, how he sounded. I thought – I thought Milo must be better than him, that there was no way things could ever get that bad for him. But seeing Samuel in that prison, so young and scared, I realised—' She buried her face in her hands then looked up again. 'He says he didn't do it.'

'And do you believe him?'

'I think he's basically a good kid who's been dealt a shitty hand, and there's a huge chance he's going to spend the rest of his life in prison because of it. But yes, I believe him.'

Caitlin looked serious. 'So if you don't think Samuel did it, who did kill Scott Jones then?'

Alex's mind flashed back to Archie, of the thought she'd had that he could have had something to do with Scott's death, but she shook it away.

'I've no idea. But Samuel reckons that Scott had a lot of enemies.'

Caitlin tilted her head. 'Course he's going to say that,' she said softly, as though she was talking to a young child.

'You think I'm being gullible, don't you?'

'Not gullible. I just...' She ran her hand over her face. 'I know you want to believe him, but I don't want you to be hoodwinked by him because you feel guilty.'

'It's not that!'

'Maybe not entirely. But clearly the police think he did it, and from what I've read, there wasn't anyone else there. He was by his side, covered in blood. It seems fairly straightforward.'

Alex wanted to be angry, but there was only concern on Caitlin's face and she knew what she was saying was right.

She did feel guilty, and she was looking for any reason to believe Samuel wasn't the man everyone seemed to think he was.

Because if he was, what would that mean for her – and for Milo?

* * *

'Are you going to tell Patrick?' Caitlin had bought a second bottle of wine and Alex could already feel the room beginning to spin. She couldn't remember the last time she'd eaten anything.

'I can't. Not yet.'

Caitlin said nothing. Then, 'And the trial? Are you still set on watching the rest of it?'

'I shouldn't.'

'But you will.' It wasn't a question but Alex nodded anyway.

'I have to.' She looked at Caitlin. 'Do you understand?'

Caitlin sucked her cheeks in, blew them out again. Met Alex's gaze. 'You should take some time off.'

'What?' She was thrown by the curveball.

'You heard me. You obviously need to be at the trial, you're going to be about as useful as a chocolate teapot if you come into the office. But I need help, so it's better if I just get someone in.'

'I can't. I'm not ready to tell Patrick yet.'

'Then don't. I won't tell him. He'll just think you're

at work, as usual.' She shrugged. Alex envied her. She was so practical, always found everything so straight-forward.

'Thank you, Caitlin. I honestly don't know what I'd do without you.'

'You're my friend. It's what friends do. Besides, if it's important to you, it's important to me.' She sipped her wine. 'Just two things.'

'What?'

'Try not to worry about Milo. He'll be fine.'

'And the other?'

'Remember whatever happens with Samuel, none of this is your fault.'

11

Milo was in the kitchen with Archie when Alex got home, the effects of the wine she'd drunk already fading. Patrick was nowhere to be seen, presumably still avoiding her.

'Hello, you two,' she said, dumping her bag on the table.

'Hi, Alex,' Archie mumbled. Milo had his face stuck in the fridge and didn't reply.

'How was school?'

'Ugghh.'

'Me-me.' He flinched at the pet name she'd always had for him, but at least it got him to withdraw his head from the fridge and look at her.

'What?'

He was so pale, his blonde hair in need of a cut. His eyes were just like his half-brother's.

'Do you want me to make you both a snack?'

'I'm not hungry.'

'But you were just looking in the fridge.'

He looked at her, bewildered, as though trying to work out why he was there.

'I wouldn't mind a snack, please,' Archie said. He was standing now, and at six foot he was several inches taller than Milo. When had the pair of them grown into men?

'Sure, what would you like? Crumpets and cheese? They're your favourite.'

Milo rolled his eyes. 'They were his favourite like five years ago,' he said and she flinched.

'Something else then?'

'Got any Pringles?'

'No. Cheese and crackers?'

Milo stared at her, then nodded. Archie bowed his head in agreement too.

'Sit down then.'

Milo slumped onto a chair and Archie sat back down beside him. They both pulled out their phones as Alex bustled around preparing their crackers and trying not to sneak glances at Milo's phone to see what he was doing. One of the conditions of Milo getting his iPhone had been that she and Patrick would check it regularly to make sure he wasn't looking at anything inappropriate, or that no one had sent him something they shouldn't have. But that had been almost four years ago now and they'd quickly let it slide, finding it easier to let him just get on with it rather than face the daily battle of trying to check his search history. She regretted that now.

She placed the plates in front of them.

'Thanks, Aunty Alex,' Archie said.

'You're welcome, love.' Alex smiled at his use of the 'aunty' that he used to call her, so incongruous with someone of his size. Milo didn't say a word, just picked up a piece of cheese and shoved it in his mouth. She sat opposite them.

'So, how was school? Anything to report?'

Milo looked up briefly. 'You've just asked that. It's fine.'

'Everything settled down then?'

He flicked a glance at Archie. What was that about? 'Teachers still hate me.'

'Oh, Milo, they don't hate you.'

'And you're there, are you, in the classroom?'

'What?'

'Never mind.'

Fuck. She'd messed that up. She tried a different tack.

'You ready for your concert tomorrow night?'

He bit into a cracker. Crumbs escaped his mouth, dropped all over his blazer. She resisted the urge to lean over and wipe them away.

'I guess.'

'Have you been practising?'

He took another bite of cracker and she waited while he chewed. 'Don't get why I have to play anyway. It's basically just all the losers who play at these things.'

He'd been asked by his music teacher to play piano in a school concert the following night. When he'd agreed a few weeks before they must have caught him on a good day, but she'd heard no evidence of any practice since then. And the truth was she was dreading it too. She knew some of the parents at school would have heard about Milo's recent problems and she wasn't sure she could face their judgement.

She also couldn't help her thoughts drifting to what Samuel had told her about being banned from playing the piano by his father. How much he would have given to have been allowed the chance to do what Milo took for granted. She swallowed down her frustration. This wasn't Milo's fault.

'It's only a couple of hours out of your life. It'll be nice to hear you play again.'

He grunted but didn't say another word.

'Are you playing as well, Arch?' Caitlin hadn't mentioned she was going but Archie used to be a whizz on the trombone.

'Nah, I gave it up ages ago.'

'Oh, right.'

She turned back to Milo.

'Fancy watching a film tonight?'

'We're going out.'

'Out? Where?'

'Just out. Park maybe.'

Alex frowned. 'It's a school night.'

'Yeah?' Beside him, Archie stared at his hands, not wanting to get involved.

'I—' She stopped. The last thing she wanted him to be doing was hanging around in the park until all hours. But she also knew that telling him he couldn't go would only alienate him further. 'I just think you shouldn't be out late on a school night.' She looked at Archie. 'Your mum will say the same.'

Milo rolled his eyes so far back in his head she thought they'd drop out. 'You're always out.'

'That's different—' she started. Is that really what he thought?

'Fuck's sake.'

'Milo!'

He stood suddenly, the cracker in his hand snapping in two and dropping onto the table. 'Forget it. I'll stay in.' Then he turned and stormed out, stomped up the stairs, his bedroom door slamming so hard the walls shook. Archie followed close behind.

Alex was still sitting at the table when Patrick walked in a few minutes later, his hair dishevelled. He stopped in the doorway.

'What's up?'

This was the first time he'd spoken to her in anything except a cool, detached tone for days and she felt pathetically grateful.

'The usual.'

'Milo?'

She nodded. He sat down opposite her in the seat Milo had just vacated and moved his half-empty plate to one side. 'I thought I heard banging. What happened?'

She ran her fingers through her hair. It needed a wash and she could see from her reflection in the darkened kitchen window that it was sticking out at all angles.

'I just don't know how to get through to him. He seems to hate me.'

'Of course he doesn't hate you.'

She looked up at him. 'How do you know?'

'What?'

'How do you know he doesn't hate me?'

'What—' Patrick seemed blindsided. But a rage had descended on her; rage that had been building over the last few days and weeks about Milo, about Samuel, and about the words Patrick had said to her a couple of weeks before – but had refused to acknowledge since.

'You clearly think he's evil and that it's my fault. So how can you claim to know anything about the way he's feeling?'

'I didn't say he was evil, I—' He stopped.

'Didn't you? What was it you were saying about us not having a baby ourselves *if it turns out like this one*?. I think those were your precise words. Or did you really think we weren't going to talk about it?'

Patrick's face paled and he hung his head. He made a low, guttural sound.

'I'm so sorry.' He looked up at her and he seemed so distraught her heart cracked a little. But she held her ground. 'I didn't mean it. I love Milo, you know I do. I was just angry. I just really want us to have a baby, Ally. Me and you. I—' He broke off, a sob choking his words.

She looked away. It would be so easy to smooth everything over. To tell him that of course they could try again. Of course they could have a baby. He'd be a wonderful father. But she wouldn't, she couldn't do it.

'I honestly don't know if I want another baby, Patrick. Not with everything that's going on here, with Milo.' This would be the perfect chance to tell him about Samuel, but she couldn't summon the courage. 'I don't want the extra debt. I don't want to be pregnant again. And you're right. I don't want to risk another child who might end up being anything like my fucking father.' She gave a bitter laugh. 'Just imagine what your mother would have to say about that.'

It was a low blow and she regretted it instantly, but it was too late to take it back. She stuck her chin out defiantly.

But Patrick didn't take the bait.

'You know I don't really think Milo is anything like him, don't you?' His voice was low. 'He's just a kid.'

She looked up at him. 'I do know that. But I also know he's a kid who's hitting and punching people and getting into fights. What happens if he starts really hurting people, Patrick? What happens if we can't stop this and he gets into really serious trouble? What if he hurts one of us?'

Patrick's voice, when he spoke, was quiet.

'You don't truly believe he'd hurt us, do you?'

Did she? A few months ago she would have said no way. Milo would and could never hurt anyone. But now?

'I honestly don't know anything any more,' she said. She rubbed her hand up and down her arm as though trying to warm herself. 'I spent so many years watching my dad dish out punches like they were sweets, and now it feels like I'm watching my son go the same way. It's got to be something in me. It's got to be. I just can't bring another child into this. I can't risk it.'

Patrick didn't move, but Alex saw the hope drain from his face, his eyes dull, deaden. From the moment they'd met, Patrick had clung to the hope that one day he would have a child of his own, his blood. And now, that hope had been extinguished, and it was like a light in him had gone out too.

* * *

The doorbell rang and Alex's heart sank. She'd completely forgotten that their friends Janie and Pete, old colleagues of Patrick's, were coming over until about an hour ago, and after the day she'd had the last thing she felt like doing was being sociable. She stayed on the bed and listened as Patrick opened the door and greeted them, shouts of laughter floating up the stairs.

It went quiet as they headed into the living room, then she heard soft footsteps running up the carpeted stairs, and Patrick's head appeared at the bedroom door.

'Are you coming down?'

'Yeah. I'll be there in a minute.'

He brought his whole body into the room. 'You're not going to ruin tonight, are you?'

'No, Patrick, I'm not going to *ruin it*. I said I'll be down in a minute and I will be.'

He lingered a moment longer and she thought he was about to say something else. Then he turned on his heel and left.

She let out a long puff of air. Why was she behaving like such a bitch? Why, when she knew she was being cruel and unfair, couldn't she stop doing it? She needed to stop pushing away the one man she knew she could rely on.

She stood, checked her reflection in the mirror and sighed. She looked tired and gaunt. She hadn't been eating properly and it was starting to show in her face, her cheekbones pronounced and her skin grey. Her trousers were almost falling down so she tightened her belt a notch, flicked some mascara on her bloodshot eyes and hoped no one would notice.

'Hey,' she said, pasting on a smile as she entered the kitchen. Janie flung her arms out and air-kissed her like a film star, then Pete gave her a more awkward hug.

'Lovely to see you,' she said. 'It's been ages.'

'I know,' Janie said, picking up her glass of wine. 'It must be what, three months?'

'At least,' Patrick said, topping both of their glasses up even though they'd barely drunk anything.

'Gosh, time goes so quickly, doesn't it?' Janie said. 'I always tell Pete we need to be better at arranging to see people.' She smiled broadly. 'Anyway, we're all here now. Cheers!'

Alex looked round for a glass, grabbed an empty one from the side and held it up to chink against theirs. She was feeling on the back foot this evening, aware she mustn't drink too much on top of the wine she'd already drunk with Caitlin. She was already so on edge. Her heart fluttered and her pulse thumped in her temple.

'Anyway, how are you, Alex? You look...' Janie's eyes swept from her head to her toes and back up again, and a frown line appeared between her brows. 'Actually, sweetie, you look exhausted. And have you lost weight?' She leaned forward and pinched Alex's cheek. 'Are you sure you're okay?'

'I'm fine, honestly,' Alex said, not daring to meet Patrick's eye. 'I've just been so busy, you know, with work...' she trailed off.

'Ah yes, Patrick said you've been working hard,' Janie said. 'Said you're always at the office.' This time Alex did glance over at Patrick with a questioning look, but his expression was impenetrable. Had he been discussing their problems with Janie? They'd always been close, Janie and Patrick, but in the last few months, she wasn't aware they'd even spoken to each other, let alone been confiding in each other. She wondered what else they'd talked about and felt a flush of shame creep up her neck.

She smiled, picked up the half-empty wine bottle from the side and filled her glass almost to the brim. 'Anyway, enough about me. It's great to see you,' Alex said and took a huge gulp. It had been a while since she'd last eaten and she felt her limbs instantly begin to relax and her head spin. The feeling wasn't unpleasant.

'Let me finish this, you all go and sit down,' Alex said, ushering them out of the kitchen.

'Are you sure you don't want some help?' Patrick said, hovering behind her. He was so close she could feel his breath on the back of her neck but he didn't make a move to touch her. 'It was my idea to invite them round tonight.'

'It's fine. You go. I'll be there in a minute.' She turned to look at him and for a second she thought he was going to ask her something. But then he clearly changed his mind, then planted a kiss on her forehead and followed his friends out of the room.

She was glad of the peace, and as she stirred the curry she let her mind drift. It was probably just as well she hadn't remembered that Janie and Pete were coming round tonight because it meant she hadn't had time to worry about it. They had been married longer than Alex and Patrick, and they'd known them since Patrick started working at his first architecture firm back in the early 2000s alongside Janie. Alex liked Pete – he was a quiet, unassuming man who didn't say much, but when he did speak you listened because it was likely to be interesting. Janie, on the other hand, she'd never been quite so sure about. She was perfectly nice, on the surface. But there was an undercurrent to her that Alex could never quite put her finger on, but that sometimes made her feel uncomfortable, like she was being studied. She wondered now whether Janie could see right through her, whether she knew that she was lying to Patrick, to her, to everyone. She felt, under her scrutiny, that Janie knew exactly where she'd been that day, that she could see into her very core. It was unnerving, and it was why she always drank too much in her company. She vowed not to do that tonight. She needed to stay in control, and she certainly didn't need a hangover tomorrow.

She thought about what Janie had said, about Patrick telling her that Alex had been working so hard. Knowing Janie, that hadn't been an innocent comment. She knew just how to plant a seed of doubt in people's minds, without it seeming as though she'd done so. Alex suspected Janie wanted her to know she had been talking to Patrick, and that he'd been complaining about her. If that had been her intention, it had worked.

Patrick had always been so straightforward. He wore his heart on his sleeve and Alex knew he struggled with the fact that she wasn't as open as he was.

'If you talk about things it helps you unburden,' he always told her. But something in her made her want to hang on to things, not to bother other people with her problems. If she kept them to herself, perhaps they'd go away. She was aware it was the road to madness, but after a childhood spent pretending everything was okay, it was the only way she knew how.

Laughter drifted through from the other room. Alex should go and join them. She put the lid on the curry, turned it off, then picked up her glass and headed through. As she lowered herself onto the sofa beside Patrick, Janie was watching her.

'What have I missed?' Alex said, taking a sip from her glass.

'We were just talking about that women's refuge that's going to have to close,' Janie said before anyone else could answer.

'Oh?' Alex hadn't read anything about it but then she'd been so preoccupied recently it was hardly a surprise.

'Apparently they just don't have the funding these days, and they're having to rely on donations more and more.' Janie took a sip of wine and almost sloshed it over the sofa.

'God, that's awful,' she said.

'The thing is, they *can* afford to fund it, but they simply don't see it as a priority,' Pete said in his quiet voice. 'Neighbours have complained about it so they're looking for any excuse to shut it down.' He sounded full of fury.

'But why would anyone complain about a refuge?'

'Apparently it's making some of the parents with young kids *nervous*.' He made air quotes with the last word. 'Although God knows what they're scared of. Sometimes people are just arseholes.'

Janie rolled her eyes. 'And obviously they've never been affected by a violent man either.'

For once Alex could find nothing to disagree with in Janie's argument. She felt indignation rise in her on behalf of all those women who just needed somewhere safe; thought about her own mother cowering under her father's fists. 'How dare they?' she said, her voice wobbling. Patrick glanced at her, concerned.

'Right, shall we eat?' he said, keen to keep the peace.

They filed through to the kitchen. Patrick served up the curry, and soon they were sitting down to eat.

'Where's Milo tonight?' Janie said, reaching over for the bowl of rice.

'He doesn't like to come out of his room these days,' Patrick said with a sad smile.

'Ah, teenagers, eh?' Janie said. 'Is he still playing up?'

Alex felt her hackles rise. Patrick criticising her to Janie was one thing, but the thought that he was moaning about Milo was something else.

'He's fine,' she snapped.

A look flitted across Janie's face and she placed her hand on Alex's arm. 'Sorry, Alex, I didn't mean anything by it,' she said. 'I know it's hard when they're this age.' Janie and Pete had two children, both now in their twenties. As far as Alex knew they'd been model children, sailing through school, and now with successful careers. At least that was the version she'd heard from Janie herself.

She gave a tight nod and spooned some curry onto her plate. Her appetite had deserted her but she didn't want Patrick to worry so she dutifully shovelled forkfuls into her mouth. It felt like chewing glue.

As the conversation flowed round the table Alex let herself drift off, going over everything she'd heard in court. Yvonne's words were stuck in her head on a loop: *He was there, wasn't he, covered in his dad's blood?* Everything she'd said about Samuel – her *son* – made him sound so cold-blooded, so evil. If Alex were on the jury and didn't know Samuel at all, would she have believed Yvonne, even though the defence had made it clear she wasn't certain at all about what she'd seen? It was impossible to tell. She felt a knot of anxiety deep in her belly.

Her thoughts were interrupted by Janie's voice, something she was saying nagging at her, tugging at her mind like a stray piece of cotton. Slowly, she tuned into the conversation going on around her.

'That bloke who killed his dad, you mean?'

'Yes, that's the one. I've been following it online this week. He smashed his dad's head open and left him to bleed to death according to what I've read on social media.' Janie shook her head. 'I don't know what's wrong with some people.'

All the blood drained from Alex's body.

'But nobody knows who actually did it,' she said. Her voice was a screech, nails on a blackboard. 'And the murder weapon was never actually found.'

Janie's head whipped up, surprised. 'Have you been reading about it too?'

Alex nodded, her jaw clenched, knuckles glowing white as she gripped her fork too tightly.

Janie frowned. 'So what makes you think he's innocent? Murder weapon aside – and it sounds like he'd have had plenty of time to hide it by all accounts – it looked like a pretty open and shut case to me.'

The words were stuck in her throat but she needed to say something. 'I—' She cleared her throat. She felt frantic, desperate to let them know that Samuel wasn't the awful person he seemed to be – but without letting them know how much she cared about it. She forced a smile. 'You just never know, do you? The prosecution lawyers will say whatever it takes to get their conviction.' She hoped nobody noticed the tremble in her voice.

'Yes, sure, but have you actually read what happened? I mean, the police found him standing over his father's body, covered in blood.' Janie smirked and Alex had to sit on her hands to stop herself from leaning over and smacking the smugness right off the woman's face. Her body shook with indignation and rage.

'You don't know that's what actually happened though,' she said, her voice harsher than she'd intended. She really couldn't afford to get into a fight about this, couldn't risk giving away that she knew more than she should. But Janie wasn't going to let it go. She leaned forward, snapped a poppadom in half and held it in mid-air.

'It's all over social media, Alex. You just need to read it.'

The roaring in Alex's ears was so loud she thought her head might explode. She mustn't cause a scene. She sucked in air, trying to cool herself down before she spoke. Luckily, Pete came to the rescue first.

'You know you can't believe everything you read online, love,' he said.

'Exactly, that's what I meant,' Alex said, shooting him a look of gratitude. Sometimes she thought he must have the patience of a saint to have been married to Janie for so many years. Probably that was *exactly* why it worked so well. Janie looked from Alex to her husband and back again, clearly decided it wasn't worth fighting about, then popped a piece of poppadom in her mouth.

'Fine,' Janie said, waving her hand in the air dismissively. 'I was only saying what I'd read. You don't need to get so wound up about it.'

Alex stared down at her plate and pushed the rice and chicken round mindlessly as she waited for her body to stop shaking. It didn't take long for the conversation to switch lanes, this time moving on to a discussion about the new supermarket that was about to open up in town and the nightmare the road closures were causing for Janie to get to work every morning. Alex let the conversation flow around her as she sat in her own bubble, smiling and nodding every now and then and hoping nobody noticed how quiet she was being.

It wasn't until sometime later, after they'd opened their fourth bottle of wine and were all feeling a bit fuzzy round the edges, that Alex realised Patrick hadn't come to her defence the way he normally would earlier. In fact, he hadn't said a single word the whole time the conversation about Samuel had been going on.

12

It hadn't been an easy decision – Alex hated lying to Patrick, for one thing – but in the end she took Caitlin's advice and went back to the court to watch the rest of the trial. Samuel had no one else there and, even though he hadn't noticed her presence yet, at least it meant he had someone on his side.

As the week wore on she began to relax about being recognised. It was clear none of Samuel and Scott's family had a clue who she was – why would they? – and more importantly nobody else seemed remotely interested in why she was there. Just another nosey member of the public.

It wasn't until the third day that Samuel spotted her and the surprise on his face was clear. She didn't have time to worry about it though, because he was being called up for questioning and she wanted to listen to every word.

'Could you please explain to the jury exactly what happened on the night your father died,' the prosecutor said. Samuel pulled himself up tall and recounted the story of how he'd come to visit his mother to borrow some money when he'd found his father lying by the fireplace, stone cold, his head smashed in. His voice was strong and clear.

'But when your mother returned home she said she found you kneeling by your father's body, covered in blood. How do you explain that?'

'I don't remember all the details,' Samuel said, and Alex glanced at the jury to see what they made of that. A woman at the front rolled her eyes but other than that none of them reacted. 'I remember finding my father lying there on the floor. I touched him, tried to feel for a pulse. But I don't remember what happened between then and when my mum came home.'

A beat of silence.

'Do you often black out like this, Mr Jones?' the lawyer said, and Alex felt a flare of anger. Surely it was a well-known fact that trauma made people block out painful memories? She hoped his defence would hone in on that later.

'No. But I don't usually find my father dead in his own house either.'

A ripple of whispers. Good boy.

'That's true, I suppose. But while it is perhaps accepted that finding your father's dead body could cause you to forget things, isn't it also true that, sometimes, it can be a convenient way of covering up the fact that you actually killed him?'

'Your honour!' Samuel's barrister leapt to his feet.

The judge nodded. 'Please try to refrain from putting words into the defendant's mouth, Mr Simpson.'

The barrister turned back to Samuel, a half-smile on his face. 'Apologies. Let me rephrase that. Is there any chance that, rather than your mind blocking out what happened after you found your father already dead, that it has in fact done the same to help you forget that it was you that killed him?'

'No. No chance because I know I didn't.'

'And exactly how do you know that, Mr Jones?'

'I just do. I just wouldn't.' Samuel looked lost and Alex wanted to run down there and hug him. She leaned forward.

'You wouldn't be that violent, do you mean?'

'Yeah.'

'I see.' He paused. 'Do you recall, Mr Jones, how on

the 23rd of December 2019, you were remanded in custody after getting into a fight in a nightclub?'

'Yeah, but—'

'And do you admit that, in fact, you caused actual bodily harm to that person?'

'Yeah, but it weren't me that started that fight.'

'But you did punch the victim several times, in the face?'

'Maybe, but—'

'So would you also admit that you can be known to be violent when provoked, which is in fact the exact opposite of what you just claimed?'

'That was different.'

Samuel sounded beaten and Alex wanted to shout down to him, tell him to ignore him, that the barrister was just trying to prove a point. On a bench in front of her, she saw the woman who'd shouted out before whisper something in the ear of her companion and Alex dug her nails into her palms.

'Thank you, Mr Jones, I have no further questions.'

Samuel looked so defeated, his shoulders slumped, head down. Alex hoped the jury wouldn't assume that just because someone got into a fight in a nightclub that it meant they were capable of murder. She tried to imagine how she might view Samuel in their position, but it was impossible to be objective.

Samuel perked up a bit when his defence barrister began questioning him and gave him the chance to explain himself. But Alex was worried that in the minds of the jurors – at least some of them – the damage had already been done.

By the end of the day she felt wretched, and knew she wouldn't be able to hide it from Patrick completely.

But as she let herself through the door, her mind miles away back in the courtroom, it wasn't Patrick she saw first.

'Hello, Alex dear, how lovely to see you.' Patrick's mother wafted towards her before she'd even had the chance to take off her coat and placed an air kiss on either side of her face. The cloying scent of her perfume clung to the back of Alex's throat.

'Hello, Nancy, it's lovely to see you too,' she managed, her mind scrabbling to work out what was going on. Patrick appeared in the kitchen doorway, his face unreadable.

'Mum and Dad have been here for ages, waiting to go for dinner,' he said, his voice stiff.

Oh *God*. Tonight was Milo's school concert and Patrick's parents, Nancy and Andrew, had insisted on coming along. God only knew why when all they seemed to do was disapprove of Milo. Alex wasn't sure she could cope with being polite to them all evening after the day she'd had.

She pasted a smile on her face. 'I'm so sorry, I got held up. At work,' she said, to clarify. 'If you give me a few minutes to get changed we can get going.'

'We've missed the booking now,' Patrick said coolly. Alex knew when he spoke to her like that he was quietly fuming and her stomach knotted. 'I made us something to eat but we need to get going in half an hour.'

She glanced at her watch. He was right, it was later than she'd thought.

'Is Milo ready?'

He shrugged. 'No idea. He hasn't been down to say hello yet.'

Alex saw Nancy's lips tighten but she said nothing.

'Fine. I'll sort him out and get changed then we can go.'

She ran up the stairs, eager to get away. She *had* totally forgotten about this evening, but even at the best of times, Patrick's parents were challenging company. Especially Nancy. It was absolutely not what she needed this evening.

She quickly got changed, slicked on some fresh mascara, trying to ignore how pale she looked, and went and tapped on Milo's door.

No answer. She knocked louder, then pushed the door open. Milo was in his usual position on his bed, headphones in, eyes closed. He didn't look very ready for his big night.

She walked over and nudged his leg and his eyes snapped open. He tugged an earphone out. 'What?'

'We're leaving in fifteen minutes, why aren't you ready?'

'I'm not going.'

'Of course you're going.'

'I'm really not.'

She took a deep breath and tried to stay calm. She sat down beside him. 'Milo, this isn't about whether you want to do this tonight. This is about learning that you can't just let people down when you've promised you'll do something.'

He pulled his other earphone out. 'But I hate the bloody piano.'

'Since when? You used to love it.'

'Yeah, when I was a kid.' He huffed loudly. 'I've got homework to do anyway.'

'Oh come on, since when did you do homework willingly?'

There was a time when Milo would have smiled sheepishly at that and admitted defeat. But there was a hard edge to him these days, and he turned his head away, towards the wall.

'Yeah, well, I need to today.'

She stood, angry suddenly. 'There are people in this world who would give their right arm to be given the opportunities you've been given,' she said, her voice raised. He looked surprised. Good. 'Now stop being so selfish and obstinate, get your uniform on, and get downstairs in fifteen minutes, or I'm grounding you.' She turned and left the room and hoped he'd do as he'd been told. She couldn't forcibly drag him there.

Downstairs, Patrick and his parents were in the kitchen with a glass of red wine each. An almost-empty bottle sat in the middle of the table. It looked expensive, which meant they'd probably brought it with them.

'Glass of Chateau-Neuf, Alex?' Nancy said as Alex walked in.

'No thanks.' She felt too frazzled to drink. 'I'll drive us to the school.'

'Is Milo coming down?' Patrick said as she popped a couple of slices of bread in the toaster.

'He'd better be.'

'It's a shame when teenagers start becoming tricky,' Nancy said, pressing her glass to her lips. 'I think it's got worse, they just don't seem to have the respect for their parents that they used to have.'

'I think teenagers have always been defiant,' Patrick said, and Alex was grateful for his support. She hadn't expected it.

'Perhaps. But I'm still convinced it's because they're so pandered to these days.'

A silence fell and Alex struggled to stay quiet. Luckily, Andrew spoke next.

'It's been a long time since we saw Milo playing the piano. I suspect he's improved significantly since then?'

I have no idea because he never bothers to play, Alex wanted to say. But instead she said, 'Yes, I expect so.'

'You always loved playing the piano when you were a boy,' Nancy said to Patrick.

'Did I? I always thought I was tone deaf.'

'Oh, don't be so daft,' Nancy said, and her tinkling laugh cut right through Alex. 'You were wonderful, it was just that you had so many other things going on and you simply didn't have time for them all.' She sighed. 'It would be marvellous to have a grandchild to carry it on one day.'

Alex bit down on her tongue so hard she almost drew blood. Here we go, the whole *my child was so wonderful, if only you would give him a child to carry on his brilliance* speech. They got a slightly different version of it every time.

'Ah well, if we do ever have a child then any musical talent will almost definitely come from Alex,' Patrick said, and Alex smiled at him. He didn't smile back.

'Yes, I'm sure. Let's just hope we get the chance to see that, shall we?' Nancy smiled sweetly, then stood. 'Excuse me a moment, I'm just popping to the loo.'

When she left Alex let out a long breath.

'Why does she always have to do that?' Patrick said, turning to his father.

'I know, I warned her before we came.' He shook his head indulgently, like it was some sort of joke. 'She never listens to me though.'

Alex was about to reply when a noise in the doorway caught her attention.

'Milo, you're ready!' she said, standing.

He shrugged. 'Yep.'

'Hello, young man,' Andrew said, holding out his hand. Milo stared at it for a moment, then took a step closer and, to Alex's relief, shook it briefly.

'Hi.'

'We're looking forward to hearing you play today. Have you been practising much?'

'Not really.'

Andrew looked thrown but recovered quickly. 'Oh well, I'm sure you'll be as wonderful as always.'

Milo ignored him and looked at Alex.

'Do I get dinner first?'

'We'll be late. Have my toast,' she said, grabbing it from the toaster and spreading butter on it. Nancy walked back into the room at that moment.

'Oh there you are, Milo, hello,' she said, pressing her hands into his arms and air-kissing him. He looked mortified. 'I do hope you've been practising, we've travelled a long way this evening to see you.'

She grabbed her handbag and wafted from the room.

Everyone followed dutifully.

* * *

Milo's first piano piece went okay in the end, although Alex suspected it was more from muscle memory than practice. She was just relieved he had got through it and hoped the piece in the second half would go as well.

During the interval, they all filed through to the school dining room for over-stewed tea and bitter coffee with plates of crumbly biscuits.

'Well, I thought that went quite well,' Patrick said. Alex could see the relief on his face.

'Yeah, he did okay, didn't he?' she said. She looked round the room for Milo. He was nowhere to be seen.

It hadn't escaped Alex's notice that several of the other parents had been casting disapproving glances in their direction since they'd arrived this evening, and even those she'd previously been quite friendly with seemed to be avoiding them. Fine, it suited her.

'I think I'd better go and look for Milo,' she said, putting her teacup on a nearby table.

'Don't worry he'll be around somewhere,' Patrick said, but she was already off, scuttling towards the music room.

'Alex, hi.' A voice stopped her in her tracks and she looked up to find one of the mums she hadn't seen for ages standing in her way.

'Hello, Claire,' she said, trying to move past. But Claire was persistent.

'I haven't seen Milo for a while, he's really grown.'

'Yes, I suppose he has.'

'And how are things? You know, with everything?' She wafted her hand around vaguely and Alex felt herself tense.

'Everything?'

'You know, the trouble you've been having... with

Milo...' she trailed off. 'I'm sorry, it's just I've been ever so worried.'

I bet you have.

'Everything's fine, thank you,' Alex said stiffly. 'I'm just off to find him now.' She indicated the corridor she'd been heading towards. But Claire hadn't finished.

'Good, I'm so glad to hear it. Only you never know, do you, where these things will end?'

Alex stopped sharp. 'What do you mean?' Her voice was cold.

Claire gave a nervous laugh. 'Well, you know. Sometimes boys, they get caught up in things they don't mean to, don't they, and end up going off the rails. I just thought... I meant...'

'Milo is fine, thank you, Claire.'

'Of course, of course. That's good then,' the other woman gabbled. 'Because you wouldn't want him going off the rails, you know. I mean, look at that kid, the one in the papers, who killed his dad... Oh gosh, not that I think Milo would ever...' she must have carried on talking but Alex had stopped listening.

Was *everyone* talking about Samuel? She'd known it was big news, but she'd under-estimated quite how big – especially among gossips.

'Sorry, I have to go,' she said, not caring how rude

she seemed as she pushed past Claire and stormed away, her whole body shaking.

Did people really think that Milo was headed the same way as Samuel? And, she realised with a lurch, how much worse would it be if they knew the truth?

* * *

The journey home was awful. After being accosted by Claire, Alex had found Milo and dragged him home despite the fact he was meant to be playing again. He seemed surprised but pleased. Patrick and his parents were confused, but she couldn't tell them what had happened. When they pulled up outside the house, Nancy and Andrew made their excuses and left. Milo went straight up to his room, and then it was just Alex and Patrick. The tension simmered.

'What the bloody hell was all that about?' he said. His voice was tight, his fists clenched by her side.

'I'm sick of it all,' she said.

'All? Can you elaborate?'

'Just... *everyone*. The bloody sanctimonious parents at school thinking they're better than me because their kids are such angels. Milo and his rudeness, you, your bloody parents—'

'My parents? What the hell are they meant to have done?'

'Oh come on, are you kidding?'

'No. I'm not.' A red patch crept up Patrick's neck and a vein bulged in his temple. 'What *exactly* is your problem with my parents?'

She shook her head in disbelief.

'They think the sun shines out of your arse, and that it's my fault we haven't been able to carry on the perfect Harding gene...' She felt breathless, but before Patrick could reply she ploughed on. 'I mean, they could barely disguise the fact that they don't think I have any good qualities to offer any child of ours, not to mention the fact that even your bloody mother seems to think there's something wrong with Milo.'

Patrick watched her, his eyes like flint. His body hummed with an unspent energy and she wondered, for a moment, what he was going to do.

Then he leaned forward so his face was right by hers, and hissed, 'Well, maybe she's right.'

The silence hung heavy in the air between them. Then before she could say anything else, he stormed out of the room.

13

If Alex had had any qualms about attending the final day of the trial, then Patrick's behaviour the previous night had quashed them entirely. His sanctimonious mother might not think Alex and her children were worthy of her precious son, but that didn't mean she was going to abandon either of them.

She arrived at the court early, and as she sat down Samuel glanced over at her. His gaze was so intense she had to look away.

Both barristers summed up their cases, then the judge told the jury to go away and make their decision. As they waited, she went for a cup of coffee in a cafe nearby. She didn't need more caffeine, she was wired enough, but she had to get out of the building.

Nursing a cooling cappuccino she switched her phone back on. Almost instantly, it buzzed with messages and missed calls.

> Where are you? School have rung.
> Ring me back. Patrick.

> Alex, ring me as soon as you get this.

> OK I'm going in. Meet me at school at 3.30pm.

Oh God.

There were missed calls from school too. Heart thumping, she pressed her phone to her ear.

'Hello, this is a message for Mrs Harding. This is Mr Pearce from Milo's school. I'm sorry to say that Milo has been in serious trouble today for aggressive behaviour. We would appreciate it if you could call us back as soon as possible to arrange a meeting with the headteacher. Many thanks.'

Guilt ripped through her. She should be there. She shouldn't be sitting in this cafe, waiting to find out whether Samuel was going to be found guilty or not. She should be at home, supporting Milo, trying to get to the bottom of whatever was bothering him.

She listened to the next message, from Patrick.

'Alex, it's me. Where the fuck are you? School have rung and want us to go in and see them at the end of the day. Milo might be suspended. For real this time. Ring me.'

And then:

'Why aren't you at work? I've rung the office five times and Caitlin's being really cagey. I don't know what the hell is going on here but your son needs you. Ring me.'

There were no more messages. She checked the time. It was just before three. If she hurried she could probably make the meeting.

She stood. Hooked her bag onto her shoulder. She was halfway along the road before she stopped dead. She couldn't. She couldn't leave without finding out the verdict. There was too much at stake.

With shaking hands, and wracked with guilt, she switched her phone onto silent, turned in the other direction and headed back towards the courtroom. She'd have to deal with the fallout of her decision later. For now, she needed to focus on the here and now.

She got back just in time, as everyone was filing back in. The jury had come to a unanimous decision.

'That was quick,' she whispered to the man beside

her who'd been scribbling in a notebook for most of the morning, clearly a local court reporter.

'Yeah, surprised me too. Probably means he's going down.'

The blood drained from Alex's face. 'Really?'

He looked at her as if she was stupid. 'Usually. A quick verdict means there's not much to discuss, decision was easy.' He shrugged. 'But don't quote me on that. Could go either way.' Alex wanted to punch the self-satisfied smirk off his face. *This isn't just a story,* she wanted to tell him. *This is a man's life.*

Alex turned to study Samuel as the jury re-entered the courtroom. His back was rigid and he was looking straight ahead, not at the jury. How was he feeling? Was he scared? Worried? Confident?

She thought about some of the things Samuel had told her and the things she'd heard in court about the way his father had treated him. She couldn't get Janie's voice from the other night out of her head either: *'It's an open and shut case, isn't it?'* What if that was the same decision the jury had come to, based on all the evidence they'd been presented with? How would she feel if Samuel was found guilty and spent most of his life behind bars?

She risked a glance around her. The same woman as before, the one who had shouted out to Yvonne, was scowling at her. She didn't break her gaze as Alex caught her eyes, and Alex looked away quickly. Who was she? A member of Samuel's family?

Her eyes wandered over the rest of the court. The atmosphere was tense, a buzz in the air. She tried to read the faces of the people in the jury, studying them one by one. The rotund middle-aged woman; the glamorous woman with a perfect face of make-up like a mask; the bald man in a scruffy hoodie. Who were these people, what was their story – and, after everything they'd heard about Scott and Samuel, what decision had they reached?

Were they about to destroy Samuel's life – or save it?

She tore her gaze from them and back to Samuel. She felt a surprising and overwhelming urge to run down there and wrap her arms around him and protect him from whatever was about to happen next.

The judge spoke and the foreman of the jury stood. Alex's hands shook.

'How do you find the defendant on the charge of murder?'

The whole courtroom stilled. The clock stopped ticking, the reporter stopped scribbling, Alex stopped breathing.

'Not guilty.'

The courtroom erupted, but Alex's eyes were only focused on Samuel. While his barrister stood up and punched the air, Samuel's shoulders slumped and his head sagged. It was as though his entire body had deflated.

Alex didn't know who the people around her on the public benches were, but most seemed shocked by the result, and a chatter of voices swelled into the air until she could barely even think. She stood up, grabbed her coat and bag and ran, head down, out of the cramped room. She wasn't sure what was supposed to happen next, so she waited in the corridor and watched everyone pile out and head towards the stairs. Nobody took any notice of her and, finally, it was quiet again, the hum of voices growing more distant.

What now?

She sat for a while, gathering her thoughts. Then, unsure what else to do, she made her way to the stairs and headed down towards the exit. But when she got there, she stopped dead. Samuel and his barrister were by the entrance to the court building. The reporter who'd been next to Alex approached Samuel, calling his name, a question already on his lips before he even reached him. There was an exchange of words she was unable to make out, then the reporter scribbled something down and followed for a few footsteps before hanging back, apparently satisfied.

Then Samuel and his barrister carried on towards the door and out through the revolving door and down the steps to the pavement below.

It was all over.

Samuel was free.

14

Alex lingered a while before she left the court, not wanting to bump into Samuel. She wouldn't know what to say to him if she did.

When she eventually emerged she looked both ways, but there was no sign of anyone she recognised. It was hard to believe someone's life had just changed in a few seconds, and yet everything else continued as normal.

She turned right and headed towards the station. Her mind was full of Samuel and what this not guilty verdict meant. Did it really mean he hadn't done it, or had he simply been lucky to get away with it? And if he hadn't done it what did this mean for her, and for Milo? Did it mean there wasn't an 'evil' gene after all?

And if Samuel didn't kill Scott, it begged the question: who did? Because it would mean the killer was still out there somewhere.

Alex was suddenly aware that she'd walked quite far and was, quite possibly, lost. Glancing round, she also realised she was completely alone. With her heart hammering, she turned and hurried back towards the court, pulling her bag from her phone as she did to let Patrick know she was on her way home. Then—

Bang!

Someone was blocking her path. Panic flooded her and she opened her mouth to scream – but then she saw a familiar pair of eyes looking down at her.

'Samuel?'

He didn't reply and she took a step back, suddenly nervous.

'What are you doing here?' Her voice trembled.

'I was gonna ask you the same thing.' His voice was quiet.

She glanced down at the pavement where her boots were standing in a dirty puddle. His shoes were scuffed, one of the laces undone. She looked back up.

'I wanted to see how the trial went.'

He studied her like a bug under a microscope. She squirmed.

'For your book, right?' There was an edge to his voice that she couldn't decipher.

'Yes. That's right.' She hitched her bag further up on her shoulder and glanced round. She didn't know this man from Adam and now she was standing in a quiet street in the deepening dusk of late afternoon with him. No one knew where she was and she suddenly felt very scared, so when he moved towards her, she flinched.

He pulled away. 'Fuck, Ally, I'm not going to hurt you,' he said, his voice incredulous.

'Sorry.' Her throat was blocked.

He stepped back. 'I really didn't do it, you know. I didn't kill my father.' He cocked his head to one side. 'Do you think the jury got it wrong?'

'No!' The word fired out of her before she could consider it.

'Good.' He smiled. Then he turned as if he was about to walk away. As she watched him she realised she desperately didn't want him to go. She wanted to talk to him for longer. She wanted him to stay.

'Wait!' she said.

He turned slowly back to face her.

'I—' She faltered.

'What's wrong, Ally? Was there something you wanted to say to me?'

She thought about walking away from here, from this moment, and never seeing him again. She couldn't do it. Didn't want to.

'There's something...' The words wouldn't come.

'Yes?' He waited, arms crossed over his chest. She looked up at his face, wondering whether to say the next words she'd been planning to say.

'I'm your mother.'

As her words settled the world slowed, the light funnelled down into one tiny spot. She couldn't read Samuel's face, or the eyes that were fixed on her. Then his lips parted and he said words she hadn't expected in a million years.

'I know.'

15

Her blood turned to ice. 'You *know*?'

He nodded.

'But how? When?'

He looked around, bewildered, and suddenly she saw a snapshot of the lost little boy she'd glimpsed before, beneath the blustery exterior.

'Can we go and sit down? Maybe have a coffee?'

She felt torn. She needed to get home, to give Milo some attention, be the mother he needed more than ever. But she also needed to speak to Samuel.

'Come on.'

They walked side by side in the gloom, their footsteps tapping out a rhythm on the narrow pavement.

Samuel shoved his hands in his pockets and sunk his head into his collar, not giving Alex any sign that he wanted to make small talk, so she stayed silent. But inside her mind was screaming, desperate to hear what he had to say.

A cafe about five minutes away was still open and quiet. Alex told Samuel to sit down and went to order coffees. She needed a couple of minutes to percolate the news and work out how to react.

'Ta,' Samuel murmured as she placed an Americano in front of him. Steam rose from it and Alex hung her coat on the back of the chair opposite and sat down. Questions piled up in her throat.

'I'm sorry I didn't tell you before,' he said.

She nodded.

He peered at her over the top of his cup. 'When I saw your name on the visitor list in Pentonville I couldn't believe it. Ally Harding. Or Alex Bailey, as you were. It was the only reason I agreed to the visit.'

All that time, he'd known. How naïve she'd been. Why else would he have agreed to let her visit?

He sipped his coffee and replaced the mug slowly on the table. The cafe was emptying and the staff were clearing up around them. She ignored them.

'How long have you known about me?'

'Couple of years,' Samuel said. 'Mum told me your name years ago, but it was only when things got really shit with Dad a while back that I decided to try and find you. It was pretty easy.' He laughed. 'I had your address and number on a scrappy bit of paper in my pocket for months but I was never brave enough to actually ring you. I mean, it's not like I thought you'd want me back all of a sudden. You gave me away for a reason, right? God knows if I'd of contacted you if this hadn't happened.'

'But why didn't you say anything when I came to the prison? Why did you let me carry on with the facade of writing a book?'

He shrugged. 'I was happy to meet you I s'pose. Didn't wanna scare you off.' He gave a bitter laugh. 'Shame I was in the nick.'

Alex didn't know what to say. Samuel drained the rest of his coffee and stood abruptly.

'I'd best get off. Ta for the coffee.' He picked up his rucksack and was halfway to the door before she shouted, 'Wait! Where are you staying tonight?'

He turned slowly. 'With friends.'

'Are you sure?' He'd been in prison for the last few months, and living in a squat before that. She was also fairly certain his mother wouldn't welcome him back to the family home with open arms given that she'd been a witness for the prosecution. She couldn't bear the thought of him being alone.

'I'm fine. Really. You don't need to worry about me.'

And before she could say anything else, he walked away from her.

16

Alex had missed a period. In fact, she'd missed two.

At first, she'd put it down to stress. She hadn't been eating properly, and her stress levels were through the roof. But now the trial was over she realised how long it had been since her last period.

She should have been happy, excited about the prospect that she could be pregnant, however small the likelihood. After all, it was what Patrick had wanted – what they'd *both* wanted – so desperately for the past eight years or so.

Except that she couldn't think of a worse possible time to have a baby than right now.

She peed on a stick and while she waited she

thought about how things had been since the day of Samuel's trial...

When she got home the night after Samuel had been freed, she was pumped full of adrenaline. But when she found Patrick sitting at the kitchen table with his arms folded, his face like thunder, she deflated in an instant.

'Good day at work?' he snarled as Alex stopped in her tracks, her heart thumping.

'Yes, fine thanks.' She dumped her bag on a chair. He just nodded.

'Patrick? What's going on?'

'Where the fuck have you been?'

Her stomach clenched.

'Work. Why?'

He smacked his fist on the table and she jumped in surprise. Patrick rarely lost his temper but it frightened her when he did because it was like he was taken over by another person. 'Are you having an affair? Is that what this is all about?'

'What? No!'

'Then I'll ask you again. Where have you been? And don't say work because when all this shit was going on with Milo this afternoon I rang the office and I know you weren't there.' He laughed mirthlessly and held his hand up. 'Although don't worry, Caitlin hasn't ratted you out. She's loyal.' He looked up at her, waiting for an answer.

What could she tell him? The truth?

'I've been in court.'

He looked as though he'd been slapped. 'What do you mean, court? What for?'

She sat down before her legs gave way.

'I went to watch a murder trial.' She cleared her throat, trying to unblock the words. 'Someone on trial for killing their father.'

She watched Patrick's face as he tried to work out what she was telling him. 'That story Janie and Pete were talking about last week? The kid who murdered his dad?'

She nodded. 'Except he was found not guilty.'

'But why?'

Silence hummed. Her body tensed, ready for impact.

'Because he's my son.'

Patrick stared. And then he laughed, a sharp bark. He must have noticed her expression because he stopped immediately. 'You're fucking kidding me, right?'

She shook her head.

'What—' He rubbed his face. 'What do you mean, he's your son?'

So, haltingly, she explained it all to him. About Samuel, about giving him away, and about how she'd tried so hard to parcel it away in her mind and tell herself he had never been a part of her life at all. She didn't know how he was going to react and when she finished she held her breath for several seconds.

'Why have you never told me any of this before? I didn't think we had any secrets.'

'I– I know. I'm so sorry. I've never told anyone.'

'I'm not just anyone though, am I?' His voice sounded like shards of glass and Alex was still waiting for the explosion.

Instead, though, as she explained to Patrick how scared she was that Samuel's violence had come from her father, through her; about the visits to prison, and watching the trial unfold, she realised he wasn't angry. He looked like a broken man.

'The thing is, I believe him, Patrick. I know he didn't do it,' she said gently.

An expression Alex couldn't read flashed across Patrick's face, then cleared almost instantly. 'I can't believe this, Alex.'

'I'm sorry.' It was woefully inadequate but what else could she say?

He looked up at her and his expression was so

pained it broke her heart. 'I suppose it does explain one thing though.'

'What's that?'

'Why you're so paranoid about Milo being evil.'

She nodded sadly. 'I was worried about Milo way before I found out about Samuel, but you're right. When I was at the prison, I kept imagining it being Milo in there instead of Samuel. I felt sick.' She looked up at him, realisation dawning. 'Oh God, how is Milo, you haven't told me what happened at school today.' How could it have slipped her mind?

'It's fine,' Patrick snapped. 'I've sorted it. He hit someone.'

'Again?'

'The other person started it, according to Milo. Kept saying things about – well, about us. You, specifically. He's been given another warning and will be in isolation for a few days. It could have been worse.'

She felt bruised, raw. 'Why is he doing this?'

Unexpectedly, Patrick reached for her hands then. She took his, grateful for even the smallest flicker of tenderness.

'He's not a bad kid, Ally. He's just a teenager.'

'Did you get into fights when you were a teenager?'

'Some. Most kids did. And then they stopped and became respectable members of society. But it doesn't mean he has an evil gene, or whatever it is you think is going on here. You said yourself Samuel's been found not guilty. And you're not evil either. So you're wrong. There is no bad gene.'

It was those words which rang in her head as she snapped out of the memory and picked up the pregnancy test from the edge of the sink with shaking hands: *there is no bad gene*. She willed them to be true as she finally dared to look at the result.

And there it was.

Two blue lines.

She stood, gripped the edge of the basin and stared at her reflection in the mirror above the sink. She looked crazy. Her cheeks were hollow, dark circles rimmed her eyes, and her hair stuck out like it hadn't been brushed for a week.

How had this happened? After all the months of trying to get pregnant, then, later, the failed IVF treatments, all the prodding and poking and injecting and undignified leg-spreading, she had, finally, fallen pregnant naturally after all. Calculating how many weeks she must be, Alex realised that she and Patrick hadn't slept together for at least six weeks. She looked down at her belly, which was utterly flat, and wondered if there was a mistake.

But she knew there wasn't. This was happening. And now she had to decide what to do.

* * *

Alex waited a couple of days to let the news sink in before telling Patrick about the baby. If she was being completely honest, she needed time to decide whether she was going to tell him at all. With everything that had happened with Samuel, plus the ongoing problems with Milo, she still wasn't convinced bringing another child into the world was a good idea.

But of course, she had to tell him eventually. She knew that. This was all he'd wanted for his whole life. Currently her marriage felt like it was teetering on a precipice. Maybe this could be what brought it back from the edge.

'Patrick, we need to talk,' she said. He was shaving and looked at her in the mirror above the sink, hand hovering, face full of foam.

'Right now?'

She nodded.

'Just give me a minute to finish here.'

She waited for him on the bed and when he emerged from the bathroom there was a tight band of worry across his forehead.

'Is this about Samuel?' he said, wiping his chin with a hand towel. 'Because I thought we'd agreed I'm not ready to talk about it yet.'

She shook her head.

'Sit down a minute. Please.'

He sat cautiously. She took his hand and threaded her fingers through his, gripping tightly. He looked surprised.

'Al, you're worrying me now. Has something happened?'

She tried for a smile but wasn't sure she pulled it off.

'I'm pregnant.'

Patrick's face drained of colour.

'Patrick?' She peered at him, and a seed of doubt began to unfurl. Was he angry? 'Aren't you going to say something?'

And then his stony face transformed, and a smile split it into two, lighting him up from the inside.

'You're not winding me up?'

'Would I do that about something so important?'

Seconds passed, then he launched himself at her so that she tipped backwards and had to steady herself against the pillow. He was saying something, but his mouth was buried in her neck, and she couldn't make out a word. Gently pushing him away, she sat back up.

He looked like an excited little boy. She wished her feelings about it were as pure as his.

'This is amazing, but – how many weeks are you?'

'I'm not sure.'

'We haven't—' He reddened.

'I know, for at least six weeks.' She looked down at her belly. 'I'm not showing yet. But after last time, I'm a bit nervous...'

'It will be okay this time. I can feel it in my bones.'

He rested his hand on her tummy, and she tried not to flinch. This meant the world to Patrick, as she'd known deep down that it would, no matter what else was going on. It was everything he had ever wanted, everything she'd ever wanted to give him.

So why did she feel as if her world was ending?

17

After weeks of not eating properly, Alex had promised Patrick she'd look after herself. The first step was making an appointment to see her GP and book a scan. In the meantime, she put her head down and got on with work, determined to make up for all the time she'd taken off. Caitlin seemed glad to have her back, but there was a distance to her, a detached coolness that had never been there before.

'Have I done something to upset you?' Alex said as Caitlin placed a steaming hot cup of tea in front of her and sat back down. She hadn't told Caitlin about the baby yet – she was waiting until after she'd seen the doctor to make sure everything was all right – so she'd simply dropped the coffee and moved to tea and hoped Caitlin wouldn't suspect.

'No, of course not,' Caitlin said. But her eyes didn't leave her screen, and she rubbed her hand across her nose. A telltale sign.

Alex got up and walked over to her desk and perched on the end. Caitlin stopped typing and slowly looked up.

'What are you doing?'

'I know there's something wrong. Is it about the time I took off? I only did it because you said you were okay with it.'

Caitlin shook her head. 'No, it's fine.' She carried on typing, but Alex wasn't about to let her get away with that. She moved the keyboard away so Caitlin was forced to stop.

'Hey!'

'Tell me what's going on and you can have it back.'

Caitlin stared at her for a few seconds as though deciding whether to say what was on her mind. Then she crumbled.

'It's Archie.'

'What's he done?' Alex thought back to the trouble Archie had been in a few years before and wondered whether he'd started playing up again. 'Do you need me to speak to him again?'

But Caitlin shook her head and couldn't meet her eye. 'I've told Archie I don't want him hanging round with Milo for a while.'

Ice dripped down Alex's spine. Their boys had been best friends since they were three. When Archie was going through his troublesome patch a few years ago, Alex had been there for him. For Caitlin. They'd worked it out together.

And this was how she repaid her?

'You're kidding, right?' Alex's voice was knife-sharp.

Caitlin looked at her, defiant. 'I'm deadly serious.'

Alex moved away quickly and sat back behind her desk. Her breath felt tight.

'I don't want this to come between us.' Caitlin's voice was reedy and Alex felt anger flare in her chest.

'I think it already has, don't you?'

'But, Alex—'

Alex stood abruptly. 'No. You don't need to explain. You think Milo's leading your precious son astray.' She picked up her bag and was about to walk away.

'You must understand,' Caitlin said, and Alex stopped in her tracks.

'What, that even though Milo and I helped Archie when he was in trouble – that I let him have a key to our house, welcomed him like a second son – you won't do the same for Milo?'

'It's not the same though, is it? You said it yourself that what Archie did back then was small stuff. Fights, skiving school. Not trouble with the police. And he was only eleven. But next year is their GCSE year and I can't have Archie distracted, I just can't. It's too important.' She hung her head. 'I'm sorry, Alex.'

The silence hung in the air for a moment, thick with all the things left unsaid.

'I'll make sure Milo stays away from him then.'

Then she left the office, her whole body shaking with fury.

* * *

Alex needed to calm down. She marched down to the river which meandered through the town and along the riverside path. She kept her eyes fixed straight ahead and focused on her breathing, trying to get her heart rate to slow and her mind to think.

At first, the rage burned inside her, the red-hot flames fuelling her. But the further she walked, the more she felt the fire cool. By the time she reached the bridge it was almost extinguished, and she stopped and leaned her elbows on the railings, staring down at the boats idling by.

Her friendship with Caitlin had always been so strong, nothing and no one could come between them. But Alex was also aware that recently she hadn't behaved very well, had taken Caitlin for granted, shut her out.

So she couldn't blame her for this, really. Yes, she and Milo had been there to help Archie when he'd been in trouble. But Caitlin was right. This was different, and not just because it was an important year at school.

The trouble Milo was in *was* different. More serious. More worrying.

More like Samuel?

No.

Her heart clenched at the thought of her eldest son. Because she knew it had to be the end of the road for their fledgling relationship. She'd promised Patrick.

After telling Patrick about the baby, he'd been more attentive than ever. They talked and agreed to concentrate on this baby and on getting Milo sorted. Nothing else. Somewhere along the way, Alex had agreed to forget about Samuel, including not talking about him, and not letting him come between them any more than he already had.

There had been no choice, when it came down to it.

After months of neglecting her marriage, which had always been her fortress against the world, it was in danger of irreparable collapse. From the outside it might look the same as ever, but inside, the cracks that had opened up over the years had split so wide that the walls could tumble down at any minute. If she didn't do something to fix it, she'd lose it forever. And then where would she be?

She needed to do everything she could to protect herself.

Head down, she walked into town. The wind had got up and the gathering dark clouds threatened rain. She shivered and pulled her coat tighter.

She'd treat herself to a decent lunch. She needed to start eating properly, and she knew Patrick would approve. As she neared her favourite cafe a few spots of rain had begun to patter onto the pavement and she picked up her pace.

Beside her, she vaguely noticed a figure huddled in the doorway of an empty shop. She glanced over – and stopped dead in her tracks.

'Samuel?'

She walked over and he looked up then quickly away, his face flaming.

'Samuel, what on earth are you doing here?'

'Nothing.'

She crouched beside him so their faces were level. He was grey and gaunt, his previously clipped hair straggly, the beginnings of a beard covering his jaw. She took in his sleeping bag, already damp and muddy at one end, and the piles of random items strewn around where he sat.

'How long have you been sleeping like this?'

He shrugged. 'Not long.'

Realisation dropped through her mind like a clear, smooth pebble. 'Have you been here since the trial?' That was a few weeks ago, and she hated the thought that he'd been sleeping rough since then. His appearance suggested it was likely.

He wouldn't look her in the eye. She knelt on a piece of cardboard that poked out from beneath his sleeping bag. There was a strong odour of tobacco and damp.

'Why didn't you tell me you had nowhere to go when I asked?'

He shrugged. 'Didn't want you to worry.'

'But I could have helped you.'

'S'fine. I'm back at the squat on Belvedere most nights.'

Her heart hurt at the thought of him sleeping on the streets or among dangerous people in the squat in a dodgy part of town. No matter what else had happened, he didn't deserve this.

An image of Milo flashed into her head. 'You can't stay here. Let me help you.'

His face was hard. 'How do you think you're gonna do that?'

Her legs were starting to scream so she sat down properly on the piece of cardboard. Rain was spitting harder now but she ignored it. She pulled out her phone.

'I'll ring a hostel. Pay for a few nights.'

He stared at her. She squirmed under his gaze. 'What?'

'Nothing. Just – they won't have anyfink. They never do.'

'There must be somewhere,' she said, frantically jabbing 'homeless hostels' into the search bar. A list of places she'd never even heard of came up. She turned the phone to face Samuel. 'Here, see? There are loads of places.'

He didn't even glance at the screen. 'Up to you.'

She had to at least try. For the next twenty minutes, she sat by Samuel, working her way down the list of hostels as the rain grew heavier and shoppers walked by them, barely noticing them. Each time she got the same response – 'we're very sorry but we're full.'

'Told ya.' Samuel was resigned.

But Alex couldn't let it go. 'A hotel then. Let me pay for a hotel.'

'I don't need your charity.'

She flinched. He was her son, not some charity case.

'Let me try one more thing. Please?'

She took his silence as a yes and rang the B&B round the corner from her office. A couple of minutes later, she ended the call.

'They have a room.'

'Right. Well. Ta.'

She pushed herself up, stood over him. 'Let me help you.' She stuck her hand out. He stood too, picked up his battered rucksack and his sleeping bag. She took the bag from him.

'Follow me.'

They walked the fifteen minutes back in the direction of her office. As they arrived at the B&B, she stopped. 'I'm going to pay for a week, then I'll come

and find you, see if we can find a more permanent so-
lution. All right?'

'You don't have to do this, you know. You don't owe
me anything.'

Oh but I do, my boy.

'I know,' she said. 'But I want to.'

Ten minutes later Samuel was safely installed in a
room, and the owner of the B&B had agreed to wash
his clothes for an extra payment.

'Thank you for this,' she said. 'I really appreciate
it.'

'If there's any trouble, he'll be out though, whether
you've paid or not. Understood?'

'Understood.' She dug in her bag and pulled a
couple of twenty-pound notes from her bag. 'Will you
give him this for me? I don't want him to refuse it.'

The owner gave her a look as she took the money
from her hands. 'Sure.'

As she walked away, a pebble of guilt lodged in
Alex's belly.

Should she have asked Samuel to come and stay
with her? It's not like they didn't have the space.

But how could she? Bringing him into their lives
had already put everything she'd worked so hard for
at risk – her marriage, her relationship with Milo.

Bringing him into her home as well was surely a step too far.

Samuel might be her son by blood, but really, she knew nothing about him other than what he'd chosen to tell her – and none of that painted him in a great light. Even just by making herself a part of his life she could be putting herself at risk: there was no way she could put the rest of her family – including her unborn baby – in danger too.

18

Patrick knew there was something wrong, but there was no way Alex could tell him about Samuel after the promises she'd made, so she gave him the only thing she could.

'Caitlin said *what*?' he said, and for once Alex was grateful Patrick was as outraged as she was.

'She says he's a bad influence, and that it's an important year.'

'She's got a nerve after everything you did for Archie.'

She slid him a glance. 'That's what I told her. But she said this was different.'

'Fuck's sake. I'm so sorry.' He slipped his arm

round her shoulders and flicked through the TV channels mindlessly.

'Patrick, can you stop doing that?' Alex snatched the remote from his hands.

'Sorry.' He rubbed his face. 'God, I'm so tired. I hardly slept last night.' He reached his hand out and stroked her belly as he had done so many times since she'd told him the news. This baby was the last thing on her mind but it seemed to be all Patrick could think about, and he seemed to have softened towards her since she'd told him about it.

She wriggled away from him. 'He's not that bad, is he? Milo, I mean.'

'He's not, love. I keep telling you that. He's just a confused kid.'

She considered for a minute. 'Do you think it's because I've worked so hard these last few years?'

'What do you mean?'

'Well, you read about it all the time don't you, kids going off the rails because they want their parents' attention. What if that's what this is all about, and it's my fault?'

'Alex, stop doing that.'

'Doing what?'

'Blaming yourself. It's as if you're determined to prove that having children with issues is all down to you. Of course it isn't. A lot of kids get into trouble. Most of them sort themselves out. God, I was a right little shit at fifteen, caused my parents all kinds of stress.'

'You didn't get into fights though.'

'Not often. But everyone's different.'

She let out a long breath. 'The thing is though, recently I've started to see my dad in him. I see the expression my father used to have on his face when the rage came, like a darkness descended, and then he's a stranger. My dad was like that and I worry Sam—' She broke off when she saw Patrick's face cloud over at the mention of Samuel's name. 'So you don't think Caitlin is right?'

'About Milo being a bad influence?'

She nodded.

'I don't know. But you can't let it come between you.'

'How can I not?'

'Just don't. You need your friends close. Always.'

She stared at him for a moment, wondering what he meant. Then he turned away, picked up the remote control again, and switched the TV back up.

* * *

Alex couldn't get the memory of Samuel sleeping rough out of her head. She saw it when she was in the shower, when she was cooking or watching TV and, worst of all, she saw it when she lay in bed at night staring up at the ceiling, her mind refusing to let her sleep. That was when images of her eldest son lying battered and beaten – or worse – filled her mind, torturing her until she had to get up and go downstairs and make a cup of tea and try to think about something else.

She was exhausted, her throat clogged with guilt.

She couldn't go on like this.

She was going to see Samuel.

She'd paid for the B&B for a few more days but she didn't know whether he'd actually still be there.

'I've no idea if he's in but you can go and knock if ya want,' the fierce landlady barked.

'Thanks,' Alex mumbled. She ran up the two flights of stairs and hovered outside Samuel's door. Now she was here she felt less sure of herself. Samuel was a grown man and, as Patrick had pointed out, not her responsibility. She pictured Patrick's face when she'd almost mentioned Samuel accidentally the other night, and knew how hurt and angry he'd be if he had any idea she was here.

No, she'd go home and—

'Alex?'

Her heart leapt into her throat as she turned. There was Samuel, right behind her, two steps down. 'Been to get some food.' He indicated the Tesco carrier bag swinging from his hand. 'You all right?'

'Yes. I—' Her hands fidgeted with the belt of her coat. 'I'm sorry, I probably shouldn't have come.' She moved towards the stairs but Samuel blocked her way.

'What do you want, Alex?'

He filled the stairwell, and she felt a sudden dart of fear. Nobody knew she was here. She glanced over his shoulder for signs the landlady was still in the vicinity, but the hallway was empty. Her pulse thumped through her body.

'Can we talk?' Her voice wobbled.

He hesitated a moment and she held her breath.

'Sure.' He stepped past her and unlocked the door, her heart hammering against her ribcage at his proximity. She followed him inside and sat on the battered armchair in the corner then, while Samuel made them both tea, she took in the tiny room: a single bed with a plain purple bedspread was butted against the back wall, faded pink curtains hung at the window and ghostly shadows of long-forgotten paintings had left their reminders on the faded wall opposite. She wondered how thin the walls were, whether anyone would hear her if she screamed.

'Here.' She jumped as Samuel handed her a mug. God, why was she so on edge?

'Thanks.' She held her tea with shaking hands as Samuel took a seat on the bed opposite her. It creaked loudly.

'So, what d'ya want to talk about?' He was clean-shaven now and it made him look younger, softer than before. She felt the knot in her stomach begin to loosen. She was fine. Samuel was fine. There was nothing to worry about.

'I want to ask you something,' she said.

He took a sip from his mug. 'Go on.'

A blast of wind made the window rattle in its frame.

'I can't stop thinking about you sleeping on the street.'

'I'm used to it.'

'Maybe. But it's keeping me awake at night and I —' She what? What was it she wanted? It slipped into her mind like a brush of silk, smooth, clean, and suddenly she was absolutely certain of it, despite previous reservations. 'I wanted to ask you to stay for a while. With me.'

Samuel's eyebrows lifted. 'Seriously?'

'Yes, but—' She took a deep breath. 'The thing is, Patrick, my husband, didn't know about you, before. That you existed, I mean. But now he does and he's – well, he's asked me not to have any more to do with you.'

'Don't blame him.'

'That's just it, you see. I agreed, to keep the peace. But I've changed my mind. I do want to see you. To help you.'

'I don't need help, I told ya. I'm good. So there's no need to upset *Patrick*. Not for me.'

Alex rubbed her face with her spare hand then looked back up. 'I'm not explaining this very well. It's not just about wanting to help you. It's about wanting to get to know you. If you want to, that is.'

Samuel didn't move or respond and Alex wondered whether she'd made a terrible mistake. She felt paralysed as she waited for him to say something. Anything.

'All right.'

'Oh. Good. I mean, great.' She put the mug down on the carpet by her feet and leaned forward. 'There is something else too. Something that could help us both.'

He nodded to indicate she should continue.

'I want to try and work out who killed Scott.'

Samuel looked surprised. 'What for? How's that gonna help?'

Alex leaned further forward. 'Listen, we know you didn't do it. But the problem is Patrick doesn't. He doesn't know you at all, and in his mind, you're a threat to us. And to Milo.' She paused. 'Your brother.'

She tried to read his reaction to finding out she had another son – his half-brother – but his face was an unreadable mask so she ploughed on. 'I just thought if we could work out who might have done it, it could help. That it might convince Patrick to let you stay.' Now she'd said it out loud it sounded mad. Samuel agreed.

'You think the police are gonna listen to a few crackpot theories from us?' He gave a bitter laugh. 'You're more naïve than I thought.'

Alex stared down at the murky surface of her tea. 'I know it sounds crazy. But even if the police aren't interested, I just thought if we can show Patrick that there are plenty of other people who could have done this, he might accept that you didn't and let you... you know, be part of our lives.'

She was clutching at straws, she knew. Samuel ran his tongue over his teeth, rubbed his cheek. Then he shrugged. 'Worth a shot, I s'pose. But I don't know what I can tell ya that I ain't already.'

'Why don't we start by going over some of the other people who might have had beef with your dad.'

Samuel barked a laugh. 'God, there were loads of 'em. Some right dodgy people hanging round the house night and day. Dealers, *associates*. Could've been any one of them. He pissed off a lot of people, my father.'

Alex's mind flashed to Caitlin and Archie.

'Can you think of anyone in particular? Someone who stands out in your mind?'

Samuel wrinkled his nose. 'Not really. There were a few that used to hang round, smoking, drinking all day an' that.' He shrugged. 'Most of the time I tried not to get involved.'

Alex sighed. She tried a different tack.

'What about that day? The day you found your dad.'

'What about it?'

'I just wondered—' She broke off, uncertain. 'I don't know. Was there anything you noticed? Anything you've thought of, since, that might be relevant?'

Samuel fixed her with a look. 'Alex, I had eight fucking months in a prison cell, I've had loads of time to go over that day. Do you really think there ain't a single second of it I haven't picked apart, looking for summat, or tried to work out if there's anyone who can confirm I wasn't at the house before I said I was?'

Alex flushed. 'I know. I just mean…'

What did she mean? What was she trying to achieve? She drained her drink and was about to leave when Samuel spoke.

'I did tell the police one thing, but they didn't take no notice.'

'Go on.' She sat back in the chair, crossed her legs.

'I thought it looked like there'd been a fight in the room before I got there cos one of the chairs was upside down and a glass was smashed on the carpet.' He shrugged. 'But the place was always a shitheap so they probably just thought it always looked like that.' He placed his palms together. 'But that's all I could think of, ever.'

Alex turned it over in her mind. Could it be something? She didn't know. But it was clear that Scott had a lot of potential enemies, and maybe that would be enough to prove to Patrick that Samuel wasn't a threat. To her, to their family, or to the baby growing inside her.

It had to be worth a go.

19

Patrick's reaction when she tentatively introduced the idea of helping Samuel told Alex everything she needed to know.

'You're joking. Right?'

She smiled uncertainly. 'Sort of.'

'What do you mean, sort of? You don't seriously feel responsible for that piece of shit, do you?' He spat the word like it was poison.

'Don't talk about him like that, Patrick. He's my son.'

Patrick turned puce, his face set like granite, and she felt a frisson of fear.

'And so is Milo. *He* should be your priority, Alex.

And our baby.' His voice shook. 'You *promised* me you'd forget about Samuel, that he was out of your life for good.' He moved so close she could make out the veins in his pupils. A beat of unease thumped in the pit of her belly.

She'd rarely seen Patrick this angry before, and never with her. In fact, until recently, the last time she'd seen him properly angry had been at a kids' football match a few years ago when Patrick thought he'd heard one of the other parents saying something demeaning about Milo. Instead of brushing it off like he normally would, that day his anger had ignited like a lit match to dry wood and he'd been on the verge of punching someone. He would have done, had Alex not stepped in and swiftly taken him away from the situation, given him space for his fury to abate. But she'd never forgotten the look on his face when the red mist had descended, and always hoped she'd never see it directed at her.

Until now, she never had.

'He's got no one else, Patrick,' she said, her voice small.

'Well, he should have fucking *thought* about that before he killed his father then, shouldn't he?' He smashed his palm against the bedroom door and Alex recoiled.

'He didn't kill him, Patrick, you know that.' Her voice shook. 'He was found not guilty.'

'Not guilty isn't the same thing as innocent, though, is it? And you seem to have conveniently forgotten that this is murder we're talking about, Alex. Not some petty crime. *Murder*.'

There was such venom in his voice Alex found herself taking a step away from him.

But then, as if all the fight had suddenly drained from his body, Patrick let out a long, low sigh. 'But if there's even the tiniest chance that he's guilty, are you actually prepared to put us all at risk to find out?'

Alex looked down at the floor and shook her head miserably. 'I don't know, Patrick. I can't just give up on him.'

Patrick smacked the door again, but more softly this time, as though he just needed to get rid of the last remaining traces of his anger.

'I know you'll do whatever the hell you want, Alex. But just don't expect me and Milo to hang around and pick up the pieces. If you do this, you're on your own.'

Then he walked out, leaving her standing there, shaking.

* * *

Once she'd calmed down, Patrick's words played on her mind throughout the rest of the afternoon and into the following day. *Not guilty isn't the same thing as innocent, though, is it?*

Was he right? Was she really being naïve, putting her family at risk out of some misguided sense of loyalty?

She didn't know which way was up any more.

Over the next couple of weeks, she tried not to think about it. Tried to put Samuel out of her mind and focus on Milo, Patrick and the baby, and forget about the fury she'd seen in Patrick's eyes when she'd mentioned Samuel. She wished she could talk to Caitlin about it – she would know what to do. But for the first time since they'd met, that was out of the question.

She needed to mend some bridges. Samuel would understand. He'd told her himself she was making a mistake, bothering with him.

But then everything changed.

It was early one morning and she was taking the long route to work to give her time to clear her head. Things between her and Caitlin were strained and the atmosphere in the office was frosty, at best. She knew they'd have to sort it out sooner or later but she wasn't sure she was quite ready to forgive her best friend just yet.

She was turning the corner onto the high street when something caught her eye. A figure, huddled in a doorway, wrapped in a sleeping bag that had probably once been blue but was now a dirty dark grey. She tried not to look, told herself it wouldn't be Samuel, not this time. He'd assured her he had somewhere to go once he left the B&B, that he didn't need her help.

But she couldn't help herself. She looked anyway.

Then the man turned to face her and her legs went weak.

'Samuel?'

As she walked towards him he pulled his sleeping bag up round his chin and turned away. But nothing could disguise the bruise that covered one side of his face, yellows and purples spreading like a stain across his cheek and up into his hairline.

'What happened to you?'

He stayed facing the wall.

'It's nuffink.'

'Samuel, half your face is black and blue, it's hardly nothing.' She crouched down, her back to the street.

He didn't reply.

'Samuel, listen. I'm sorry I didn't come back and find you. Patrick, he—' She stopped, unsure what to tell him. *Patrick doesn't want me to have anything to do with you ever again?* Samuel twisted his body further away as though he couldn't bear to even look at her, or for her to look at him.

'Are you hurt anywhere else?' she said gently.

He didn't turn round but his shoulders lifted in a shrug. She reached out to touch his arm but he flinched and pulled it away. Tears gathered behind her eyes and she swiped at them roughly. This was about Samuel, not her.

She was desperate to help him, but if he refused to even speak to her, what more could she do?

She stood, her shadow falling across Samuel's horizontal form.

'I've got to get to work now, but if I come back later will you at least let me get you something to eat? We can talk?'

Nothing.

With a heavy heart she turned and walked away, towards the office. Her head felt like an explosion of conflicting thoughts, all firing in different directions.

She'd promised Patrick she'd forget about Samuel, that she wouldn't let him back into their lives. And he was right – she hardly knew Samuel, he could very well be dangerous, and she couldn't put the people she loved at risk.

On the other hand, it was clear that Samuel was hurt, possibly badly, and it would almost certainly happen again. He had nothing and no one else. How could she just leave him at the mercy of the streets?

Her footsteps slowed until she was almost at a halt. She caught her reflection in a shop window and almost didn't recognise the woman staring back at her. Wild eyes, ghostly face. But there was a flash of something else there, something tugging at her mind. And then she caught it and she knew.

They were also Milo's eyes staring back at her.

And Samuel's.

He was her blood.

Swivelling on her heel she marched back to where she'd just left Samuel. He was still facing away from the street. She crouched down beside him.

'I'm not leaving you here,' she said. It wasn't clear whether he was even listening, but she hoped he was. 'I want to help you. More than I have. I...' She rubbed her face and rocked back on her heels. 'The offer's still there for you to come and stay with me. With us.' She waited, watching his prone body, hoping if she waited long enough, he'd respond.

Eventually, just as she was about to give up and leave again, he turned his head. The bruises were dark, as if they'd worsened in the last five minutes. Who had done this to him?

'Samuel, can you hear me?'

A tiny nod. She took it as encouragement.

'So... will you consider it?'

Slowly, he twisted himself round to face her. He was obviously in pain and it was clear it was more than his face that had been injured.

'Why?'

'Because—' She let out a long breath. 'Because you're my son.'

When it was clear he wasn't going to say anything else she stood again. The street was busier now, the sun was peeking through low-lying clouds and making the wet pavements shimmer.

'Let me get you something to eat. What would you like, a sandwich? Something hot maybe? A coffee?'

He looked up at her, squinting in a shaft of sunlight. 'I could eat a sausage roll?'

'Okay great, sausage roll it is.' She backed away, then turned and scurried to a nearby cafe and ordered a sausage roll and a coffee for Samuel and a mint tea for herself. As she waited for the drinks to be made she held her hand against her still-flat belly.

What the hell was she doing? She hadn't planned to ask Samuel to stay again, but when she'd seen him lying there, his face swollen and bruised, there really hadn't been any choice. Samuel didn't have anyone else: his family thought he was a murderer, and any friends he might once have had had run a mile after his arrest. There was no way she could abandon him again, no matter what damage it caused between her and Patrick. She could deal with that later, but this couldn't wait.

She hurried back to the spot where she'd left Samuel, praying he wouldn't have disappeared. When she saw he was still there, relief flooded her.

'Here you go.' She handed Samuel his drink and a paper bag and he slowly sat up, flinching with every movement. His left hand was curled into his side but she could see deep purple bruising and a greying piece of cloth wrapped round his fingers.

'Ta.'

'Who did this to you?' she said.

He shrugged. 'Don't matter. It happens.'

'To everyone? Or this just about you?'

He shrugged again. She said nothing else, just waited for him to eat his sausage roll. He devoured it in a few bites, as though he hadn't eaten for a week, then picked up the coffee and held it to his face. He looked older somehow, haunted, and she fought the urge to reach out and give him a hug.

'I mean it, you know,' she said, as he took a sip from his takeaway cup and watched her from under furrowed brow.

'About me staying with you?'

'Yes.'

He shook his head and grimaced in pain. 'I can't.'

'But you exactly can't stay here.'

'Why not? Lovely accommodation, great company...' he trailed off, the joke lost.

'Please, Samuel.'

He looked away, down at the floor. 'Can I ask you summat?' His voice was so quiet she had to lean forward to hear him above the chatter from the street behind her.

'Of course.'

'Do you trust me?'

'What?'

'If I'm going to even think about coming to stay with you then I need to know you trust me. I've had a lifetime of people thinking I'm scum. I can't do it again.'

'I don't think you're scum. I never would.'

'But your husband does?'

She shook her head. 'He doesn't know you.'

He nodded. 'So you do trust me?'

Did she? Who knew. She didn't really know him either. But she did want to help him.

'Of course I trust you.'

He nodded again then, finally, he looked up, his eyes heavy. 'Then okay. If you're totally sure I ain't fucking up your life, I'll come.'

20

Patrick was getting dressed the following morning when Alex finally summoned up the courage to tell him what she'd done. Her whole body thrummed with fear as she waited for him to react.

'Aren't you going to say anything?' Her voice wobbled.

He pulled his T-shirt over his head and tugged it down, then stepped into his trousers and slowly buckled them up. He didn't look at her once, and Alex was beginning to think he was never going to speak to her again.

'What do you want me to say, Alex?' His words were pure ice, and fear trickled down her spine.

'I... hoped you might say you were all right with it.'

He turned away from her again, started putting his watch on. Feeling nausea rising in her throat, she perched on the edge of the bed.

Patrick's face, when he finally looked at her, was unrecognisable.

'I've told you my feelings on the subject, Alex. I'm not sure I could have been any clearer.'

'I—' She had no defence.

'I'm assuming you don't really expect me to tell you I think it's a great idea?'

She looked down at her hands. Her nails were chipped, skin coming away on her thumb. She brought it to her mouth and chewed on it until it began to sting.

'The thing is, Samuel hasn't done anything wrong.'

Patrick's eyes blazed. 'Really? How did you work that one out?'

'You know he didn't kill his dad. There were loads of other people it could have been. He told me—'

'Ohhhhh, here comes the truth.' Patrick's voice was loaded with sarcasm. 'Samuel has fed you a line about all the enemies Scott had, and you've swallowed it hook, line and sinker. Am I right?'

'No, that's not how it was. I just asked him who else could have done it, because someone must have. Scott had loads of enemies, Samuel reckons—'

'I don't give a *fuck* what he reckons, Alex.'

Alex recoiled as Patrick stepped closer to her, towering over her. Her eyes were level with his belly and she looked up at him.

'This isn't you, Patrick.'

He looked up sharply. 'What isn't me?'

'This – maliciousness.'

'Malicious? Are you kidding?'

She shook her head. 'No, I'm not.' She took a long, shuddery breath and stood, on more level ground now. 'The thing is, I saw Samuel yesterday. He'd been badly beaten up and had nowhere else to go. I'm not saying you have to welcome him with open arms, but a bit of compassion would be nice.'

'Compassion.'

'Yes.' She shook her head. 'You manage it for everyone else.'

The fight seemed to go out of Patrick then, and he slumped onto the bed beside her. He leaned his elbow on his knees and stared down at the carpet.

'You promised me, Alex. You promised you were going to forget about Samuel. Look to the future. To this baby.' He gestured at her belly. 'And now you've invited him to *stay*?' He let out a bitter laugh. 'Do you realise with your need to help this man, you're putting all of us in danger?'

'But I've told you, Samuel's not dangerous.'

'Isn't he? How do you really know that?' He stood again, abruptly. 'This is your decision to bring him here, Alex. Your decision to bring this *situation* into our lives. If you can't see how stupid you're being then I don't know what else to say to you. So, you do what you want, but remember that if anything happens, it's on your head.'

Before she could reply he'd left the room.

* * *

She couldn't get Patrick's words out of her head.

You're putting all of us in danger.

If anything happens, it's on your head.

Fear lodged in her throat like a stone. She couldn't bear the thought of putting any of them in danger, especially Milo. Was she being totally naïve?

But it didn't matter. It was too late now. Because although Samuel was back at the B&B for now, he was coming to live with them in two days' time.

She still needed to tell Milo the news. But what the hell was she going to say? 'Hello, Milo, how was your day? Oh and by the way you've got a brother I've never told you about and he's moving in with us.'

What was she doing?

Milo was playing on his Xbox when Alex went to find him, lost in a virtual world. 'Can we talk, love?' she said, pushing his bedroom door closed behind her. He didn't look up or reply so she sat on the end of his bed and waited. Eventually, he looked round. 'What?'

'Can you pause that for a minute?'

'I'm in the middle of a game.'

'This is important.'

'So's this.'

'Please, Milo.' Alex's voice was harsher than she'd intended but it worked. He put the controller down and spun his chair round to face her.

'What?' he asked again.

'I need to tell you something and I don't know how you're going to take it.'

He didn't reply. Alex swallowed.

'The thing is, years ago, way before you were born, I had a baby. A little boy.' A frown creased Milo's forehead, the only sign he was actually listening. She ploughed on. 'I was very young and someone convinced me that my little boy would be better off being brought up by someone else so... I gave him away.' The words felt thick on her tongue.

Milo stared at her from beneath his lowered eyebrows, reminding her of Samuel who had given her the exact same look.

'I haven't told anyone about it because – well, because it was too painful.'

'So why are you telling me now?' Milo asked.

Alex swallowed. 'Because I've found him again. And the thing is, he's got nowhere else to go so I've asked him to come and stay with us for a while.'

The silence hung in the air, heavy. Alex felt like she couldn't get enough air into her lungs. She'd been prepared for Milo to shout, to stomp around. She hadn't expected this stony silence. Then he shrugged and swung back to face his game. 'Fine.'

'Fine?'

'Yep.'

'Is that all you have to say? Don't you have any questions? Don't you want to know anything about him?'

'Not really.'

'For God's sake, Milo, please.'

He threw the controller on the floor and swung round again. The look in his eyes scared her. He looked empty. 'So I've got a half-brother I've never met and you've decided to ask him to come and stay with us. What do you want me to do about it?'

'I just wanted to make sure you were all right with it.' The words sounded weak even to her ears.

'I said I was fine. I couldn't really give a shit.'

Alex didn't know what to say. She'd have preferred histrionics, endless questions. Anything but indifference. She stood, brushed imaginary crumbs from her trousers. 'Well, he'll be moving in the day after tomorrow. I can't wait for you to meet him.'

Milo didn't acknowledge her, or even flick his eyes away from the screen. She let herself out and closed his door quietly. She'd succeeded in alienating her husband and her son with the decisions she'd made.

She just hoped she wouldn't live to regret it.

* * *

Alex closed the front door behind her and listened to the silence of the house. Milo was at school and Patrick had made himself scarce, which she was glad about.

'Let me show you where you'll be staying,' she said, taking Samuel's battered rucksack and heading towards the kitchen. They had a small room at the back of the house that had previously been her office. It had been full of junk but she'd cleared as much as she could and made up the sofa-bed.

'Here you go,' she said, opening the door. 'It's not much but I'm afraid Patrick works in the spare bedroom.'

Samuel stepped inside.

Alex hovered for a moment. She felt so nervous in this man's presence. Would she ever start to relax around him, or would he always make her feel on edge?

'The bathroom's here if you want to freshen up, otherwise, well, let me know when you're settled and I'll show you where everything else is.'

He nodded and she turned to leave.

'I know this a lot for you,' he said. 'For your family. But you don't know what it means to have someone who cares enough to do this for me.'

The words were unexpected and she didn't know what to say, so she just gave a slight nod.

'Make yourself at home.'

She returned to the kitchen and sat at the table, head in her hands, and let out a long, exhausted breath. Ever since she'd picked Samuel up she'd had a sense of dread hanging over her like a cartoon dark cloud. What the hell had she done, inviting him to stay? Patrick was furious, Milo barely speaking to her, as usual. Not to mention Patrick's words that kept churning over in her mind: *You're putting all of us in danger.*

He was right that she barely knew this man she'd invited to live in her home. But then again, just because they didn't know who'd killed Scott, that still didn't mean Samuel had done it. Did it?

'Mind if I sit here?'

Alex was so lost in her thoughts she jumped, and looked up to see Samuel waiting for her to reply.

'Sure.'

'Sorry, didn't mean to scare you.' He pulled out a chair opposite her and sat down stiffly, his ribs clearly giving him some pain.

'Sorry, I'm just a bit jittery.' He'd showered and changed and looked much brighter, less like a vagrant than he had before despite the bruising on his face turning from purple to a sickly shade of yellow. His left hand was still bandaged but clean now, at least. She smiled at him. 'Everything okay?'

'Great, ta.'

'Need anything?'

'I couldn't have summat to eat, could I? I'm starving.'

'Yes, of course.' How could she not have thought to ask? 'Shall I make us both something? I could do with some lunch too.'

'Thanks.'

She stood and started pulling things out of cupboards and the fridge. She felt unhinged, slightly hysterical. Tension rippled through her body. She needed to calm her nerves. This wasn't doing anyone any good, least of all the baby growing inside her.

'Can I help?' Samuel appeared beside her and she flinched away from him.

'Sorry. I'm just...' Just what? Afraid of her own son? She rubbed her face. 'I'm just tired. It's been a tough few days.'

'Cos of me?'

'Partly.' She sighed. 'It's not your fault though. None of it is. I—' She dropped the knife she'd been using to chop the tomatoes. Tears fell freely and she almost threw herself into her chair before her legs gave out completely. Samuel moved behind her and anxiety thumped low in her belly.

The front door slammed and they both looked up guiltily as Patrick appeared in the kitchen doorway. His face was a mask. 'You're here then.'

'I am.' Samuel lifted his chin. 'Don't worry, I won't stay long.'

'Oh, I'm not worried.' Alex hated the scorn in Patrick's voice. These last few days she'd seen a side to her husband that she didn't like all that much.

'I'm just making us something to eat, want to join us?' she said. Patrick slowly turned to look at her. His body hummed with tension. 'No thanks, I've eaten.' He turned and left the room, then she heard him running up the stairs before his office door slammed.

Alex's face burned with shame at his rudeness. 'I'm sorry,' she said. 'He'll come round.'

Samuel shook his head. 'It's fine. I get it. I wouldn't want me here either, if I was him.' He shrugged. 'I should probably just go.' He turned to walk towards his room.

'No, don't!' He spun round, a question on his face. 'Please, Samuel. Please stay.' She sounded desperate.

'I don't want to cause no problems.' He nodded his head towards the doorway where Patrick had just been standing. 'The guy clearly ain't happy about me being here.'

'It's fine. I'll talk to him again.'

The air thrummed, then he gave a small nod. 'Okay. But if he's still this angry in a couple of days, I'm out of here. Okay?'

She nodded. 'Understood.' She turned back to the counter and picked up the knife again, and beside her, Samuel plucked a knife from the stand and helped her.

* * *

Patrick was one thing, but Milo was another obstacle entirely. As four o'clock approached Alex felt her shoulders hunch and her stomach swirl with worry.

Finally, she heard his key in the lock. She stepped into the hall.

'Hi, love.'

'Huuh.'

'Good day?'

'Yep.'

He started to walk up the stairs.

'Hang on. Please.'

He looked down at her from a couple of steps up and she was aware how much he'd grown over the last few months. How more like a man he was, no longer her little boy. Stronger than her too.

'What?' His voice was low.

'Will you come and meet Samuel?'

'I've got stuff to do.'

'What stuff?' He stared at her for a moment, challenging.

'Homework.'

She almost laughed but didn't want to provoke him.

'Just a few minutes. Please, love.'

He hesitated another minute, then with a huge sigh he dropped back to ground level and followed her to the living room where Samuel was waiting. As they walked through the door, Milo stopped.

'Milo, this is Samuel. Your—' She hesitated. She'd been about to say 'half-brother' but decided it was best to skirt over that for now. 'Samuel, this is Milo.'

Samuel shoved his hands in his pocket and nodded. 'All right, Milo, nice to meet you.'

'Yeah.' Milo hovered like a storm cloud in the doorway. The silence crackled.

Samuel broke it first. 'Do you like football?' Samuel said. 'Arsenal are my team.'

'Not really.'

'Milo, you do!' Alex said. She looked at Samuel. 'He used to love football but doesn't really talk about it as much any more, do you, love?'

Milo gave her a withering look. 'S'all right.'

'Fair enough.' Samuel rocked on his heels and stared at the carpet.

'Can I go now?' Milo mumbled.

'I guess so. But we'll eat dinner together tonight, okay?'

Milo stared at her for a moment, then nodded, turned and stomped up the stairs.

'He don't seem very happy to see me,' Samuel said. An understatement.

'Sorry. He's having a tough time.'

Samuel waved his hand in the air. 'I'm only kidding. Can't blame the poor kid. Who'd want a brother like me waltzing into his life?' He sat down. 'I really ain't sure this is a good idea you know. I can go back to the squat.'

'No, please don't. Patrick and Milo will come round. It just might take some time.'

He gave a small smile. 'If you're sure, then thanks.'

Yet again she hoped she wasn't making a massive mistake.

* * *

The oven was broken. Alex had wanted to cook something special, a sort of welcome meal to help Samuel settle into the family. It wouldn't be the same if they sat down to a dinner of sandwiches.

Maybe they should go out. A chance to build bridges, but somewhere it would be harder to cause a scene. Yes, that was a good idea.

Alex rang the little Italian restaurant she, Patrick and Milo loved, then ran upstairs to tell Milo.

'I guess I have to come, right?'

'I hoped you might, yes.'

He shrugged. 'Whatever.'

It was the best she could hope for.

At seven o'clock on the dot, they left the house. Patrick had refused to come so it was just the three of them. Alex wondered whether they'd see anyone they knew, or if anyone would ask who Samuel was, or recognise him from the news. If they did, what she would tell them?

Enzo, the maître d' Patrick and Alex had known for years, ushered them to their favourite table and handed them menus before making himself scarce. Alex had hoped for a bit of conversation, some tentative getting to know each other. Instead, they sat in stony silence.

The place was still quiet and Alex was relieved. Hopefully they could eat dinner and get out of there quickly. It was already beginning to feel like an ordeal.

Enzo took their orders, and they still hadn't spoken. By the time the drinks were brought over, she'd had enough. She took a gulp of her elderflower cordial, wishing it were wine.

'So, Milo, tell us about your day.'

He sat with his arms crossed and glowered at her.

'Same shit as usual.'

'Milo, come on.'

He looked away. 'It was fine. Nothing happened. Except I had to apologise to Mrs McCarthy for not staying for the second half of the concert.'

'Oh. Was she okay about it?'

'Dunno.'

She turned to Samuel. 'Milo was in a school concert the other night but we had to leave early.' She didn't tell him that it was because someone had been talking about him and she hadn't been able to stand it another second.

'What do you play?' Samuel said.

Milo didn't reply.

'He plays piano,' Alex said, and as soon as the words were out of her mouth she regretted them. Remembering what Samuel had told her about not being allowed to play, she didn't want him to think she was rubbing his nose in it.

She tried to think of something else to talk about. She couldn't bring up the court case, or his father – Milo knew the basics, but nothing more, and now wasn't the time to fill him in on the details. She didn't want to talk about the problems Milo was having either, that would be unfair. What else was there? She barely knew Samuel, and Milo was pulling away from her more and more.

She wished they'd stayed at home.

Just as she was considering leaving, the food came. At least it gave them something else to do other than talk. Or not talk.

As they ate in silence, the restaurant began to fill up and Alex glanced round occasionally. Had anyone seen them? Were people wondering who Samuel was?

She was being paranoid. Why would anyone care?

The plates were taken away, and Alex was about to suggest they went home when a figure appeared at the side of the table. Her heart sank. Just what she needed.

'Hello again, Claire,' she said. It was the school mum who had brought up the subject of Samuel at the concert a couple of months before. The reason they'd left early. She prayed Claire wouldn't recognise Samuel.

'Fancy seeing you again so soon,' she said. Her face flickered in the low light.

'Yes, fancy,' Alex said. She hoped she'd get the hint and leave.

She didn't, of course.

'We missed you after the interval at the school concert,' Claire said, turning to Milo. 'Was it because of the trouble you and Archie got into?'

Milo reddened and Alex froze. 'What?'

Claire swivelled her head to look at her, eyes wide.

'Oh gosh, sorry, I assumed you would have been told about it.'

'Clearly not.'

Alex refused to look at Milo who seemed to have slumped lower in his seat.

'Well, it's not really my place to say...'

'Please, Claire, tell me what happened with Archie,' Alex said, a smile that looked more like a grimace on her face.

Claire hesitated a few seconds, then couldn't help herself.

'Well, it was just I heard that Archie has been bullying a boy in the year below.' Her eyes flicked to Milo who was staring at his knife. Samuel was watching Milo.

'Go on.'

'Well, I don't really know any more than that,' Claire said. 'Just that something happened that night and Milo was covering for him and I thought...'

The air was still, the candle casting shadows across their faces.

Alex wouldn't look at Milo, and in the silence that followed Claire turned her attention to Samuel.

'Well, it's lovely to see you out anyway. And who's this?' She smiled at Samuel.

'This is Samuel,' Alex said, without explanation.

'Hello, Samuel, it's lovely to – oh!' The exclamation was loud and a couple of heads turned. Claire's hands fluttered to her mouth.

'Everything okay, Claire?' Alex was in no mood for this and just wanted her to leave.

'This is... That man... The one who...' Her mouth puckered like she was sucking a particularly sour sweet.

'Nice to meet you.' Samuel held his hand out and smiled sweetly. Claire ignored it.

'Why is he...' She glanced behind her. 'What is he *doing* here?' She hissed the words.

'He's staying for a while.'

Her eyes widened. 'With you?'

'Yes.'

'Right.' She glanced from Samuel to Milo. 'And you're okay with that, with everything going on with Milo, are you? Having a *murderer* in the house.'

'I think we're done here.' Alex stood, and Claire reared back. She opened her mouth as if to say something else but, seeing the look on Alex's face, quickly changed her mind. She turned and walked away without saying another word.

Alex felt the fury rise like flames from her belly.

'Come on. We're going home.'

* * *

They were home just over an hour after they'd left. Samuel made himself scarce and when Milo tried to head upstairs, Alex lost her temper.

'I think you and I need to talk,' she said, her voice razor-sharp.

Milo stopped dead. 'What about?'

Alex waited, arms folded over her chest. She'd spent too long pussy-footing around. It was time for some answers.

'Come into the kitchen please, Milo. It's an order, not a request.'

She headed into the kitchen. Samuel's door was firmly shut. She waited at the table.

For once, Milo must have known she meant business, and he skulked into the kitchen and slumped into the chair opposite her. He trained his eyes on the table and picked at a loose piece of skin on his thumb. He looked, Alex thought, like a troublemaker. Where had her sweet little boy gone?

'Look at me please, Milo.'

He flicked his gaze up and away again.

'Are you going to tell me what's going on?'

He didn't move. Rain pattered against the window and a dog barked somewhere. She waited.

Finally, Milo looked up. His pupils were pinpricks in the overhead light and a trail of spots ran from his chin towards his ear.

'There's not much to tell.'

She leaned forward onto her elbows. 'Milo, I'd like to know what's been going on with you and Archie.'

Milo shifted in his seat but still said nothing.

'What did Claire mean when she said you were covering for him?' Her hands shook and she laid them flat on the table.

He shrugged.

'Milo!'

He looked up sharply, his eyes unreadable. 'I can't tell you.'

Worry forked through her. She leaned forward, her voice gentle this time.

'Milo, if Archie is getting into trouble and dragging you into it as well, I need to know.'

A pause, then, 'She was right. What she said.' He twisted his hands in his lap.

'Claire?'

He nodded.

'Archie's been bullying someone?'

'Yeah.'

'Who?'

He shrugged again. 'Just this kid in the year below.'

'And what exactly does it entail, this bullying?'

Milo squirmed. 'He beat him up the other day.' His eyes snapped up. 'He was suspended.'

A surge of anger swept through Alex. This had all been happening and Caitlin had had the gall to tell her Milo was a bad influence on Archie?

'I'm assuming Caitlin knows about this?'

He looked up then. 'I think he told her it was my fault.'

Oh God.

'Milo, why have you been covering for him? You should have told me.'

'Archie said—' He slouched even further down in the chair as though he was trying to hide himself. 'He said he'd do something worse and make sure I got the blame. And after everything I – I couldn't risk getting into any more trouble...' he trailed off.

Alex let that settle for a minute. Milo seemed to be scared of his oldest friend. But why?

She cast her mind back to the fights Archie used to get into when he was younger. They had been quite nasty, turned him into a tiny, little ball of aggression. But because he was only small back then, nobody had been too worried. After all, wasn't this just what boys did when they were growing up, becoming men? And then the fog had lifted and the Archie they all knew and loved was back. But was there still another side to him, a malevolent side that he managed to hide most of the time?

And if so, what had happened to make him so angry this time?

Alex's mind flicked back to what Caitlin had told her about Scott ripping her off. What was it she'd said? *It nearly broke poor Archie when he found out we might have to sell the house.*

She thought about how big he'd got, how she'd felt she didn't know him as well any more; how he sometimes made her feel intimidated.

'I don't want you to spend any time with him, okay? Not until I've spoken to Caitlin.'

Milo looked up in horror. 'You can't!'

'What do you mean?'

'He told me not to tell anyone. He doesn't want his mum to know, says she's been really stressed recently.'

Has she? Was it down to her or was there something else going on that Alex didn't know about?

'Please, Mum, I promised.'

Alex let out a sigh. 'Okay. But I'm not keeping it quiet for long. Caitlin needs to know what Archie has been up to.' She gave him a look. 'And tell him if he drags you into this again, I'm telling her straight away, no questions asked.'

''K.'

* * *

Alex was shaken by what Milo had told her. Everything was so muddled in her mind – Patrick's anger, Caitlin barely speaking to her, Samuel living here against everyone's wishes, Milo keeping secrets, and now Archie getting into trouble for being aggressive again. It felt like her whole life was falling down around her ears.

Which is why it took her so long to notice that Patrick wasn't home. By eleven o'clock, though, she felt a niggle of worry.

She went to bed and lay in the dark, eyes wide open, her mind a scribble of thoughts. Sleep was an impossibility. This was the first night in the house with Samuel here and, with Patrick out, she felt on edge. She'd reassured Patrick that she trusted Samuel implicitly, but the truth was she didn't know him at all. And now, as she lay wide-eyed in the darkness, every little creak and bang made her heart hammer and her palms sweat. Were they footsteps outside her door, or just the ghost of them in the floorboards from earlier in the day? Should she go and check on Milo?

God, Patrick had been right all along, she was an idiot to invite this stranger into their home. Who *did* that?

By the time she heard the front door opening and closing again at around one in the morning, she was frozen with terror. Slowly though, as she listened to Patrick moving around downstairs, the tension seeped out of her.

He had obviously been drinking because he was noisy, clattering plates and cups around the kitchen and humming to himself. She wondered whether it would wake Samuel up, and hoped the two of them wouldn't have a late-night meeting in the kitchen.

Finally, she heard him walking upstairs. The landing light was still on and Alex held her breath as she waited for the door to open. She wasn't planning on an in-depth discussion at this time of the night, she just wanted a cuddle, and to let Patrick know she still loved him. They could talk in the morning.

But the door didn't open. She strained her ears and heard the office door opening and closing. Was he going online before coming to bed? She listened for a few more minutes. Heard a few bangs and a scraping sound.

Curiosity piqued she climbed out of bed and crept upstairs to the office. She stood outside, debating whether to go in. All was quiet in there now, so she tapped gently on the door and pushed it open. The light was out.

'Patrick?'

He didn't reply.

'Patrick, are you in here?'

'Uh-huh.' He sounded sleepy.

Alex pulled her phone from her dressing gown pocket, switched the torch on and shone it into the room. As her eyes adjusted, her heart plummeted. Patrick had pulled the rarely used sofa-bed out and curled up on it in an old sleeping bag.

'What are you doing?'

He lifted his head from the pillow and squinted at her. 'Going to sleep.'

'In here?'

'Yes.' He dropped his head back to the pillow.

'I thought—' I thought what? That he'd miraculously forgiven her? That they could forget it all and move on?

'I'm staying in here.'

'Tonight?'

He opened his eyes again. 'Until you sort your priorities out.' Then he closed his eyes, turned his back on her, and went to sleep.

21

There was no chance of sleep, the events of the day churning round in her mind.

Patrick not being beside her was one thing. But there was also Samuel downstairs who her husband believed was a danger to them all.

Then, across the hallway, there was Milo.

She couldn't stop thinking about what Milo had told her. How Archie had told him to cover for him, had threatened him into silence. Something didn't sit right. Was there more to this than Milo had admitted? Could he be covering up something bigger than a few playground fights?

By the time morning came, Alex's eyes felt like they were filled with grit. She stumbled through breakfast, Patrick staying well out of the way, and gave Milo strict instructions to steer clear of Archie for a while. Samuel said he was going out, which was a relief. Who knew what would happen if he and Patrick were left alone in the house together.

She was dreading going into the office and facing Caitlin but she needed to. Things had been frosty between them to say the least and, quite apart from how they'd left things, Caitlin was her friend.

Caitlin was already there when she arrived, sitting at her desk. Alex had stopped for a drink and a cinnamon swirl for them both on the way in, and she lay one of each on Caitlin's desk then sat down. When she looked over Caitlin was still staring at the screen, but her fingers hovered above the keyboard.

Finally, she looked over at Alex.

'What's this for?'

Alex shrugged her coat off and hung it on the back of her chair. 'A peace offering.'

Caitlin studied her for a minute, then pulled the coffee and the paper bag towards her. She peered inside and Alex saw a smile twitch her lips. 'Thank you.'

'I don't want to leave things like this between us, Cait.'

'Me neither.'

A silence fell. There was so much Alex needed to say that she didn't know where to start.

'Samuel's come to stay with us and I'm afraid I've made a terrible mistake.'

Caitlin was in the middle of taking a sip of coffee and almost spat it out. She slammed her cup down, a burst of liquid erupting through the gap in the lid and splashing onto the desktop.

'What the actual *fuck*, Alex? How have you not mentioned this to me before?'

'Things haven't exactly been great between us, have they? But anyway, he only moved in yesterday.'

'Fucking hell. This is—' She stopped, then stood up and walked over to Alex's desk and perched on the end. 'How does Patrick feel about it?'

Alex looked down at the desk. 'He's moved out of the bedroom and won't talk to me.'

'Oh. That's not good.' She let out a puff of air. 'You can't really blame him though, can you?'

Alex looked up again. 'Do you think I've made a massive mistake?'

'I don't—' She ran her hand over her face. 'I don't really know how to answer that. I mean, Patrick didn't want it, I can't imagine Milo's thrilled about it and...' she stopped.

'What?'

'Well, you hardly know this man. He could be dangerous, Ally.'

'You're as bad as Patrick.' She didn't want to admit she'd had similar thoughts in the middle of the night too.

'Maybe. But we're right. I know Samuel was found not guilty, but he was still accused of *murder*. And I know you want to believe him and that's great, but to invite him into your home? I mean, I can't...' She shook her head. 'What were you thinking?'

'He was...' She swallowed. 'He was sleeping rough. And he'd been badly beaten up. I couldn't just leave him there.'

Caitlin studied her for a moment, then stood and walked back to her desk, picked up her coffee and pulled her pastry out of her bag.

'Let's just hope he's not such a scumbag as his father.'

Something occurred to Alex then, something Samuel had said.

'Exactly how much money did Scott actually take from you?' They'd talked about it at the time, when Scott Jones had just been a faceless builder who'd ripped Caitlin off. But even then Caitlin had been cagey about the details and now Alex wondered why.

'What has this got to do with anything?' Cait's voice was sharp.

'I don't know,' Alex said carefully. 'I just... I can't help thinking that there's something I'm missing. If Samuel is innocent, then someone else must have killed Scott.'

'You...' Her eyes were wide. 'You think it's *me*?!'

'God, no, of course not!' Shit, she was messing this up. 'No, I meant, maybe there were other people he conned who wanted revenge too.'

'Oh, I have no doubt about that.'

'So how much did you lose, Cait?'

Caitlin put her cup down gently. 'Why are you pushing this, Alex?'

Why was she? She couldn't say exactly, she just knew she had to know more.

'I just wondered why you never told me.'

Caitlin sat, frozen for a moment. Then she stood, palms face-down on the desk.

'Can we go somewhere else?'

'Where?'

'The pub? I'll tell you everything, but I need a drink.'

Alex didn't need asking twice.

The pub round the corner from the office was quiet at this time of the morning, the only people in there the hardened drinkers who propped up the bar at all hours, red faces shining as they downed pint after pint, and a couple of tables of people having brunch, egg and chips and pints of orange juice.

'You find a seat somewhere quiet, I'll go to the bar.'

Caitlin trudged off, looking like she had the weight of the world on her shoulders. Alex ordered a vodka for Caitlin and a tonic water for herself. It was still early but Caitlin seemed like she needed it. She wasn't planning to tell Caitlin that hers was just tonic. She'd tell her about the pregnancy soon but today didn't feel like the right time.

'I got doubles,' she said, placing the glasses on the table in the corner where Caitlin was sitting, looking worried.

'Thanks.' Caitlin tipped half of it down her throat before Alex had even sat down. She slid onto the bench opposite and leaned her elbows on the table, and waited.

Caitlin stared at a spot on the table. She seemed to be trying to work out what to say.

'You know I nearly lost the house?'

Alex nodded. 'You told me that bit.'

She raised her eyes to look at Alex. 'That bastard Scott Jones took everything, Ally. He wiped me out completely, then he fucked off and left my house in a complete state, half done, and I had no money to fix it. Archie's bedroom didn't even have a wall for over a month. Well, you saw it.'

'Oh my God, Cait. Why did you never tell me it was so much money?'

Caitlin shook her head. 'I was too ashamed. I felt like such an idiot. I mean, who does that? Just hands over twenty-five grand just like that?'

'Twenty-five *grand*.'

It was worse than Alex had imagined.

'I know. I'd saved for years to get that loft conversion. I just wanted to give Archie a space of his own. I thought—' Her voice broke and she swiped a tear away furiously. Alex reached out and cupped her hands round Caitlin's.

'I can't believe you didn't tell me how bad it was.'

'I know. I'm sorry. It just – it became a nightmare. I had no savings left and any spare penny I had went back into the business. I had to practically beg the bank to let me pay back my mortgage arrears in the end.'

'I could have helped you.'

'No.' Caitlin shook her head furiously. 'I didn't want that. I didn't want to be so fucking useless. I thought if I could sort it out on my own then everything would be fine.'

'You nearly lost your *house*, Cait.' Something occurred to her then, a snatch of conversation in the back of her car. 'Archie knew about it, didn't he?'

'I always thought he didn't. I thought I'd kept it from him. But then one night he said he wanted to kill the builder for making me so stressed so I clearly wasn't handling it as well as I thought.'

'Oh, Cait.'

'I know. But I couldn't blame him. Because I wanted the man dead too.' She looked up at her. 'I'm just glad someone else did it for me.'

Before Alex could respond Caitlin downed the rest of her drink. 'Want another?'

'Oh, no. I'm good, thanks.'

Caitlin slipped out of the booth and headed towards the bar. While she was gone Alex took a moment to try and gather her thoughts which were like tangled wires in her mind.

Caitlin had almost lost everything because of Scott Jones.

Archie had known about it and wanted him dead.

Could he—

Before she could get any further with that thought, Caitlin placed another glass in front of her.

'I got you another one anyway.'

'Vodka?'

'Double.'

Alex stared at it.

'I know it's early, Ally, but I really need it.'

'Yeah, no, I know. It's fine. Thanks.'

Alex ran her finger round the rim of the glass and wondered whether Caitlin would notice if she didn't drink it.

'So, when did Archie find out about what Scott did?'

Caitlin shrugged, her hands wrapped around her glass. 'A year or so ago. Just before he died I guess.'

Alex tried to keep her face neutral. She clearly wasn't doing a very good job.

'Why are you looking at me like that?' Caitlin said.

'Like what?'

Caitlin peered closely at her. 'Weird. Like you've got a bad taste in your mouth.'

Alex tried to rearrange her features and forced a smile.

'I don't know. Sorry.' She stared at her drink. 'I just thought talking about it might help work out who killed Scott.'

'You thought that talking about Scott ripping me off might help you work out who killed him?'

'I just— I thought that if he ripped you off that

badly, then he must have done it to lots of people and...' she tailed off.

Caitlin crossed her arms and studied Alex. 'Why are you so bothered about this, Alex? I mean, I get it, Samuel's your son and everything, but what exactly are you trying to prove here?'

Alex let out a long puff of air. 'It sounds stupid but I just keep thinking that if I can figure out who did kill Scott then perhaps Patrick will finally believe that it wasn't Samuel and accept him.'

Caitlin sat back. 'Do you really believe that's the only reason Patrick doesn't want Samuel anywhere near you?'

'I don't know, I...'

'Come on, Ally, you're not stupid. You spring a secret child on Patrick that you'd kept from him for what, the last twelve years, tell him he's been accused of murder, then move him into your home against his wishes, and you expect him to be happy about it?'

'Not happy, no. I just want—'

'Patrick's never going to welcome Samuel with open arms. You do know that, right?'

'But he doesn't know him, Cait.'

'Neither do you.' Caitlin leaned forward and took Alex's hands in hers. 'Just... Don't let Samuel manipulate you. Get to know him, sure. But be careful. Because you never really know people.'

Alex thought about Archie again, about what Milo had begged her not to tell Caitlin, and felt a flash of guilt. She should tell her. It wasn't fair to keep it—

'Anyway, aren't you going to drink that?' Caitlin broke away and pointed at Alex's untouched drink.

Alex peered down at it. 'I– I'm not sure I really fancy any more alcohol this early.' She fidgeted in her seat.

'Oh my God.' Caitlin gasped, her eyes wide, and Alex knew the game was up. Caitlin could read her like a book. 'You're pregnant, aren't you?'

Alex nodded, her face burning. 'Yeah.'

'Oh, this is—' Caitlin broke off. 'This is great news. Isn't it?'

'It could be better.'

'But... this is what you've always wanted, Ally. What you've both been trying for, for years. I don't understand.'

Alex sighed. How could she explain it without sounding like she was going mad? She took a deep breath. 'I'm scared.'

'Scared? What of? I know Patrick isn't happy right now, but surely he's thrilled about this at least?'

Alex shook her head. 'It's not that, it's—' She hesitated, unsure whether to say it out loud. 'I can't help thinking, what if there's something wrong with me that makes my children bad? I don't know whether I want to risk it again.'

Caitlin stared at her for so long she began to wonder whether she'd even heard her. But then she spoke. 'You're not seriously still worrying about that, are you?'

Alex nodded. 'I haven't stopped thinking about it since I found out about Samuel.'

'But I've told you before, it's absurd.'

'Is it? It doesn't feel absurd.'

'Because of your father?'

'Partly. Mostly.' Alex rubbed her face. 'Caitlin, what if this is in their genes? What if it's me, and I make another baby that goes the same way?'

'But I—' She stopped, then reached for Alex's hands, her manner softening. 'Please listen to me, Alex. This is not your doing. Milo will be fine. And this baby growing inside you will not be born evil. Nobody is. It's just – it's a matter of upbringing. Personality. Circumstances. Bad luck.' Alex tried not to think about Archie again. Caitlin was looking at her until she was forced to meet her eye. 'Nobody is born evil, Alex. You believe me, don't you?'

Alex nodded. She wanted to believe her.
So why was she finding it so hard?

22

Every time Alex thought about how complicated her life had become in just a few short weeks, terror scuttled round her body like a beetle trapped in a bath. Her heart raced, her head span and her legs began to shake. It was unnerving. And definitely not made any easier by the knowledge that she'd brought it all on herself.

She didn't have to get involved with Samuel. She could have done what she promised Patrick she would do and put it all in the past, closed up in a little box marked 'done and dusted.' It would have been the sensible thing to do. Then she could have concentrated on helping Milo and getting excited about this baby with Patrick.

Instead, she'd let a man she barely knew, and who had recently been accused of murdering a family member, come and live in their home.

It wasn't hard to see why everyone was so angry with her. It wouldn't be hard to put right.

And yet.

Despite her doubts and Caitlin's warning, having Samuel back in her life was the only thing getting Alex through the days. Patrick had distanced himself from her, Milo felt unreachable, Caitlin thought she was mad to risk everything, and she had no headspace at all to concentrate on work. Plus there was the nagging worry that by keeping Archie's secret she was doing more harm than good.

And yet there Samuel was. Hers. How could she let that go?

The truth was, she hadn't known there was anything missing from her life until he came back into it. Now, though, she felt like a jigsaw puzzle that had been completed, the final piece slotted in. The trouble was, her unborn baby now felt like an extra, a piece of the jigsaw that had accidentally been put into the box from another one. Un-needed. Unwelcome.

What an awful thing to think. But it made her cling to Samuel like a lifeboat on a stormy sea even more.

'You're becoming obsessed with him,' Patrick said. He'd stayed out of Alex's way since moving into his office, and they were like ships that passed in the night. Part of her was relieved, glad she didn't have to deal with worrying about keeping him happy too. This morning, though, they'd met in the kitchen by accident just after Milo had left for school. The atmosphere had been frosty as they manoeuvred awkwardly round each other.

'I'm not obsessed, that's ridiculous,' she'd said as the coffee machine ground beans noisily.

'Right.' She hadn't missed the jaw tightening as he'd taken a bite of his toast.

The coffee machine stopped abruptly and her next words came out too loud. 'Jealousy doesn't suit you, Patrick.'

He almost choked on his mouthful, crumbs flying out of his mouth in all directions. 'You think I'm *jealous*?' His eyes were like saucers.

'Why else are you being like this?'

He took another bite of toast and studied her as he chewed. She poured steaming coffee from the pot into her mug and she held it in front of her face like a mask while she waited for him to answer. Finally, he swallowed.

'Forget it. There's no talking to you.' He started walking towards the kitchen door.

'That's right, run away like you always do.'

He stopped dead and turned slowly to face her. His plate was balanced in his hand, and anger flashed in his eyes.

'You seriously want to do this now?'

'Yes, Patrick, I do. You've been avoiding me ever since Samuel moved in and it's not exactly the grown-up way to handle it, is it?'

He placed the plate carefully on the worktop and folded his arms. 'And you think you're handling things really well, do you?'

'Well, no. But—'

'I don't want him here, Alex. I've made that perfectly clear. But you've moved him in anyway. It's clear what your priorities are, and they don't include Milo, and they *definitely* don't include me. Until that changes I don't particularly want to be around you. And I certainly don't want to be around *him*.' He almost spat the last word as if it tasted bitter on his tongue.

'But you don't know him—'

'How many times do I have to say it – neither do you.' He took a step towards her and tipped his head to one side. 'How certain are you that he didn't kill his father?'

She took a step away from him, heart thumping. 'Not this again.'

He barked a laugh. 'Of course this again. I'm hardly going to forget about it, am I?' He took another step towards her until he was towering over her and she stood her ground, her body tense.

'A jury found him innocent, Patrick.'

'Not guilty.'

'What?'

'Like I said before, they found him not guilty. Not innocent.'

'It's the same thing.'

'Is it?' He took a deep breath. 'You've betrayed me from the moment we met by not telling me about him, and now he's tearing us apart. I can't do this any more.'

He turned and walked out of the room. Shortly afterwards his footsteps disappeared up the stairs and his office door closed behind him.

Feeling wobbly, Alex lowered herself onto a dining chair.

She wanted to ignore him, tell herself she did know Samuel. That she knew he couldn't have killed Scott.

She trusted him.

And yet Patrick's words kept gnawing a little hole

of doubt in her certainty, asking *what if he's right? What if I'm being taken for a fool?*

'Everyfink all right?'

Alex jumped and turned to find Samuel behind her. He was wearing pyjamas she'd bought for him yesterday and his eyes were bleary as though he'd just woken up.

How much of that had he heard?

She stood, smoothed her hair down, wiped her eyes. 'I'm good, thanks, Samuel. I hope we didn't wake you.'

He shook his head.

'Do you want something to eat?' She moved across to the fridge, pulled the door open. 'Eggs? Bacon?'

He shook his head. 'I'm good, ta.'

'Are you sure?'

'I'm not hungry. Thank you.'

She felt her face flame. She was trying too hard. 'Right, course. Sorry.'

He went to move back to his room and she was suddenly overwhelmed by the desire to keep him there, to keep him talking to her.

'Clothes!' she shouted, and Samuel stopped.

'What?'

'I– I wondered if you needed any clothes? If you want to go shopping?'

He glanced down at himself. 'Nah, I'm good.'

'Right.'

'But—'

'Yes?' She took a step towards him.

'Well, there is summat I need.'

Anything, she wanted to shout but stayed quiet.

'A phone. You know, just a cheap one.'

'Oh yes, of course!' Her voice was overenthusiastic and she tried to rein it in.

'It don't have to be anything fancy, but...' he tailed off. 'I don't like to ask.'

'Don't be silly, of course you need a phone. Do you want to go and get one now?'

He glanced back over his shoulder again and she wondered what he was looking at. 'Sure. If you've got time?'

She was meant to be at work, of course. 'Fifteen minutes?'

'I'll just shower.'

While Samuel got ready Alex forced herself to eat some toast. She'd lost her appetite recently and was aware her clothes were feeling loose. With a baby growing inside her, no matter how she felt about impending motherhood right now, she had to look after herself. The bread felt like sawdust in her throat.

Half an hour later Samuel and Alex arrived at the

shopping centre in town. As they made their way towards the phone shop Alex wondered what people
saw when they looked at them. Did they assume they
were an ordinary mother and son out shopping together? Or did they see something else, a trace of the
turmoil they'd both been through to get here?

She longed to talk to Samuel, to ask him questions,
find out a bit more about the rest of his life – the
things he liked, disliked, his favourite food, films,
music – but she didn't want to pry. She hoped in time
she'd get to know him almost as well as she knew
Milo.

'I'm sorry,' he said out of the blue.

'What for?'

'I know Patrick don't want me at the house.'

'I'm sorry he's being like this.'

'S'alright. Why wouldn't he? I'll find summat else
soon, I swear.'

Alex stopped dead and Samuel stopped a couple
of steps ahead and turned back to her. 'What?'

She reached out to touch his arm but changed her
mind at the last minute and stood with her hands
hanging limply at her side. 'You're welcome to stay as
long as you want. It's my house as well as Patrick's.'

'I don't want to cause no problems.' He glanced
down at his feet and she noticed how scuffed his

trainers were. He might look like a man, but Alex could see the lost little boy behind the six-foot body – the little boy who'd always been told he wasn't good enough.

'You're not causing problems,' she said, her voice clear, certain. 'I want you to stay.'

'Thanks,' he said, after a split second's hesitation.

They spent the rest of the morning buying Samuel all the things he needed, at Alex's insistence: the new phone he'd asked for, some new trainers, jeans, a suit for job interviews. She didn't care that it was costing her a fortune. She needed to show Samuel what he meant to her, how much she wanted him around.

'Tell me more about you,' she said as they collapsed into chairs in a cafe a few hours later.

'Ain't much to tell,' he said, fiddling with the sugar packets. Alex was reminded of the man she'd met all those months ago in prison, with his defences up. They'd come so far since then.

'Tell me anything. I mean, I know all about your childhood, and how your dad treated you.' She shrugged. 'But I don't know any of the everyday stuff. You know—' she picked up a menu from the table and glanced at it '—what's your favourite food? What would order from this menu?'

He looked at her askance. 'You wanna know what my favourite food is?'

She put the menu down and leaned on her elbows. She felt frantic, her heart racing inside her chest. 'I just want to know who you are,' she said.

He frowned. 'I'm not that interesting, really. I'm just a bit of a fuck-up with no prospects, whose dad hated him and who's now sponging off the mum what gave him away.'

His words felt like bullets, and she recoiled. Of course he felt like this. Stupid, stupid her.

'Samuel, I need to tell you more about your adoption. I need you to know I didn't want to give you up. I was just told it would be for the best.'

'You don't owe me an explanation.' He was sullen now, and she was worried she'd lost him again.

'No, I do. I want to.' The waitress arrived and took their order. When she left Alex turned back to him. 'I was only just seventeen when you were born. My parents thought it would be best if I gave you away. Their friends Scott and Yvonne... They wanted a baby and everyone thought you'd be better off being brought up by them. And I agreed. I mean, I was a kid. But then you were born and I...' she trailed off, hit suddenly by a tsunami of emotion, dredged up from the deepest depths of her soul. She thought she might faint. 'I changed my mind. The instant

I saw your face, held you in my arms, I thought I was going to burst with love. But then you were gone and I didn't think I'd ever get over it. I did though. Sort of.' She looked him in the eye. 'But I never forgot about you. Ever.'

It was impossible to read his expression. When Milo was angry, he developed a little crease above his left eye that showed Alex he was holding in his feelings. When he was sad, his eyes were downcast, when he was excited, he bounced from foot to foot, even now, at fifteen. She could read him, she knew him, even if he didn't want to talk to her.

But Samuel? She didn't know him at all. But if she had to guess she'd say her intensity was freaking him out.

She was being too much.

They finished their coffee and cake in silence, gathered up their carrier bags, and drove home. It was only mid-afternoon but heavy clouds made it gloomy and by the time they pulled into the driveway, the lights were on upstairs in Milo's room. The house was cold and Alex shivered.

She turned on the heating and tried to listen for any sounds of life. Just as Samuel gathered up his bags of shopping, Patrick appeared on the stairs like a ghost. Alex was glad to see him, despite the tension that still hovered between them. At least it meant he was still here.

'Been shopping?' He eyed the carrier bags with suspicion.

'Samuel needed a few things.' Her heart thumped against her ribcage.

'Looks like you've spent a lot.'

She flinched. How dare he? 'Not that much.'

'Right. Generous of you.' He didn't look at Samuel once, but continued down the stairs and stopped at the bottom. 'Your son needs you.' He put the emphasis on the 'son' as he nodded upstairs.

'Milo? Is he okay?'

He shrugged. 'I don't know, he wouldn't say. He asked where you were but I couldn't tell him. Perhaps you should go and see him.'

Alex knew what he was doing, and she refused to rise to it. If he wanted to say something, he could say it directly, rather than making snide comments. She turned to Samuel.

'If you take those things to your room, I'll be back in a bit to make us a drink.'

He nodded and Alex ran up the stairs, her heart in her throat, to see what trouble Milo had got into now. What sort of mother was she, that her heart sank at the thought of a simple conversation with her fifteen-year-old son?

* * *

'You've what?'

'Fuck's sake, Mum, it's no big deal.'

'You're kidding me, right?'

Milo had been caught selling weed to a boy in year eight. It was outside school grounds, but the head was coming down hard on him. Understandably. Her instinct was to scream and yell and tell him what a fool he was being, that he was going to ruin his life. But she knew from experience that would do more harm than good. She took a moment to compose herself.

'Milo, look at me.'

He reluctantly slid his eyes from the duvet where he was watching his fingers pick away at a loose thread and met her gaze. He might look defiant, but she could see the fear in those big brown eyes.

'What's going on, sweetheart?'

He shrugged but said nothing.

'Has this got anything to do with what's going on with Archie? Because I don't think I can keep it from Caitlin any more if—'

'No!' The word shot out like a bullet. 'This is nothing to do with Archie. It's just me.'

She studied him for a moment. Was he telling the truth or was he still covering for his friend?

'You know this is really serious, don't you?'

'I guess.'

She let out a lungful of air and tried to relax her shoulders. 'You could be thrown out of school for this.'

'So?'

'You don't mean that.'

'I do.' His voice wobbled.

She reached for his hand but he snatched it away. She let hers rest on the duvet between them. 'Is this because of Samuel?'

He shook his head.

'Because if it is, you need to talk to me.'

'It's not about Samuel. It's not about anything. I just sold some weed.'

'But why?!' The question exploded from her before she could control it and she regretted it instantly. Any chance she might have had of wheedling out the truth had dissipated into the air with those two words. He sank back into his pillows and crossed his arms over his chest. Alex sighed.

'Where did you get the weed from, Milo?'

'What?'

'Where did you get it from? I mean, how do you even know people who sell it?' She studied him, trying to see what was going on behind those eyes. She knew his face as well as she knew her own, the gentle curve of his chin, the dimple in his cheek when he smiled. He was still her little boy. Except he wasn't really, was he? He was a man now, his face becoming harder, more defined.

How had she let things get so bad? How had she let him drift so far away from her?

'I just do. It's not difficult.'

'Listen. Here's what going to happen. We'll sort this out with the school, try and get them to let you stay. But you have to promise to keep away from the people selling you this stuff. Promise?'

'Yeah.'

'Milo.'

'What? I said yeah.'

'With conviction, so I believe you.'

He stuck his chin out. '*Okay*.'

'Good.'

'Can I go now?'

'Go where?'

'Out.'

'Of course not. You're not going anywhere. You're grounded.'

And before he could argue, she stood and left the room.

23

Alex bundled through the front door laden down with carrier bags and dumped them on the hall floor as she slipped her shoes off. She stood in her socked feet for a moment, straining her ears for any sign of life. But the distant hum of the boiler and the creak of a long-forgotten floorboard were the only sounds to break the eerie silence. Where was everyone?

She shivered, then bent and slipped her fingers through the handles of the bags and heaved them up. The plastic dug into her fingers and she shifted them slightly, a bottle banging against the wall with a clang. She looked down. Red liquid seeped out of the bottom of the bag, spreading across the carpet.

'Shit!' She quickly put the bags on the kitchen

worktop and reached for a tea towel, the closest thing to hand, and began dabbing furiously at the red wine stain. She seemed to be making it worse rather than better and tears of frustration gathered behind her eyes. She swiped at her face with the back of her hand.

The sound of the key in the lock made her heart leap into her throat. She turned towards the front door, straightening up as the door swung open, then froze as a familiar figure stepped over the threshold.

'What are—'

'Oh!'

They stood staring at each other for a few seconds, Alex's heart hammering in her chest, before Archie held his hands up as if in surrender. 'Sorry, Alex, I—'

'What are you doing here?' Her voice was sharp.

He glanced at his hand where her spare key still swung. She'd forgotten he still had that. 'Me and Milo are doing a science project, he said it would be all right.'

Oh did he? And since when did Milo worry about homework?

Archie took another step into the hallway and she stepped away from him.

'You scared me.' She looked up then, puzzled. 'Milo's meant to be grounded though and—' She stopped. She felt so confused she couldn't remember what she was supposed to know and what was meant to be secret.

'Yeah, sorry. I didn't know you were going to be here.'

Clearly.

The air stood still for a moment, then Archie pointed at the stain by her feet. 'Something's leaked.'

'Yes, I know. Thanks.'

She crouched down to carry on wiping up the mess she'd made, hoping Archie would just go upstairs. But suddenly he was standing right in front of her and she leapt up so they were facing each other. He was taller than Milo, sturdier, and he towered over her these days. Her heart thumped in her temples at his proximity, her hand resting instinctively on her belly.

'I need to just...' She turned quickly and went back into the kitchen, keen to put some space between them.

'Do you want some help clearing it up?'

'No, it's fine, I'll finish it later. Thank you.' She could still feel him behind her as she started unpacking the shopping. 'What's this science project about then?'

'Just something we've got to finish for tomorrow. A presentation.'

'Milo didn't mention it.'

'Right. Well, can I just—' He gestured toward the stairs.

She should tell him to go home. She'd made it quite clear to Milo he wasn't welcome, but she couldn't bring herself.

'Sure, go,' she said, waving him away. 'He's probably on his Xbox.'

He didn't need telling twice, practically running up the stairs, and she stood for a few seconds in the peace of the kitchen, letting her fists unclench and her shoulders relax. She shook her head at how ridiculous she was being.

This was the boy she'd known since he was three years old and had needed bedtime stories to stop him being scared of the dark; who she'd watched grow and laugh and fight. Even when he'd been in serious trouble, she'd always loved him practically like her own.

So why was he making her feel so uneasy?

And then it hit her.

Despite what she'd said to Caitlin, the niggle she'd had that Archie might somehow have been involved in Scott's death had grown into more than that – had expanded until it was now more than just an unlikely explanation, a vague possibility. Archie had good reason to hate Scott, and she'd seen first-hand how he could react when someone upset him. Not to mention the fact that Milo had admitted Archie was being aggressive again, bullying some poor boy. Could he, in some misguided attempt to get revenge, have let things get out of control?

Scott had been a huge man, though, used to fighting. If what they'd heard in court was true, surely there was no way someone Archie's size would be able to overpower him? She pictured him now, as he'd loomed over her in the kitchen. He was so big, so strong. Almost a man himself.

Plus she also knew how fiercely loyal Archie was to Caitlin. It had always been just him and her against the world. And Archie had known about the money Scott had stolen, how it had almost broken his mum. She knew Archie well enough to know that he would do everything to protect the only family he had.

That was what was bothering her: that it was the only logical explanation she could think of – and it didn't bear thinking about.

* * *

'Milo, dinner's ready.' Alex stood at the bottom of the stairs and waited for some sort of response. Almost thirty seconds passed before she heard footsteps and Milo's bedroom door opened.

She walked back into the kitchen and waited for him to appear.

When he did, he was silent, just slumped into a chair at the table, staring at his phone.

'Milo.' He looked up but said nothing. Alex pulled out the chair opposite him and sunk into it. 'I need to talk to you.'

'I thought you said dinner was ready.'

'It will be in five minutes.'

He rolled his eyes. 'What?'

'It's about Archie.'

Milo stiffened. 'I know you said you didn't want me hanging round with him but we really did have a science project to do for tomorrow.'

'It's not about that.'

'Oh.' He seemed to deflate. 'What then?'

Alex took a deep breath. 'Did Archie tell you much about the man who ripped his mum off? Apart from that one time in the car.'

Milo frowned. 'What?'

Alex leaned forward. 'In the last couple of years, has Archie ever talked to you about the fact that his mum was ripped off by someone and that they almost lost their house?'

For a few seconds Milo said nothing and Alex thought she was wasting her time. But then he gave a tiny nod. 'A couple of times maybe.'

Alex stiffened. 'Can you remember when?'

Milo shrugged. 'Last time was about a year ago I s'pose. Maybe a bit more.'

Alex nodded. 'Can you remember exactly what he said?'

'Just that. That some bloke had taken all his mum's money.'

'And how did he seem?'

'What do you mean?'

'Did he seem angry? Upset?'

'How would I know? It was ages ago.' He picked at a ding in the table. 'Why are you asking me this?'

'Caitlin only told me about it recently, and I was just wondering whether Archie had said anything about it to you.'

Milo studied her for a moment as though trying to work out whether she was lying. Then he shrugged again. 'We didn't really talk about it much. He was pissed off but then he would be.'

'So that's all he said?' She didn't want to push Milo too much and make him clam up but she was determined to find out whether her theory could be right.

'He didn't say whether he knew who the bloke was or anything?'

'Dunno.'

'Milo, please try and think. This is important.'

'I don't know! He never said.' He folded his arms across his chest and it was clear she wasn't going to get anything else out of him tonight.

She stood, then walked across the room and rapped gently on Samuel's door. It opened almost immediately and she wondered whether he'd been standing on the other side of it listening to her and Milo's conversation, and if so what he made of it.

'Dinner's ready if you want some.'

'Oh right. Ta.'

She served three plates of pasta and sat. The tension at the table hummed.

'Do you know where your dad's gone?' Alex asked Milo as he forked pasta into his mouth as though he hadn't been fed for a week.

Milo just shrugged. 'Out.'

'He didn't say where?'

'Nope. He's never here though, is he?'

'No, love. No he's not.'

Milo was right. Patrick spent so much time out of the house or hiding away in his room that he might as well not live there. She knew he was trying to punish her, but with the baby coming this should have been a time when they were closer than ever, not being torn further and further apart. It was as though he couldn't stand the sight of her.

'It's my fault,' Samuel said. 'He hates me being here.'

Milo looked at Samuel, then across to Alex.

'Oh. Right.'

Then he continued to fork spaghetti into his mouth as though nothing had happened. Alex was once again reminded of how young he really was.

They finished their dinner in silence.

* * *

Later, with Patrick still out and Samuel and Milo in their rooms again, Alex stood by the bedroom window and stared out into the street, thinking about the scan she'd had the other day. It was the first time she'd seen an image of her baby, the first time it had felt real, and Patrick hadn't even been there to share it with her. How had it come to this?

She sighed. She'd always loved this house, it felt like her sanctuary, a place to be with the people she loved most in the world, her family. But over the last few days, it had begun to feel as though four completely separate people were living here, living four completely separate lives, and the house felt colder, less welcoming as a result.

In fact, if she was honest, it was making her feel more than a little on edge.

The creaks from the ancient floorboards in the middle of the night that had never bothered her before now felt sinister; the large, high-ceilinged rooms that she'd always loved for their character now felt empty and if she was alone in the house she found herself listening for noises, her heart fluttering in her chest.

The street outside was quiet, the sky a deep navy blue, almost black. She wondered where Patrick was, and when he would be back. She couldn't hear any sounds coming from Milo's room and assumed he was gaming as usual. She had no idea what Samuel was up to, or even whether he'd gone out. The beech tree across the road rustled in the wind, and the whiny hum of a scooter zipping down the street made her heart gallop.

She reached up to pull the curtains closed when something caught her eye. A movement, over the road by the park. She half-hid behind the curtain and wished she didn't have the light on because she felt exposed all of a sudden. She squinted out into the road, trying to work out what had caught her attention. A fox, a cat, or nothing at all. She needed to pull herself together, this was ridiculous.

She took a couple of deep breaths – then stopped again. There it was. She ran across the room and switched the light off and peered out into the darkening street once more, into the shadows between the trees and the dustbins and the cars. Something was moving out there – some*one*? – she was sure of it. Her mouth was dry and her palms were damp and she wiped them on her jeans and swallowed. Her eyes darted around, following every tiny movement. And then she saw him: a man, standing by the fence to the park. Who was he and why was he watching her?

She wanted to call out for Milo, or Samuel, but she was frozen. Besides what would she say? There's a man outside? So what?

She looked again. Was he even watching her? It was impossible to tell.

A car drove past slowly, the headlights illuminating the shadows, and by the time it had passed she couldn't see anything else. She stood there for a few more minutes, waiting, watching.

The slam of the front door made her jump and she stepped back from the window. Her throat felt tight and she couldn't suck in enough air and oh God she wanted to call out but there was no sound and—

'Alex?'

A familiar voice. She stood on wobbly legs and walked over to the bedroom door and pulled it open.

'Patrick, you're home.' Relief flooded her body like a warm bath.

'Yeah. I wondered where you were.'

'I was just—' She indicated the bedroom but couldn't bring herself to admit how terrified she'd been just a few minutes before. It felt ridiculous, unhinged.

Patrick was watching her and she longed to throw herself into his arms and tell him everything – that she felt she was going mad, that she was scared all the time, that Milo had confessed that Archie had been lying to his mum, about her suspicions about Archie. Normally he was the person she told everything but right now, as he stood on their landing with that look on his face, she realised he was another reason she was currently feeling so unsafe. Because right now she barely recognised him at all.

24

There was money missing from Alex's purse. She knew for certain there was – about £100 – because she'd taken it out to give some cash to the plumber who was coming to look at a leaky tap in the kitchen. Cash in hand he'd said, for a small job like that.

It wasn't the first thing that had gone missing either. Alex hadn't been able to find the gold necklace Patrick had bought her for her thirtieth birthday. At the time she'd assumed she'd just misplaced it, even though she always left it in a box in her dressing table drawer when she wasn't wearing it. But this time, she was 100 per cent certain the money had been taken.

At first, she'd assumed it must have been Samuel.

But she'd bought him so much and he knew he only had to ask for whatever he needed. Why would he take from her?

Then a nugget of worry wormed its way into her belly. Archie had been here the other day, and he knew his mum was still struggling for money. But would he really steal from her?

If not him though, it only left one other suspect, and as much as she tried to push the thought away, it wouldn't leave her alone, like an insistent wasp at a window.

Milo had had a new phone the other day. She hadn't twigged at the time because it looked so similar to his old one, but now she wondered where he'd got it from.

Surely, though, he wouldn't steal from her either?

There was only one way to be sure.

Heart in her throat, she ran up the stairs and tapped on Patrick's office door. A creak and the slide of wheels against wood told her he was coming, and she felt nervous. Then there he was, his solid frame filling the doorway. 'Everything okay?'

She pressed her fingers to her temples and looked up. 'Patrick, have you borrowed some money from my purse?'

'What?'

She swallowed, her throat dry. 'Some money has gone missing from my purse. I just wanted to check it wasn't you.'

'Of course it wasn't me.' He leaned against the doorframe but still didn't let her in. 'It was probably Samuel.'

Alex shook her head. 'No, I don't think it was.'

Patrick cocked his head to one side. 'Oh really? Why not?' Alex wasn't sure she liked the new tone he used with her these days.

'I just don't. Why would he when I've already bought him everything he needs?'

Patrick's laugh was loud, bitter. 'Wow, he really has done one on you, hasn't he?'

'What do you mean?'

'Oh come on, Alex. Who do you really think took that money, the Tooth Fairy?'

'Don't be sarcastic, Patrick.'

He rubbed his hand over his face, suddenly exhausted, and stepped to one side. 'Look, why don't you come in.'

She hovered in the doorway, unsure whether she wanted to actually have this conversation. *For God's sake Alex, he's your husband.* She inched inside and perched on the edge of the sofa while Patrick walked back to the other side of his desk. She tried to ignore the bedding piled up on the floor, an indicator of the chasm that had opened up in their marriage. Patrick shuffled some papers to one side and slid them beneath a folder, then sat down, elbows resting on the table. She felt as if she was being interrogated.

'How much money has gone missing?'

'About a hundred pounds. Not much.'

'Enough.' His eyes slid to his computer screen then back to her. 'Is that all? Has anything else been taken?'

'My necklace,' she admitted.

'The heart one?'

She nodded, felt a lump in the back of her throat and her eyes began to prickle. She was on the verge of tears and hated herself for it. She swallowed. 'I'm worried it might be Milo.'

'*Milo?*' Patrick sounded genuinely surprised.

'Yes.'

He studied her for a moment and she wondered what he was thinking. She knew she looked terrible: her hair was in desperate need of a cut, and her dark roots were showing. There were bags under her eyes, and a trail of spots across her chin – a sure sign of stress.

'Why would you accuse Milo over Samuel, Alex?' His voice was soft, but there was an undertone.

'I just don't think Samuel would risk it.'

'But you think Milo would?'

'Samuel's got no reason to. Plus Milo's got that new phone.'

Patrick shook his head. 'Have you ever thought you might be the problem here?'

Her blood ran cold. 'What do you mean?'

'Listen to yourself. Money was taken from your purse, and rather than assuming it's the man you hardly know who has just come to live in our home – who's recently spent time in *prison* – you decide it's more likely that your fifteen-year-old son has taken it.' He crossed his arms. 'Now tell me, why would he do that?'

'I don't know, Patrick, but it's not as if his behaviour has been exactly exemplary recently, is it?' She felt her hackles rising.

'And why do you think that might be?'

'What are you getting at?' She froze. 'Are you saying this is *my* fault?'

He lowered his gaze. 'Don't you think it's weird that Milo's behaviour has got worse since you brought Samuel into our lives? I mean, you're spending all your time with him, you buy him things endlessly—'

'He needed clothes! And I'm always here for Milo. He just never wants to be anywhere near me.'

'Of course he does.' He let out a long breath, his cheeks puffing out with the effort. 'He's a good kid, Alex. He just wants his mum back, and not have to make do with the scraps of your attention.'

Bile rose in her throat. Had she been neglecting Milo since Samuel had come back into her life?

'But he was behaving like this way before he knew about Samuel,' she said, her voice laced with doubt. 'Before all of this.'

'Maybe. But even you've got to admit it's been worse since you brought *him* into our lives.' He shrugged. 'And that's all on you.'

Fury burned through Alex and she stood so abruptly her head span. She'd heard enough.

'I'm a good mother, Patrick.'

'And no one is saying you're not. I'm just saying that before you accuse him of anything, maybe have a good long think about who is more likely to have been stealing from you. Because if you accuse Milo of taking this money there may be no coming back from it.'

Right at that moment Alex hated Patrick. She hated his face, his calmness, the way he could make her feel so small, so wrong. She ran from the room and pounded down the stairs, her heart hammering, her legs weak.

Patrick could tell her Milo was innocent all he liked, but she knew it was only because he hated Samuel and wanted her to tell him to leave. And she wasn't about to give him the satisfaction.

* * *

When Milo was little he'd been happy to let her come into his room whenever she liked. They used to snuggle on his tiny single bed and read bedtime stories until they both fell fast asleep, or cuddle up under his duvet and make a den, giggling in the torchlight. Then, it had been a warm, welcoming room, with framed Batman pictures on the walls, a soft nightlight to stop him getting scared, a small white wardrobe filled with neat rows of the shirts and trousers and jumpers she'd lovingly picked out for him. Now, it felt like a stranger's room – clothes piled on an ancient beanbag in the corner, some dirty, some clean; bare walls apart from a couple of dog-eared photos Alex had stuck up years ago and he'd obviously forgotten to take down; a screwed-up duvet and a distinct smell of old socks.

She knocked on the door gently, even though she

knew he was still at school. Patrick's office was only one flight up and she didn't want him to hear her going into Milo's room, so she pushed the door open gently and carefully closed it behind her. She stood on the threshold for a moment. If she did this now, she'd have crossed a line she vowed she'd never cross from the moment Milo had become a teenager.

'I promise you'll always have your privacy,' she'd told him when he turned thirteen. It had been important to her, something she'd never had herself, her father always assuming the right to barge into her room whenever he liked. Now, though, she was going back on that promise, and it didn't feel good. But needs must.

She took another step inside and surveyed the room, trying to work out where to start. A floorboard creaked beneath her foot and she stopped, listening. When she was sure it was safe she hurried over to the bed, dropped to her hands and knees and shone her phone torch into the cavity. There wasn't much under there. A couple of battered boxes of long-forgotten Lego, a plastic box of old single sheets she hadn't wanted to throw away, a few old socks, a pair of scrunched-up boxer shorts and an ancient pair of pyjama bottoms Milo hadn't worn for years. Everything was covered in dust and she realised how long it must have been since anyone had cleaned under there. She pulled the dirty underwear out and threw them towards the door, then stood and brushed the dust off her trousers. Where else? She headed to the wardrobe, one door of which was flung open, revealing drawers with sleeves trailing out, and endless empty coat hangers where the clothes they were meant to house had given up clinging on and had slumped to the base of the wardrobe. She opened the other door and shone her torch into the bottom. She pulled open the couple of drawers and ran her hand round the edge, then knelt and ran her hand round the base of the wardrobe, pulling the clothes out as she went. Her hand hit something hard at the back and she leaned further in and dragged it out. It was an old shoebox, covered in a thick layer of dust. It didn't look very promising, but she pulled the lid off anyway, just in case. There was no point breaking Milo's trust and then only doing a half-hearted job. She needed to know either way if he'd taken her money, even if only to put her mind at rest.

Fat chance.

The box contained dozens of old photos, some random Lego instruction books with their covers ripped off, a handful of plastic animals, some toy cars and a few torn football magazines from three years ago.

No sign of any cash. She hurriedly replaced the lid and shoved it back to the back of the wardrobe. She doubted Milo even knew it was here, he was unlikely to notice she'd tampered with it.

Next she went back to the bed and pulled open the drawers of the bedside table. She was nervous about what she'd find, but in the event, it was almost empty, just a couple of old chocolate bar wrappers, half a packet of sticky sweets and a tatty paperback with a water-damaged cover. She closed the drawer. There was only one place left to look. She walked over to the chest of drawers and pulled open the top one. Clean pants and socks were thrown in willy-nilly, but there was nothing else. She pulled open the next one – then stopped in her tracks. Tucked down the side of his T-shirts was a white envelope. She removed it carefully and, with shaking hands, lifted the flap and peered inside.

Notes. Dozens of them, a fat wad of five- and ten-pound notes. There must have been at least two hundred pounds here.

Bile rose in her throat. As much as she hadn't wanted Samuel to have been stealing from her, she'd definitely prayed it wasn't Milo either. Because that would mean she couldn't trust him at all.

She let herself sit back onto the floor and sucked in some air, trying to steady her breathing. Her head spun and she felt nausea swirl in her belly. Surely there was no other explanation for her missing cash?

The question was, what the hell was she going to do about it?

25

In the end, she did nothing. What *could* she do? Confronting Milo would only make things worse – between the two of them as well as between Alex and Patrick. If they could get much worse.

Instead, she just kept her purse with her all the time, and kept a closer eye on Milo.

How had it come to this?

She felt dizzy and sick most of the time. Although she knew it was partly down to the baby growing inside her, the stress of her ever-spiralling home life was undoubtedly exacerbating it. She just wished she could talk to Patrick about it. But now he was part of the problem.

Instead, she buried her head in the sand and tried

to carry on as normal. Patrick spent most of his time in his office, only coming down for food and drinks, while Milo, who was still grounded, was either at school or sulking in his room. Samuel spent much of his time holed up in his own bedroom or out of the house. She couldn't help feeling that her plan to bring her whole family together had spectacularly backfired.

So she turned to the one thing that always brought comfort when she was frazzled: she cleaned. It had started when she still lived at home. On the days when she could hear her parents arguing and she knew it was likely to end in her father giving her mum a smack, or worse, she lost herself in chores. Dusting, hoovering, scrubbing the bathroom – anything to distract herself from what was going on in the other room. It didn't work then, and it wasn't likely to work now, but she needed to do something to busy herself, to stop the trembling of her hands.

She stuck in her headphones, gathered together some cleaning products, and set to work, starting at the top of the house. She vacuumed under beds – including Milo's – dusted surfaces, scrubbed skirting boards. She shook out rugs, cleaned sofas, polished woodwork. Then she started on the bathrooms, scrubbing them until they gleamed. She wasn't sure what she was trying to achieve, but at least it was keeping her busy.

And then she found something.

A plastic bag, down the back of the toilet beside Samuel's room. She pulled it out and stared at it for a moment while she waited for it to sink in.

It was a bag of drugs.

Small blue pills.

Fuck.

She yanked her headphones out of her ears and shoved the bag in her pocket. Then she went into the kitchen, sat down at the table and put her head in her hands and let the tears she'd been holding back for so long come. Tears for her, for Milo, for Samuel, for Patrick – it all came out as she sat there, soaking the tabletop. She cried until the tears ran dry, until her eyeballs felt scratchy and her breath came in short, raggedy bursts.

That's where she was, head in her arms on the table, when Samuel came in, bringing in a waft of cold air and cigarette smoke with him.

'What's happened?' he said, sitting down beside her. He didn't touch her – he never did, and she was glad. She reached her hand into her pocket and pulled out the bag and threw it on the table. It sat between them for a few seconds, a wordless accusation.

'What's this?'

'You tell me.'

'You think it's mine.' It was a statement, not a question.

She looked him directly in the eye. 'Who else's is it?'

He shrugged. 'No idea. But it don't belong to me.'

She studied his face, trying to work out if he was lying. If he was, he was bloody good at it. She shuddered, suddenly nervous. She didn't know this man at all, and she was kidding herself if she thought she did. She wondered whether Patrick would hear her if she screamed.

'I swear on my life, Alex. These pills are nuffink to do with me.' He picked them up. 'Where d'ya find them?'

'Behind your toilet.'

He nodded. 'Right.'

'What?'

He let out a long breath. 'Where do you think Milo would hide them if he didn't want you to find them?'

'You think these belong to Milo? He's fifteen!'

'He's already been caught dealing weed, hasn't he?'

Alex gripped the edges of her chair, her knuckles white. 'He— It can't be him. Where would he even get something like this?' And yet even as she said the words out loud she realised that the tiny seed of doubt she'd been trying to ignore had begun to bloom, spreading its tendrils out wider and wider until she couldn't ignore them any more.

Milo was stealing money. And he was dealing drugs.

She felt as if her insides had been scooped out. She stood abruptly, the chair clattering to the floor behind her.

'I can't—' She pushed her hand through her hair. She felt frantic, untethered. Her hand fluttered to her belly. Her baby. What was the stress of this doing to her unborn child?

How could she even think about bringing a new life into the world when the ones she'd already created had brought so much trouble?

* * *

'We need to talk.'

Alex waited until Milo got home from school and followed him up the stairs to his bedroom. He looked at her with such disdain when she stepped towards his open door she was glad looks couldn't kill.

'What about?'

She held up the bag and watched as he registered

what she'd found. But the look on his face wasn't what she'd been expecting. Rather than guilt, or anger, or surprise, he just looked puzzled.

'What's that?'

'It's a bag of pills.'

'Right. And?'

'Do you know anything about it?'

She watched as his face dropped and his eyes widened. 'You think they're *mine*?!'

'Yours or Archie's,' she said. Milo hesitated a fraction of a second, tears shining in his eyes, before slamming his bedroom door shut. And Alex knew in that instant that she'd made a terrible mistake.

Whatever these pills were and wherever they'd come from – even if they were Archie's – she was absolutely certain that Milo knew nothing about them. And now, just as Patrick had predicted, there was no coming back from the fact that she'd accused him.

What had she done?

26

Alex knocked on Milo's door. No answer. He was often late for school but today it was almost eight thirty and there was no sign of him at all. School started in twenty minutes.

She rapped again, irritation rising in her throat. 'Milo!'

Nothing.

She pushed the door open and poked her head round it – and stopped dead.

His bed was empty.

The duvet was pulled neatly up, which was un-heard of, and his curtains were closed. Heart thumping wildly, she flicked the overhead light on and ran over to his wardrobe. Yanked the doors open.

There was nothing missing. His blazer was still hanging there; the rest of his uniform lay crumpled over the back of his gaming chair.

'Milo!' she yelled, even though it was clear he wasn't in here. She ran back to the bedroom door and out onto the landing. 'Milo!'

She sprinted down the stairs, almost tripping over her own feet, into the lounge. Nothing. Kitchen. Nothing. Downstairs loo. He wasn't there either. 'Milo, where are you?'

She was frantic now, her whole body charged with adrenaline.

Samuel poked his head out of his bedroom door. 'What's up?'

'Have you seen Milo?'

He shook his head. 'Not since last night. Why?'

'I can't find him.' She spun round. 'He's gone.'

'I'll help.' He stepped into the kitchen. 'Where first?'

'You check the back garden,' she said. 'I'll go upstairs.' She ran at breakneck speed up the first flight, poked her head round the bathroom door then carried on up to the top floor. When she burst Patrick's room unannounced he looked up in surprise.

'Have you seen Milo?'

'No. Why?'

'He's gone. I can't find him anywhere.' She was breathing heavily and she put her hands on her knees and dropped her head until the spinning stopped. By the time she was upright again, Patrick was halfway down the stairs, calling Milo's name. For the first time in weeks, Alex was grateful that Patrick was here. He might not like her very much right now, but he loved Milo and would never want to see anything happen to him. She followed him.

When they were both sure Milo was nowhere in the house, and Samuel had confirmed he wasn't in the garden, they needed a plan.

'I'll ring school, you ring Caitlin,' Patrick instructed.

She did as she was told. Never mind everything else that was going on with their boys, Caitlin was her best friend.

As expected, Caitlin was horrified.

'I'm coming over.'

Alex tried Milo's mobile endless times as well as the Find My app, but his mobile seemed to be switched off. She spoke to the police who assured her someone would ring back.

'What do you need me to do?' Caitlin said the second she arrived, taking her coat off and hooking it over the back of a chair.

'I don't know,' Alex said. Tears were threatening and her voice wobbled.

'We'll find him.' Caitlin pulled her in for a hug as Alex nodded mutely. 'I'll start with social media.' Caitlin whipped her laptop out of her bag and within seconds was trawling through Facebook. 'Archie gave me some names to try before he left for school, so I'll start with them.' Alex was so grateful for her efficiency.

'Drink this,' Patrick ordered, plonking a cup of herbal tea in front of Alex. Samuel was hovering somewhere behind her and it hit her that this was the first time the four of them had been in the same room together – and the first time Caitlin had met Samuel. Not ideal circumstances, but at least they were all here trying to help her find Milo.

Alex sank back into her chair, and Patrick rubbed her shoulders as she tried to relax. She was hollow with exhaustion, her eyes filled with sand and her heart was jumping all over the place. She took a sip of her tea and tried to take a couple of deep breaths.

'I don't know what to do next,' Alex said, her voice scratchy. She hadn't smoked for fifteen years but right now she craved a fag. She drummed her fingers on the table. Caitlin grabbed hold of her hand and she stilled.

'We'll find him.'

Alex's breath hitched in her chest as she suppressed a sob. 'But what if we don't?'

'We will,' Patrick said, pressing his thumbs into the soft hollows of her shoulders. They were solid with tension and she winced. 'You've got to look after yourself as well though.' He leaned down to whisper in her ear. 'And the baby.' He was right. Getting worked up wasn't doing her – their – baby any good at all.

'I'll go out and look for him,' Samuel said, striding towards the front door. Alex stood, desperate to go with him.

'Where will you look?'

He stopped. 'Dunno. But I've gotta do summat.'

Before she could reply, he left. When the front door slammed Alex felt as though she'd been punctured, the air pouring out of her like blood.

She needed to be doing something too. Staying here was hopeless.

'Where are you going?' Patrick said as she strode towards the front door.

'I don't know. Anywhere. I—' She stopped. 'Where the fuck is he, Patrick? Where's my boy?'

Her legs gave way and she gripped the back of a nearby chair. She felt as though her insides had been scraped out. This was her fault. All of it. She should never have invited Samuel to stay without making sure Milo was really okay with it first. And she should never have accused him of hiding those drugs. No wonder he didn't want to be anywhere near her. Why should he trust her ever again?

'Let's try some of his friends,' Caitlin said gently, guiding Alex to sit back down again.

'He doesn't really have any friends apart from Archie,' she said, and her heart clenched. 'Not ones I know of, anyway.' Who *was* he hanging around with these days? Gone were the days when Milo and Archie lived in each other's pockets, even before Caitlin had asked Milo to stay away from him. Why hadn't she thought to find out who he *was* hanging around with?

'I've got a few numbers from Archie,' Caitlin said. 'We might as well give them a ring and see if they've heard from him.'

'Okay,' Alex agreed. It was better than doing nothing.

Caitlin made the calls as Alex scrolled through local Facebook groups again trying to find out if anyone had seen Milo. A few minutes later she realised Caitlin had gone quiet and she looked up to find her friend watching her apologetically.

'No one's around so I've left messages. Sorry,' she

said. 'Perhaps we could ring the school and ask to speak to them?'

'Maybe.' Alex rubbed her hands over her face, trying to scrub away the image that kept sliding into her head of her boy, lying somewhere, beaten and bloodied, hurt and scared... She squeezed her eyes tight and tried to close her mind to it.

She didn't know how much time had passed, but the sound of hammering on the front door broke the silence. Alex almost sprinted to the front door and slung it open.

'Milo!' she sobbed, throwing herself at him, not caring that he didn't respond, his slim, narrow body stiff as a tree, his arms straight by his sides. She squeezed him tightly as relief flooded her. She felt as bruised and battered as if she'd been in a physical fight. Finally, she pulled away and let him step inside the house. Samuel followed him.

'You found him?'

He nodded.

'Where was he?'

'At the park. Just sitting on one of the swings.'

She followed Milo into the kitchen where Patrick had him in a tight hug. Alex was shaking and her face was wet, as though the tension was leaking out of her.

'Where did you go?' Patrick said gently.

'Have you been out all night?' Alex said at the same time.

Milo looked from Alex to Patrick and back again and shrugged. Frustration rose in her, from her belly to her throat. She wanted to shout and scream; she wanted to hug him. She did neither of these things, terrified of scaring him off again. Instead, she stood, helplessly, waiting for him to speak to her.

'I just went out.'

'All night?'

He shrugged again.

'Milo, come on, your mum's been worried sick. We all have,' Patrick said, and Alex was grateful to him for taking control.

'I'm fine though, aren't I?'

'You're also only fifteen, you can't just spend all night out and not expect us to be worried. And why was your phone turned off?'

'Ran out of battery.'

Alex doubted that – Milo was addicted to his phone, it was rarely far from a charger. Which meant he'd deliberately switched it off to punish her.

'Milo, I'm so sorry,' she said, stepping towards him. He didn't move away. 'I didn't mean what I said before. I never really thought the drugs were anything to do with you.' She didn't dare look at Caitlin or Patrick, neither of whom knew about the drugs.

'You did. But it's fine. It doesn't matter.' He looked round. 'I'm starving, can I get some food?'

She wanted to keep talking to him, to beg him to forgive her. But she also knew pushing him was the least likely way to get him to open up.

'Sure, what do you want? Bagel? Bacon sandwich?'

'Bacon sandwich would be good.'

She busied herself frying some bacon while Patrick and Caitlin cajoled Milo into taking a shower and getting some fresh clothes on. He was meant to be at school but she was going to let him have the day off. She needed him here, to make sure he was safe.

As the bacon sizzled she remembered a day many years before, just before she met Patrick and it was just her and Milo. He was only about two and half, and they'd been playing hide and seek in the garden, when he'd completely disappeared. For the first five minutes, Alex had been impressed at his hiding skills. But as the minutes had ticked by and there was no sign of him, and he wasn't responding to her increasingly fraught calls, the panic began to overwhelm her. She'd been frantic as she'd dashed around the garden yelling his name. In the end her neighbour, a kind woman in her seventies called Margaret, who loved

Milo, had heard Alex shouting and came out to find out what was going on.

'Milo's disappeared,' Alex had said, the words gushing out between gasps of breath.

'Stay here and keep looking, I'll go and look out the front,' she'd said. It must have only been about ten minutes later that Alex heard a little voice shout 'Mummy!' and she turned, to be barrelled over by a small figure throwing itself at her from the other side of the garden.

'He said he'd wanted to do the best hiding, so he'd gone to the churchyard to hide behind his tree,' Margaret had said, smiling. The churchyard was at the other end of their street, across a busy road where cars flew down far too fast, and where anything could have happened to him in those two or three hundred metres, and her heart clenched as she squeezed him tighter. 'Mummy, you're hurting me a bit,' he'd said, his voice muffled from pressing into her chest and she'd let go, but only a little bit. Then, she'd been able to explain to him why he mustn't go anywhere without Mummy, why she'd been so scared. Now, though, even though the terror felt exactly the same to her, she didn't know what to say to her son, now almost an adult himself, to make him understand how much she loved him. How terrified she was of losing him.

The terror never diminishes. And neither does the guilt.

She was brought abruptly back to the present by a movement at her elbow, and she turned to find Samuel standing there with a look of concern on his face. Everyone else had disappeared to help Milo.

'Sorry, did you say something?' she said, blinking to focus on his face.

'I wondered if I could have a word,' he said. He looked serious.

'Sure. Just let me turn this off.'

She set the bacon to one side and they sat at the table, facing each other. 'Thank you for finding Milo,' she said, her voice cracking.

He shook his head, dismissive. 'S'nothing.'

'It's not. It could have been hours before he came home if you hadn't thought where to look.'

'You won't thank me when you hear what I'm gonna say.'

Her heart shrivelled. 'Why? What do you mean?'

'It's my fault he ran off.'

'Of course it's not!' she said. 'I was the one that asked you to stay. You must never think that.'

But he shook his head again, his hands clenched in front of him. 'No, not that. I—' He swallowed, and a sense of dread prickled Alex's neck. He looked her in the eye. 'Them drugs you accused Milo of hiding? They were mine.'

Confusion swept over her. 'But you said they were nothing to do with you.'

He bowed his head. 'I know. I didn't want you to throw me out, so I panicked and said it were Milo. But that was a stupid thing to say.'

Her head swirled as she took the words in. 'But—' She didn't know how to phrase it. 'Are you sure? I mean, you're not just saying that to protect him?'

'No, I swear!' He stopped again. 'I get it if you want me to leave. I'll be out by lunchtime.'

'Of course I don't want you to leave.' The words were out before she'd even given them any thought. Did she really want someone she couldn't trust in her home, putting her vulnerable teenage son and her unborn child at risk, not to mention the marriage that was falling down around her ears? What was she thinking, when he'd given her an easy route out, a way to get back to how things had been before?

But she also knew she couldn't let him live back on the streets again. This was her chance to make it up to him once and for all.

'Are you sure?'

She nodded. 'Positive.' She heard footsteps on the stairs and she stood abruptly and started buttering some bread. 'Thank you for telling me. I'd appreciate it if you didn't say anything to Patrick about this.'

'I won't. But—'

She whipped her head round to look at him. 'Thank you, Samuel. I'll handle it.'

He hesitated a fraction of a second, then nodded and headed to his room. The door clicked shut just as Milo and Patrick came back into the room, closely followed by Caitlin who had a pile of clothes bundled in her arms. 'I'll just shove this lot on for you then I'll get out of your hair,' she said, heading to the utility room.

'Thanks, Caitlin,' Alex said, then handed Milo a plate. 'Your sandwich is ready, love.'

'Thanks.' He took a huge bite before he'd even sat down. It took all her effort not to throw her arms around him and cover his face in kisses.

'Did you talk to him?' Alex whispered to Patrick instead.

He nodded. 'He's fine. I told him he could have the day off, I hope that's okay?'

'Yes, course.'

'I'll ring school, shall I?'

'Please.' He nodded but didn't leave. 'You okay?'

He flicked a glance towards Milo, then back at her. 'What was that about drugs you mentioned earlier?'

Her heart plummeted. 'It's nothing. It was just a

misunderstanding, that's all.' She hoped he'd leave it, for now at least – and to her relief, he seemed to take her word for it. As he went to ring school, Alex sat down at the table and watched Milo.

'What?'

'Nothing, love. I'm just glad you're home and safe.'

'I'm not a little kid any more.'

'I know. But I'm still your mum. And I'm sorry for not believing you, about the pills. I know it wasn't you. Okay?'

'Okay.' He took another bite and chewed. 'Is Samuel allowed to stay still?'

She hesitated. Would he welcome him, or be angry? She watched him carefully as she replied. 'Yes. Is that okay?'

He nodded. 'Sure. He's cool.'

Relief flooded through her. It was only tempered when she turned her head and saw Patrick standing in the doorway, his face like thunder. But by the time he'd come back into the room, it had cleared, and she wondered whether she'd imagined it after all.

27

Alex needed to go into the office. Work had always been her focus, and she was so proud of the business that Caitlin and she had built up. She loved her work, but she also knew she'd badly neglected it recently.

To thank Samuel for his help finding Milo she also wanted to give him a chance to get back on his feet, so she'd asked him to come and do some admin for them. Only she hadn't told Caitlin, or even asked her. Because she would have said no.

They arrived early, before Caitlin's usual start time.

'You sit there,' Alex told Samuel, pointing to the desk beside hers. They didn't have a spare desktop computer so she'd lent him her laptop, and he opened it up expectantly.

'Are you sure this is cool with Caitlin?'

'It'll be fine,' she said, ignoring the swirling in her belly that belied her confidence.

'Thanks. For trusting me,' he said.

'You don't need to keep thanking me.'

'I know. But, like, it means a lot. People don't usually trust people like me.'

She dipped her head to compose herself. 'Give me a minute and I'll have something for you,' she said, settling behind her screen. She waited while her emails loaded, dreading seeing how many she'd need to plough through before she could crack on with her day.

'Shall I make some drinks?'

Alex glanced up. 'Great, thanks, Samuel. Tea for me.'

She got stuck in, deleting junk messages and replying to the most urgent emails. She was so engrossed she didn't notice Caitlin was in at first. So when she spoke, Alex almost jumped out of her seat.

'What's he doing here?'

Alex looked up, heart hammering. She'd known the confrontation was coming, but she still felt unprepared. She stood, legs like jelly. 'I've asked him to come and help for a few days.'

'And you didn't think to ask me?'

'I—' she started. She had no justification for not warning Cait and she knew it. 'I'm sorry. I didn't want you to say no.'

Caitlin looked away then lowered herself into her chair stiffly and switched on her computer. The hum of it warming up was the only sound in the room.

'Can we talk about it?' Alex said, unable to bear it any longer.

Caitlin's head snapped round. 'What is there to talk about?'

'I just—'

'We run a nursery business, Alex, in case you've forgotten,' she said, her voice steel. 'What do you think would happen if the parents found out we had someone like him helping us?'

Alex's blood turned to ice in her veins. 'What exactly do you mean by *someone like him*?'

'Someone who was recently accused of murder, as if you really need me to spell it out,' Caitlin spat.

Fury rose in Alex, encircling her neck like a python. 'He was found not guilty. As you well know,' she said, her face burning. 'And it's not as though your son is so bloody perfect, is it?'

The air stilled, the words hanging in the space between them. Then slowly, Caitlin turned to face Alex.

'What do you mean by that?'

Alex wanted to backpedal, to claim she hadn't meant anything at all. But she couldn't go on pretending that everything was fine.

'Milo told me something.' She looked down at her hands. 'He begged me not to tell you.'

'Go on.'

'He said—' She swallowed. Why was this so hard? 'He said Archie has been bullying someone at school and that he's been covering up for him.'

Caitlin didn't speak and Alex glanced up at her. Her face was grey and, despite everything, she wanted to run over there and throw her arms around her friend, comfort her, the way she always had. She stayed still though and waited.

Finally, Caitlin looked up at her. 'Why didn't you tell me before?'

'Milo begged me not to.'

'But why would he do that?'

'He... he said Archie had threatened him.'

'Oh my God.' Caitlin's shoulders slumped. Alex pushed herself away from the desk and walked over and wrapped her arms round her friend. Caitlin didn't shrug her off, and she stayed there until a movement in the doorway disturbed them both.

'Sorry, I'll come back later.' Samuel hovered, a mug in each hand, looking awkward, then left again.

Alex pulled a chair over and sat down beside Caitlin. 'I'm sorry for not asking you about Samuel. And I'm sorry for bringing this up now. But I couldn't keep it from you any longer. It was killing me.'

Tears filled Caitlin's eyes. 'Why do you think Archie is doing this again?' She sniffed. 'I thought we'd sorted things out years ago, he's been good as gold since.'

'I know.' Now definitely wasn't the time to mention her suspicions about Archie's involvement in Scott's death. It wasn't as though she had any concrete evidence to show her, and they were on shaky enough ground anyway. 'It's hard being a teenager, you know that. None of them are perfect.' It sounded trite but what else could she say?

Caitlin looked at her then. 'I'm so fucking sorry for being such a bitch about Milo.'

Alex shook her head. 'It's okay.'

'No. It's not.' She wiped her nose on her sleeve. 'I feel so ashamed. I've let you down, Ally. And now I'm doing the same with Samuel. I mean, you're right, Archie sure as hell isn't perfect. I don't know why I kid myself he is.'

'Did you...' Alex paused. 'Did you know about Archie's behaviour?'

Caitlin sniffed but kept her gaze trained on the

middle distance. 'I had my suspicions but I was too afraid to talk to him about it in case I didn't like the answer. Some mother I am, hey?'

'You're a brilliant mother.'

'So brilliant that my son is a bully?'

Alex crossed her arms. 'You told me nobody is born evil, and that how my children behave is not my fault. Do you remember that?'

Caitlin nodded miserably.

'Well then, if that's true for me, it's most definitely true for you.'

Caitlin gave a sad smile. 'Thank you, Alex. I don't deserve you.'

Alex didn't reply, but couldn't help thinking that if Caitlin only knew the truth she wouldn't be so sure.

* * *

Caitlin agreed they could afford to have Samuel working for them for a while, but they also both agreed it was probably best for Alex and Samuel to work from home for now. The arrangement suited Alex fine because it meant she could spend more time with Samuel and keep an eye on both Milo's and Patrick's movements.

Patrick wasn't thrilled about Samuel being there

all the time, but to Alex's surprise, Milo seemed happier about having his half-brother around than she'd expected.

'Shall I make some lunch?' Samuel said, looking up from the spreadsheet Alex had given him to fill in.

'I thought I'd make sausage sandwiches,' she said, leaping up to open the fridge.

'Ta, they're my favourite.'

'I know.' She pulled the packet from the fridge and turned on the hob.

'You don't have to keep buying things for me, you know.'

She felt herself blush. She hadn't realised it was that obvious. 'I know. Sorry. I just—' The words caught in her throat. 'I just really want to make you feel welcome.' What she really meant was that she wanted to make up for lost time but it didn't feel like the right thing to say.

'I do feel welcome.' He stood up and moved behind her. She felt her body tense. But to her surprise when she turned to face him he held his arms out and wrapped her in a hug. It was the first time they'd had any physical contact since he was a tiny baby and as she pressed herself against his chest Alex swallowed back tears. They'd missed out on so much. They had so much lost time to make up for.

She pulled away and looked up at Samuel's face. But before she could speak, the kitchen door opened and they both jumped apart guiltily.

'Hi, love,' Alex said as Patrick came into the room. He usually stayed away when he knew Samuel was here so she was surprised to see him.

'Don't mind me, I'm just getting some lunch.' He didn't even acknowledge Samuel's existence.

'I'm making sausage sandwiches if you want one,' Samuel said.

'No thanks, I'm not keen.' He still didn't look at him.

'How's your day?' Alex said, trying to keep things light as Samuel started heating oil in a pan.

Patrick shrugged. 'Fine.'

'Are you sure you don't want to eat lunch with us here?'

Patrick froze, the fridge door half open. Alex wondered if he'd heard her. Then he closed the fridge door, turned, and walked away. 'I'll get something out.'

The front door slammed and shame washed over her.

'I'm so sorry—'

'Don't worry. I don't blame him.' Samuel turned the hob off and turned to face her. 'I don't have to live here to spend time with you, you know,' he said. 'I could move somewhere else, like we agreed if Patrick still weren't happy, and still see you.'

'I know. I just—' She stopped. She just what? What did she think she was going to achieve by having him staying here? 'I'll sort it out. I promise.'

He shook his head. 'Don't ruin your marriage for me, Alex. I ain't worth it.'

* * *

For the next few days, nothing changed. Patrick stayed well away from the kitchen where Samuel and Alex were working, only coming to get drinks and food when absolutely necessary. He ate meals in his office which was also now his bedroom, and in the evenings Alex usually watched TV alone. Samuel sometimes joined her although he often went out until late – she didn't dare ask where – or spent time in his room. Milo only joined her when Samuel was around.

She was still trying to work out how to bring Patrick round to the fact that Samuel was staying. It felt as though their marriage was hanging on by a thread and she didn't want to be the one to sever it completely.

Then one evening, Samuel and Alex were packing up for the day when there was a loud bang and the front door flew open. Patrick appeared in the kitchen doorway.

'We need to talk.'

'What's happened?' Her heart fluttered in anticipation of his next words.

'Alone.' His eyes flicked to Samuel.

Alex bristled at his manner but gave Samuel a nod. 'Do you mind?' But he was already halfway out of the door. She turned back to Patrick. 'That was bloody rude.'

'I seriously couldn't care less.' He came further into the room and stopped halfway between Alex and the door. He had a look on his face she couldn't read. 'Have you seen what your precious *son* has done?'

'Milo? What's happened now?' She walked towards him but he shook her off angrily.

'No, not Milo. Although of course you would think that immediately.' He laughed bitterly.

'Patrick, why are you being like this?'

He folded his arms across his chest. 'I guess you haven't seen what your beloved Samuel has done then? Or maybe you have and you've decided to forgive him for that too?'

'Patrick, I have no idea what you're talking about. Just tell me what's going on.'

He leaned forward. His eyes flashed with menace. 'Your car, Alex.'

She flinched. 'What – what's happened to my car? Where is it?'

He nodded towards the door. 'Go and take a look for yourself.'

Unease wound itself around her belly as she plucked the keys from the hook by the door and headed outside. It was almost dark but even in the gloom she could see the huge scratches down the driver's side door, the dent that buckled the metalwork. She ran her fingers along it.

'When did this happen?'

'No idea. I just came out this evening and there it was. Totally fucked.'

She swung round to face him. 'You think Samuel did this?'

'Where was he last night?'

'In his room.'

'Did you check?'

She thought back to the previous evening. She'd been on her own all night, mindless TV the only company she'd had. But she'd seen Samuel go to his room around nine o'clock, and she was fairly certain he hadn't come out again. 'No, but...' she trailed off. 'He wouldn't have done this.'

'Christ, Alex, you really do think the sun shines out of that boy's backside, don't you? It's just a shame you don't have the same blind faith in me or Milo when something goes wrong.'

Alex shivered as if she'd been doused with freezing cold water.

'But why would you think Samuel has done this? You have no reason other than the fact you don't want him here.'

Patrick sighed and shook his head slowly. 'I'm sorry, Alex, I didn't want to have to tell you this. I saw Samuel take the spare keys the other night.'

She felt unsteady and reached out to the car to stop herself from falling over.

'When? When did you see him take them?'

'When you were watching TV. I came down to get a beer from the fridge and I saw him putting the keys in his pocket. He didn't notice me, and I didn't say anything because I thought maybe you'd told him he could use the car. But clearly you didn't...'

'Well, no, but I wouldn't have minded—'

'Sorry, Alex, I wish I'd have told you at the time. It's hard though. You don't want to hear anything bad about that man. I always end up being the baddie.'

She stared at Patrick. Was he smirking? Was he *pleased* about this?

'I don't believe you,' she said, her voice a whisper.

'What?' His voice was cold, flinty.

'I think you're just making this up so I'll tell Samuel to leave.'

Patrick's eyes widened and his face turned red. The temperature had dropped and she wrapped her arms around herself for warmth. Out of the corner of her eye she spotted a movement and looked up to see Milo's curtain closing. They were making a scene. She started walking towards the house.

'I can't believe you'd even think I'd do something like that.' Patrick stood in front of her, blocking her way.

'You'd do anything to get rid of him.'

'True. But I didn't make this up, Alex. How else do you think the damn car got damaged?'

'I don't know. Vandals?'

Patrick shook his head. 'Christ, he's really got you good and proper, hasn't he?'

'What's that supposed to mean?'

'You'd trust him over your own husband, over your own son.'

'He *is* my son. I have to trust him. I owe him.'

Patrick barked a laugh. 'Ha! You think that cooking him a few meals and giving him a bit of work to do is enough to make up for giving him away?'

Her breath left her. She'd never known Patrick to be cruel, no matter how angry he was.

'No. I—' She couldn't speak. She tried to swallow but something was blocking her throat. She felt tears burn her eyes and she blinked them back furiously. Suddenly, she found her voice again.

'Let me past, Patrick. I need to go inside.'

He stood for a moment longer, then stepped to one side. As she passed he said something, and she stopped, turned. 'What did you say?'

'I said, I'm moving out.'

'You're leaving me?'

He shook his head. 'It depends on what you do next, Alex. It's your move.'

28

Patrick moved out that evening into a flat across the other side of town that he'd rented from an old school friend. In the days that followed Alex felt hollowed out, as though an empty space had opened up inside her that she didn't know how to fill. Milo was furious with her for driving Patrick away, and any progress they might have made towards being close again had disappeared in a puff of smoke. They weren't just back to square one, they were way beyond that.

And although things with Caitlin were better, there was still an underlying tension between them that simmered, unspoken. It would take some time to cool completely. Besides, she also knew Caitlin was more likely to agree with Patrick than her this time, and she didn't want to hear it.

In the meantime, though, Alex knew she had to tell Samuel what Patrick had said – including about him taking the car keys.

'Thanks for trusting me,' he said, when she reassured him she believed it wasn't him. She hoped she wasn't making a huge mistake.

Over the next few days she was like a shadow, getting on with work, eating – for her baby, not for her – and, when everyone else was out, she cleaned the house furiously.

She stopped sleeping. She lay awake most of the night, tossing and turning, trying to get comfortable in what felt like a huge bed without Patrick in it. Even though he'd moved out of the room weeks ago, knowing he was no longer in the house made her feel unsettled. She was fixated on the slightest noise, and even when she did manage to snatch a few hours in the deepest depths of night she'd wake up after a fevered dream, heart thumping wildly, a sheen of sweat coating her skin. Was this what it felt like to go insane?

At her next routine check-up, she asked the doctor for something to help her sleep. Given her pregnancy, he could only give her some mild sedatives, and they barely touched the edges of her insomnia.

It was worse when she was alone in the house. At least with Milo and Samuel there she felt as though there was some layer of safety. Alone though, when Samuel was out and Milo was staying with his dad – something he increasingly did despite the fact Patrick was only renting a small one-bedroom flat – she felt open, vulnerable. She'd never lived alone, and it turned out she didn't know how to do it.

'I'm going to Dad's,' Milo said one evening. Samuel had gone out and Alex had no idea what time he'd be home – or whether he would be – and it was already getting late.

'At this time of night?'

Milo looked at her with a challenge on his face. 'Yeah.'

'You've got school in the morning, love, can't you just stay here?'

'Dad's is closer to school.'

Her stomach tightened. It wasn't just that she didn't want him to choose Patrick over her. It was that she didn't want to be on her own. She needed to keep him close, safe from harm.

'Please, love. Stay here.'

'You can't make me. I've told him I'm coming.'

Before she could argue, he left. The slam of the door felt like the final straw and she let the tears come.

She stayed up late. She was desperate for a drink but she couldn't do that to her unborn baby. She held her hands to her belly to see if she could feel anything, a sign that they were there, but there was nothing. She felt so detached from this being growing inside her she wouldn't have been surprised if she'd imagined the whole thing, except that she'd seen it on the screen with her own eyes.

It occurred to her then that if things between her and Patrick didn't get any better, she'd be bringing yet another baby into a broken relationship. First Samuel, then Milo, and now this baby. And look at how they had turned out: one had been in prison accused of murdering his father, while the other was getting in fights and dealing drugs at just fifteen.

She thought back to her father. The endless nights when she'd hide in her bedroom, Walkman turned up to maximum to drown out the sounds of his shouting and, later, the thumps and bangs that would inevitably follow. The bruises her mother tried to hide, the fake remorse he showed afterwards that her mother always chose to believe. It was clear there was something wrong with the men in her family. If this was another boy, what chance did this poor baby have?

Maybe it wasn't too late to change her mind.

* * *

Alex finally dragged herself up to bed, her eyes like grit. She lay listening to the sounds of the house: the creaks of floorboards, bangs from the boiler, cars passing on the street outside. Sleep felt a long way off, but she must have eventually dropped off because the next thing she was aware of was a tapping sound.

She froze, her body paralysed with fear, then peeled one eye open and peered out into the blackness. The looming shapes of the wardrobe, the dressing table, the chair in the dim light from the landing were menacing now, fearful creatures of the night. She held her breath and listened, ready for the slightest sound.

Just as she was about to relax, there it was again. And this time there was no denying it. Someone was in her room.

She waited, frozen, hovering in a place just outside her body.

And then a figure loomed into her vision. Blood roared in her ears and it took everything she had to remain completely still. If she could pretend to be asleep, maybe she'd survive this nightmare.

She watched, horror-struck, through half-closed eyes as the shadow moved towards her bedside table. Whoever it was, was tall, taller than Milo. Patrick? But no. Patrick was stockier, surely? And anyway, he was with Milo, at his flat over a mile away. Samuel then? But he'd lived here for weeks now, what reason would he have to suddenly start creeping around her room in the middle of the night?

An image came into her mind then of another figure looming over her just a few days ago, someone who she'd noticed had grown in recent months, bulked out. Someone she suspected might even have stolen from her already. *No.* Even through her fear she knew Archie would never do this to her. He wouldn't.

Which meant it had to be someone she didn't know. And that was way, way worse.

She needed her phone. If she could just get hold of it where it was charging on the bedside table, maybe she could alert someone. But the short distance felt like a yawning canyon, completely unreachable.

She watched through half-closed eyes where the intruder still stood by the dressing table and opened her jewellery box and picked out a few things. He stuffed them in his pocket, then pulled open a drawer where she kept her more expensive jewellery – a ring she'd inherited from her maternal grandmother, a necklace Patrick had given her for their tenth anniversary – and pulled those out too. If he was just after jewellery, maybe she would be okay. Perhaps he would leave without hurting her.

She concentrated on keeping perfectly still as she watched the figure move swiftly from the dressing table to the chest of drawers. He rummaged through the top drawer, discarding pants and bras, then paused, as if listening to something. Alex held her breath as he cast a quick look behind. He had a hood pulled up and she couldn't make out his face in the darkness. The moment stretched out and Alex dared not move. Then as quickly as he had arrived, he left, pulling the door closed behind him.

She lay perfectly still as she listened to footsteps creep down the stairs. Then slowly, as the adrenaline drained from her body she leaned over the edge of the bed and vomited onto the floor.

Suddenly galvanised into action, she swung her legs out of bed and walked shakily to the bedroom door. The taste of vomit was still in her mouth. She stood for a few seconds, listening. She couldn't hear anything. She gently pulled open the door and stepped out onto the landing. Milo's door was slightly ajar and she crept over, pushed it open and flicked on the main light. Empty. She did the same with the bath-room door. Nothing.

She crept towards the top of the stairs and listened again. It was deathly silent.

And then, there it was. The swish of a door opening and closing, followed by a click, then the sound of the downstairs toilet door opening and the light being switched on.

Samuel! It was just Samuel, getting up for a wee.

Relief flooded her body. He'd been here all this time! She raced to the bottom of the stairs and into the kitchen. Flicked on the light and waited for Samuel to come out of the bathroom so she could tell him what had happened while he'd been asleep. Perhaps he'd been disturbed too?

Her heart pounded in her head.

Then Samuel emerged from the toilet and when he saw her, he stopped dead.

'Samuel?'

'Alex?'

They stared at each other for a split second. Some-thing about the situation wasn't right, but for a mo-ment Alex couldn't work out what.

And then it hit her. Samuel wasn't in his pyjamas, as she'd been expecting. In fact he didn't look as though he'd been to bed at all. He was fully dressed. In black. With a hoodie.

Vomit rose back up her throat again and she swallowed it down.

'It was you?' she whispered. Her voice was scratchy.

'What? Was what me?' He took a step towards her but she stepped back, suddenly aware of how vulnerable she was in this house, in the middle of the night, alone with his man. She tugged her pyjama top tighter round her. Her feet were freezing against the cold kitchen tiles. An image flickered into her mind, of the tall figure in her room only moments before. Hood up.

Tall.

Slim.

Samuel.

'Don't,' she said. Her voice shook.

'Alex, what's going on?'

'I need you to leave.'

Confusion flickered across his face. 'Are you still asleep?' He waved his hand in front of her face and she flinched.

'No. I'm wide awake. As are you, I see.' She looked pointedly at his fully dressed state. He glanced down at himself.

'Yeah. I've just got in.' He frowned again. 'I don't get what's happening.'

Terror had flooded her veins now, she felt out of control. 'I know it was you, just now.'

'Just now what?'

'Just get out,' she screamed, her legs shaking.

'But—'

'Now!'

He froze and for a fraction of a second she wondered whether she'd made a mistake. But then fear kicked in again and all she was certain of was that she needed him to get away from her as quickly as possible. She didn't care that it was the middle of the night, or that until now she'd trusted him. Right here, right now, it was clear how wrong she'd been about him. He'd been in her *bedroom* for fuck's sake.

He turned, went into his room, and moments later re-emerged with his bag. 'I ain't got a clue what's going on here, Alex, but whatever it is you think I've done, I'm sorry.'

Then he left, closing the back door softly behind him.

Alex thought her legs were going to collapse beneath her, but before she did anything else she plucked the keys from the hook by the door and locked the door. Her hands shook uncontrollably, and as soon as it was secured she moved away, then turned and sprinted back up the stairs, grabbed her mobile from the bedside table, avoiding the pile of vomit on the carpet, and rang Patrick's number. She didn't care that it was the middle of the night, she didn't care about anything. She just needed to speak to him. It rang and rang and rang and just when she thought he wasn't going to answer, he picked up. 'Hello?' His voice was muffled, sleepy.

'It's me.'

'Alex?'

'Please come home.'

29

Patrick was back. Still sleeping in the spare room for now, but at least they were talking again. It felt as though they'd reached a truce – an uneasy one, but it was a step in the right direction.

He'd come back early this morning after he'd calmed Alex down over the phone.

'He was in my room,' she'd sobbed, disbelief mingling with the fear.

'Is he still there?' Patrick had said, and she was grateful he hadn't said *I told you so.*

'No, I told him to leave.'

'Good.' Alex heard him swallow. 'Stay where you are and Milo and I will be over as soon as he wakes up.

I don't want to scare him by dragging him over there in the middle of the night.'

She glanced at the clock. It was already 5 a.m., she could wait another couple of hours.

'Thank you,' she croaked.

True to his word, Patrick and Milo had arrived just after 7 a.m., Milo looking confused and half-asleep.

'Thanks for coming,' she'd said.

'Why couldn't I just have gone to school from Dad's?' Milo grumbled.

'I told you,' Patrick had replied. 'Mum needed some help with something. I said I'd drive you to school, didn't I?'

'Huh,' he grunted, and Alex was so grateful they were both there she didn't even pick him up on it.

'Go and jump in the shower and I'll take you in an hour or so, okay?'

Milo stomped up the stairs without a reply and Alex led Patrick into the kitchen. She turned to face him.

'Thank you for coming.'

'Of course I came. I love you, Alex.'

'Do you?'

He sighed and rubbed his face with his hand. When he looked at her she could see the hurt in his eyes. 'I've always loved you. I just—' He stopped. 'I hated what you were doing. With him.'

'With Samuel.'

He nodded. 'It just wasn't you, to be so... so *needy.*'

'You think I was needy?'

He raised his eyebrows and her face flushed with shame. 'I just thought – I still think – that you clung to Samuel the way you did because of what was going on with Milo.'

She didn't reply. Because what could she say? She'd assumed that Patrick hadn't liked Samuel because he was jealous, or angry with her for not telling him about Samuel when they'd first met. But now it was clear that Patrick had been right about him from the very beginning, whereas Alex had been too blind to see his true colours.

Patrick sat at the table and gestured for Alex to do the same. 'I know you told me what happened on the phone but tell me again. Slowly this time.'

She repeated the whole thing. About waking up and finding a hooded figure in her bedroom. About the terror she'd felt and the relief when she'd realised he'd only wanted her jewellery. About how she'd gone downstairs once she was sure he'd left and realised Samuel was in after all. And about how Samuel had been fully dressed, wearing a dark hoodie. How she freaked and told him to get out. She omitted to mention she'd briefly wondered if it was Patrick.

'I feel so guilty,' she said. 'What if I'm wrong? What if it wasn't Samuel?'

Patrick looked serious. 'Ally, I know you desperately want to believe he's good. But you know it must have been him, right? I mean, were there any signs of a forced entry? Anything to suggest someone else had been in the house?'

She shook her head miserably. 'I just don't understand why he'd feel the need to do this. If he'd needed anything, he could have just asked me, and I would have given it to him. Surely he knew that?'

Patrick reached out and covered her hand with his. 'I know, love. But you know what a hard life he's had. He's never been able to trust anyone. He was bound to deceive you sooner or later. I'm just sorry I wasn't here to protect you.'

She looked up at him. 'Does this mean you're coming home?'

He hesitated. 'Do you want me to?'

'I do.' A tear rolled down her face. 'I really do.'

* * *

Just when Alex thought things were getting back on an even keel – she and Patrick living in the same house, things with Milo settled at school – everything blew up again.

Alex was back at work, even though she still felt like she was walking on eggshells with Caitlin, and was still nervous about upsetting things with Patrick. Her nerves were shredded as she wavered between wanting to call Samuel and tell him she was sorry, and being terrified that he would come back, unable to shake the image of the figure in the dark hoodie in her bedroom.

Having Patrick working from the kitchen for much of the day helped ease her nerves a little. She tried not to think about what would happen if Samuel tried to come in and found Patrick there. She hoped for both of their sakes he'd stay away. At least for now.

She was unpacking the shopping a few days after Patrick moved back home when the phone rang. The landline rang so rarely it made them both stop in their tracks.

'Want me to get it?' Patrick said. Alex nodded. She didn't know why but she had a bad feeling about this call.

'Hello?' Patrick said. Alex listened, trying to work

out from his end of the conversation what was happening. He wasn't giving anything away.

'Shall we come in now?'

Her stomach dropped. Milo? Or Samuel? School or the police? She waited impatiently as Patrick wrapped up the call, then stood as he hung up.

'What's going on?'

'That was the school,' he said, and her stomach dropped even further. 'Milo's been fighting again. This time he's really hurt someone. They need stitches.'

'What?' She felt shame welling up in her as she remembered the bruises that had always covered her mother's body. Her father's vile temper was rearing its ugly head again, and this time it was ruining her boy's life.

She grabbed her bag and started heading for the door. 'Wait!' Patrick called. She turned. 'We'll go together.'

'You don't need to. This is my problem to deal with and you've got work to do.'

'Alex, for the last few weeks Milo has been more or less living with me because he's been so angry with you. If you think this is just your problem then that's up to you, but he's more likely to speak to us if I'm there too.'

She wanted to cry. Patrick was right. Her infatua-

tion with Samuel had damaged her and Milo's relationship so much recently that he preferred to spend
time with his stepdad than his own mother.

'Okay then.'

It only took them ten minutes to get to school.
Patrick drove because Alex didn't feel she could right
now. When they arrived they were hurried straight
to the head's office. Milo was already there, huddled
on a hard plastic chair, staring at the floor. He
looked so young. Alex wanted to promise him everything was going to be all right. He didn't even
look up.

'Thank you for coming at such short notice, Mr
and Mrs Harding,' Mrs Kingston said, shaking both
Alex and Patrick's hands. 'Please, take a seat.'

Alex perched on the edge of the one closest to
Milo. She tried to catch his eye but he refused to look
at her. His leg bounced up and down, his neck buried
inside his coat like a turtle. Beside her, Patrick seemed
much calmer.

'As we mentioned on the phone, Milo was caught
fighting with another pupil at lunchtime, and the
other pupil has required stitches at hospital,' Mrs
Kingston began. Alex tried to focus on a spot just
above her shoulder.

'Who was the other pupil?'

Mrs Kingston steepled her fingers. 'I'm afraid I'm not at liberty to say.'

'Are they being dealt with too?' Fury thumped in her belly.

Alex looked at Milo. 'Milo, was this something to do with Archie?'

Milo flinched but said nothing. Alex tried to search out the truth in his eyes but he kept his gaze trained on the floor in front of him. Then he shook his head.

Mrs Kingston continued.

'As you know, we have been concerned about your son's behaviour for some time, which is why we thought it important that we speak in person.' She cleared her throat. 'I'm afraid in this instance I have no choice but to suspend Milo for a week.' Alex nodded numbly. 'But as you know, we don't like to just hand out punishments without trying to find out more about what is causing such behaviour.' She leaned forward onto the desk. 'Milo has always been a well-behaved young man. It's only during the last year or so that he has caused us any problems at all. I wondered, Mr and Mrs Harding, whether there is anything going on at home that might be causing some disruption?' She had the grace to look uncomfortable, and Alex pitied her having to ask parents questions like these.

No doubt she was expecting a tale of divorce, or a bereavement, which often went some way to explaining a teenager's disruptive actions. Alex couldn't help wondering what she'd make of their story – long lost son, prison, a murder trial...

'I can't think of anything,' Alex said, her voice cracking.

'Huhhh.' A muffled sound came from Milo and they all looked at him.

'Milo? Is there something you'd like to say to your parents?'

For the first time since they'd arrived, Milo looked up. Dark circles framed his eyes and his skin was pale. Alex's heart broke. What had she done to her beautiful boy? Where had he gone?

Finally she caught his gaze. His look was challenging and Alex thought for a minute he was going to tell Mrs Kingston exactly what had been going on at home. But then he must have thought better of it, and he tore his gaze away and stared at a spot somewhere in the centre of the desk.

'No.'

Silence hummed between them all for a moment. Patrick stood. 'Right, well, we'll take him home now then, if we may?'

Mrs Kingston looked up, surprised, and stood too.

She was tall, with high cheekbones and lips painted a dark red. 'Yes, of course. We will see Milo back here in a week's time then, but if there's anything you'd like to discuss in the meantime then please do get in touch.'

'Of course. Thank you.'

'And please be aware that if anything like this happens again, we'll have no option but to take further action.'

They filed out of the room. Alex felt as if she'd been on trial herself and been found failing as a parent. Which was fair enough.

She just wished she had a clue how to get through to Milo and find out what was really going on in that mind of his.

* * *

'I'll talk to him,' Patrick said, once they were home and Milo was in his bedroom.

'Don't you think we should do it together?'

'I just think he might be more likely to speak to me.' Patrick rubbed her upper arms. 'Besides, I don't want to put you through any more stress. You've got the baby to look after.' Guilt pierced her. She'd been so preoccupied with Samuel and Milo she'd hardly had time to think about the baby. 'At least let me have a go?' he added.

Alex was suddenly overwhelmed with gratitude that Patrick was back and helping her to deal with this. She felt too fragile. She was certainly in no fit state to try to get through to a belligerent teenage boy who didn't want to speak to her. She also wasn't sure she wanted to know what secrets Milo was hiding.

'Okay, thank you, Patrick.'

'We'll sort this out, okay?'

She nodded. Then Patrick went upstairs to speak to her son and left her standing in the kitchen, alone.

30

Alex rapped lightly on Milo's door. When there was no answer she poked her head in. He was lying on his bed with his headphones in, eyes closed. His usual position.

'Milo!'

No answer. She walked over and nudged him on the arm. His eyes snapped open and he pulled an earbud out of his ear. 'What?'

'I'm going to paint the hallway. Do you feel like helping?'

'No.'

She sighed. It was the reply she'd been expecting but she was still disappointed. Milo had been at home for three days now and had spent most of that time in his room. She'd thought that helping her with some decorating might cheer him up.

She should have known better.

'Well, I'll be downstairs if you fancy giving me a hand later, okay?'

'Yep.' He stuck the earbud back in and rolled away to face the wall. She headed back down the stairs. The paintbrushes and dust sheets were in the garage so she pulled her jacket and boots on and unlocked the door that led from the kitchen. Flicking on the light she looked up, trying to remember where she'd put everything last time she'd decorated.

She dragged the step ladder into position, climbed up and reached for the box at the top of a shelving unit Patrick had put together a couple of years ago. It was heavier than she'd expected and she almost toppled backwards as she freed it from the shelf and lifted it back down the steps. She placed the box on the dusty garage floor and went back up to get the dustsheets which were rammed into the corner. As she tugged them towards her something caught her eye, half hidden behind a load of old painting rags. Something silver, glinting in a shaft of light.

She stood on her tiptoes to reach for it, and finally got a grasp and tugged it towards her. It got caught on a nail and she pulled it harder. It went flying out of her grasp and clattered to the ground. Shit.

She climbed down the steps and bent to pick it up. It was a trophy of some sort. She studied it, frowning. Neither Patrick nor Milo were particularly sporty, at least not competitively, and as far as Alex was aware neither of them had ever won a trophy. It certainly wasn't hers. It was too dark in the garage despite the dim overhead light to make out the words engraved on the gold plaque.

Something tugged at the back of her mind but stayed just out of reach.

She threw it on top of the box of paintbrushes, then carried the whole lot through to the kitchen, dumped it on the table and filled the kettle. A cup of mint tea might go some way to easing the tension that thrummed through her body.

While the kettle boiled she turned back to the box and pulled the flaps fully open. She tugged out dozens of paintbrushes, some of them wrapped in cling film with remnants of old paint still clagging up their bristles, a roller, a plastic paint tray, some cloths and a bottle of white spirit, and emptied it all onto the table. The kettle clicked and she poured the water onto the teabag then turned back to the box and picked up the trophy. The dust was thick so she wiped it away with her sleeve and peered at it.

Player of the Year 2002: Scott Jones

Her hand flew to her mouth. *Scott Jones*?

Samuel's father?

Samuel's *dead* father.

She gripped the trophy tightly in her hands as her brain whirred, memories of the court case tumbling through her mind thick and fast.

Yvonne's claim that there must have been a trophy missing from the shelf.

Her certainty that it had been used as the murder weapon.

The fact it was never found had been one of the main reasons Samuel had been found not guilty.

And now it was here, in Alex's house.

What the fuck was it doing here?

31

She dropped the trophy onto the table with a clatter and sat, her legs unable to hold her any longer, trying to calm her thoughts. Surely there had to be some reasonable explanation for this to be here.

But if there was, she couldn't see it.

This was the suspected weapon that had killed Scott Jones.

In her home.

The only question was, who could have put it there?

Her mind spooled back over the last few days, weeks, months. Dozens of people had been in her house. But how many of them would have had the opportunity to hide something there?

And more to the point, how many would have had a reason to?

Milo and Patrick were here all the time, but even if she did think they were capable of something like murder, neither of them had known Scott. The only other people who would have had the opportunity to do it were Archie and Caitlin – but these were people she knew, that she loved. Did she *really* think they were capable of something as premeditated as this?

She held her head in her hands and shook her head, trying to dislodge the only other thought that seemed to have settled there.

Samuel.

Her blood chilled in her veins. She'd trusted Samuel. She'd invited him into her home, her heart. She'd put everything she loved at risk for him. But he'd broken that trust when he'd broken into her room and stolen from her. Now there was this.

Oh, Patrick, you were right all along.

She stood suddenly, the movement making her head spin. The last thing she felt like doing now was decorating so she bundled everything back into the box and took it into the garage where she threw it back onto the shelf. She grabbed one of the rags the trophy had been hidden in, wrapped it back up, then went back into the house and stuffed the whole thing in her bag.

What was she supposed to do now?

Should she tell Patrick about this?

He'd want to call the police immediately. But something was telling Alex to keep this from Patrick for a while. Previously, she could have predicted how he'd react, but right now she wasn't so sure. Anything to do with Samuel seemed to stoke the fire of his fury.

No, she needed to find out a bit more first. Because if she was wrong about this, then she could be ruining Samuel's life all over again – and this time nobody would believe he was innocent.

And if she was right? It didn't bear thinking about.

She dug out her mobile, dialled a familiar number, and waited.

* * *

Caitlin came immediately, and now she and Alex were standing side by side, staring down at the trophy which sat accusingly on the table in front of them.

'And you found this hidden in your garage?' Caitlin said, peering at it more closely. They'd agreed that, although it was probably too late for any incriminating fingerprints to still be on there, they probably shouldn't touch it any more than Alex already had.

'Up on the top shelf.'

Caitlin straightened up. 'Fuck. Have you told the police?'

'No. I—' Alex stopped. She knew she should have done of course. 'I want to find out a bit more first.'

'But surely they can do that?'

Alex nodded but didn't reply.

'If you're hoping to find out that this was nothing to do with Samuel, I think we both know you're going to be disappointed,' she said, and Alex was grateful to Caitlin for getting to the point.

'But surely there *must* be another explanation?'

Caitlin looked at her with pity. 'Such as?'

Alex racked her brain, trying to work out what possible other reason there could be for this trophy to be hidden in her garage. 'Well, first of all Samuel didn't know me then, so following your logic it could only have been in my house since he lived there. So where was he keeping it before? Where was it when he was in prison? Or living on the streets? It doesn't make any sense.'

Caitlin rubbed her chin. 'Where was he living after the trial?'

Alex tried to think back to what Samuel had told

her about the weeks following the trial. He'd been on the streets a bit, but not the entire time. 'I think he said he was in a squat on and off.'

'Right. So it could have been kept there?'

'Maybe. But what about immediately after the murder? If he'd killed Scott, where would he have hidden it?'

'His mum still lives at the family home, doesn't she?'

Alex nodded.

'Well, he could have hidden it anywhere. There could be a hiding place he knows about that the police didn't find. Or his mum could have hidden it for him.'

'But she testified against him. There's no way she would have helped him out.'

Cait's voice was gentle now. 'Sorry, Alex, but the truth is you don't know these people at all. Anything could have happened.'

Alex felt her heart harden. They might have had their differences recently, and she might not fully trust Archie still, but Caitlin was right. All Alex knew about Samuel was what he had told her, and what she'd heard in court.

'Will you help me?'

'Of course I will. What do you want me to do?'

Alex took a deep breath. 'Will you come with me

to find the squat Samuel lived in? Someone there might know something.'

'Are you sure? This could be dangerous, don't you think it would be better to speak to the police and let them deal with it?'

Alex thought about it. She could see why Caitlin might think that. But she didn't want to get the police involved while there was still a chance she could be wrong about this. What if Samuel had simply brought it with him as something to remember his dad by? Even though it was an unlikely suggestion given what she knew about his feelings towards his father, and given how the trophy had been hidden, she owed him this much at least.

'Let's just try. Then I'll go to the police, I promise. Please?'

Caitlin studied Alex for a split second, then nodded. 'Okay. Where do we start?'

* * *

Alex finally remembered the name of the street Samuel had told her the squat was on: Belvedere. She'd noticed it at the time because it was a notorious area of town for trouble – not somewhere she ever fancied going alone. She hoped it would be obvious which house it was when they got there.

'Shall we go then?' Caitlin said, grabbing her coat from the rack.

'What, now?'

'No time like the present. It's not like we're going to get any work done today.'

Alex stood too. Her legs felt wobbly. What on earth did she think she was doing, taking matters into her own hands? What if Samuel was at the squat? And what if he – or someone else there – was dangerous?

But what other choice did she have?

'Let's go.'

Caitlin drove because Alex was too jittery. They didn't speak on the short journey through town, and while Caitlin listened to the satnav directions, Alex let her mind race ahead to what they might find. Would Samuel be there? Likely, given that he didn't have anywhere else to go. What would she say to him? Would he be furious with her? She thought about the way he'd reacted when she'd accused him of hiding drugs in the house, and how he'd convinced her they weren't his, even though he'd later admitted they had been. He'd had her fooled more than once, it seemed. She wasn't hopeful that this was going to be any different.

She only noticed the car had stopped when Caitlin spoke to her.

'Looks like it might be that one,' she said, squinting at the run-down terraced house in a row of relatively neat homes. A ground-floor window was boarded up, and newspaper covered the rest. The white plastic door was grubby, the overgrown lawn filled with weeds. There was an air of sorrow about the place, of neglect, and her heart hurt at the thought of Samuel slumming it here. It looked like a place where hopes and dreams came to die.

Alex opened the door and climbed out. A blast of frigid air hit her and she shivered. How cold must it be inside? She stood staring up at the house for a few seconds before she felt Caitlin tugging at her sleeve.

'Shall we go in then?'

Alex looked at her friend in her stripy bobble hat and beautifully made-up face and wondered what she must look like standing beside her. Her hair was lank and unwashed, her nails bitten and the dark circles under her eyes had started to turn into bags.

'Come on.'

Caitlin marched ahead and by the time Alex reached the door Caitlin had already tried to peer through tiny cracks in the paper over the window. Giving up, she walked to the front door and did the same with the glass panels there. They were still intact but a large crack ran the length of the right-hand pane.

'I can't see anything.' She tugged her hat off in exasperation.

'It doesn't look like we can get round the back either, there's no access.'

They both looked up at the top windows. There was no paper covering them, but no curtains hung at them either. There was no sign of life.

'I'm going to knock.'

'No!' But before Alex could stop her, Caitlin was hammering on the grubby plastic. A few moments passed, but no one came.

'For God's sake, it shouldn't be hard to break into a squat, the people who live here managed it,' Caitlin said, walking back to the windows and pressing against them with her palm.

'Caitlin.'

'What?' she whipped round.

'Be careful.'

'You want to get in there and see if they know anything about Samuel, don't you?'

'Yes, but—'

'Can I help youse?' A deep voice made them both spin round to see a man letting himself through the broken gate. His hair hung in dark blonde dreadlocks, and a days-old beard covered the lower part of his face. It was hard to say how old he was, but Alex would guess he was a few years younger than her, but well-worn. He was clutching a plain white carrier bag in one hand.

'Oh, hi.' Alex stayed where she was, not daring to step any closer. She'd learned not to trust anyone. The man looked from Alex to Caitlin and back again.

'Are youse looking for someone?' He had a strong Geordie accent and his voice was gruff, a smoker's rasp.

'We are, as a matter of fact,' Caitlin said, and she held out the photo of Samuel they'd printed out before they left. 'Do you know him? He's called Samuel.'

'I do, aye. Posh boy.' Alex's heart caught in her throat. He looked up. 'Why, what's he done?'

'Does he live here?' Alex asked, ignoring his question.

'He did. Left a few days ago though.'

Her heart plummeted. 'Do you happen to know where he went?'

He shook his head. 'No idea.' He must have seen the disappointment on her face because he added, 'Sorry.'

'Are you sure you don't have any idea where he might be?' Caitlin pushed.

'We don't really share stuff like that.' He shrugged. 'You know how it is, easy come, easy go.'

She didn't but nodded anyway.

He must have taken pity on them because he said, 'D'youse want to come in and take a look, see if you can find owt that might help?'

Alex glanced at Caitlin. She nodded.

'If you don't mind...' she trailed off.

'Haway then. I'm Paul, by the way, but everyone calls me Antun – you know, on account of Ant un Dec being Geordies, like.' He grinned and his teeth were surprisingly straight and neat. Alex wondered what circumstances had brought him here, to this squat hundreds of miles from home.

They approached the door and he pressed his palms against the wooden section between the panes of glass and gave it a firm shove. The door creaked open. 'Not exactly high security but it's not like we have owt worth nicking.' He stepped inside. 'Come in.'

As they followed him into the dim hallway Antun heaved the door back into position and Alex was glad she hadn't come alone. She wondered what Patrick would think if he knew where she was.

They followed Antun along the hallway. The walls

had once been white but now they were a grubby grey, smeared with years of uncleaned streaks, scratches and fingerprints. The floor underfoot had probably once been covered with carpet but now there were only a few tatty threads left stretched across the floorboards, and some of the wooden boards were bowing and cracked. It felt like a death trap. It was also icy cold. Alex shivered and pulled her coat tighter.

'This is the kitchen, and I sleep in that room,' Antun indicated as they entered a vast space. Someone had clearly once spent a lot of money on this house and Alex wondered what the story was behind it falling into disrepair. Cupboards lined the walls but most no longer had doors, and they were all empty.

'We have to keep all our food in our own rooms, or else it gets swiped,' Antun explained as if reading her mind. A few pots sat on the side, and there was a small gas stove on part of the worktop that wasn't broken. Otherwise there was little sign that this was used for preparing food.

Antun turned to face them. 'Posh boy was upstairs, I think he shared with another lad up there. Front room.'

'Can we go up?'

'Help yourselves.'

'Is there anyone else in?'

'No idea but no one will bother youse if that's what you're worried about. We're used to people coming and going round here. Can't really complain when you're living somewhere for free, eh?' He gave a sort of grimace and Alex felt a pang of sympathy for this man-boy who had found himself living in such depressing circumstances.

'Right, come on then,' Caitlin said.

Alex turned to Antun. 'Do you think there's any way Samuel could have hidden something here? For a few weeks maybe?'

'Something valuable, you mean?'

Alex glanced at Caitlin. 'Not necessarily. Something... important. To him.'

He considered me for a moment, then shook his head.

'Nah. Nobody leaves owt in this place unless they want it to get nicked.'

'Even if it's something of no value to anyone else?'

'Everything's got a value to someone.' He ran his hand over his beard. 'Anything you don't want to get found, you keep on you all the time.' He held up his hands which were still clutching the white carrier bag. 'As you can see, I have nowt worth nicking, like.'

Alex smiled sadly at him.

'Did you know him well?'

'Posh Boy? Not really. None of us know much about anyone else here. We don't ask too many questions.'

'So you don't know what he was like?'

'Not really. Although—'

'What?'

He shook his head. 'Nah, it's probably nothing.'

'Please.'

He stared at her for a minute. 'Well, he could be quite – what's the word? Fiery.'

'Fiery?'

'Yeah. Ya nah. Lost his temper easy.'

Alex glanced at Caitlin. 'Did he ever lose his temper with you?'

'Nah, not me. But he could be handy with his fists when he was, you know, off his face.'

Although Samuel had admitted he could lose it sometimes, it was something Alex hadn't witnessed herself. She forced a smile.

'Right, well. Thank you. That's really helpful. And thanks for letting us in.'

'Any time.'

Antun disappeared and Alex turned to Caitlin.

'What do you make of that, then?'

'I guess it's not a huge surprise, given what we're here for.'

Alex hung her head. 'I guess not.'

Keen to get on and get out of there, they headed towards the staircase. Caitlin ran up fearlessly, but Alex hung back, her heart beating fast in her chest. What if they were caught? Would someone try and hurt them? She had no idea who lived here, what kind of people ended up living in a place like this. She doubted they were all as helpful or as generous as Antun.

'What's up?' Caitlin stopped at the top of the stairs and peered back down at where Alex hovered.

'I'm not sure about this.'

Caitlin put her hand on her hip. 'There's nothing to be scared of. Anyway, we're here now, we might as well *try* and find out something.'

Alex let out a breath. 'You're right.' She strode up the last few steps, taking care to miss the wonky ones. 'Although you heard what Antun said. There's no way Samuel could have hidden anything here.'

'Don't be such a defeatist.'

'I'm not. I'm being realistic. I really don't think we're going to find anything.'

She shrugged. 'You don't know until you try.'

They stood at the top of the stairs and peered into

the gloom of the landing. The house was in a slightly better state of repair up here, although floral wallpaper still sagged from the corners, dislodged by damp, and the carpet was worn and patchy. All the doors were shut except one right at the end which allowed a sliver of wintry light to filter onto the landing.

'I think it might be that one,' Caitlin said.

Before Alex could change her mind she set off towards the chink of light. Her pulse roared in her ears. She screamed when a door to her right swung open and a figure appeared, silhouetted.

'Oh.' The woman watched them, her mouth open. She looked as shocked as Alex felt.

'Sorry,' Alex said, her legs feeling as if they were about to collapse beneath her.

The woman studied her a second longer, then shrugged, shut the door behind her and headed down the staircase.

Alex didn't dare breathe again until the woman was out of sight and she heard the front door slam shut.

'You look like you've seen a ghost,' Caitlin said from behind her.

'Sorry. I don't know what's wrong with me.' What *was* she so scared of?

'Come on. Let's just get this over and done with.'

They stalked to the end of the corridor and pushed the door fully open. Net curtains sagged at the window, there were a couple of dirty mattresses on the floor and a rickety-looking wooden chair in one corner but other than that the room was empty.

'It doesn't look like there's anything to find in here,' she said, trying to hide her disappointment at their lack of progress.

Caitlin bent down and prised up the corner of the mattress closest to the door and shone her phone torch under it. Nothing. She did the same with the other one as Alex looked on helplessly from the doorway. Caitlin let it drop, clouds of dust puffing out from underneath.

'Nothing there. Although I suppose it might be a place he could have hidden the trophy for a while.' She looked doubtful.

'I suppose so.' Alex cast her eyes over the rest of the room. Although there was very little furniture, there were some cupboards built into the wall that she hadn't noticed at first. She walked over to them and pulled the doors open. There was very little on the shelves apart from a few measly items of clothing, and a stash of tobacco.

'Brave of someone to leave that here,' Caitlin said, peering over her shoulder.

'There's nothing here,' Alex said despondently.

'Hang on.' Caitlin pulled the flimsy wooden chair over to the cupboard and stepped up onto it. It wobbled beneath her feet and Alex grabbed onto her hips to stop her toppling to the ground. She shone her phone torch along the top shelf, and the one beneath that, and ran her hand over the surfaces of each. She turned to Alex as she stepped down, wiping the dust from her hands onto her jeans. 'Nope. Nothing. Sorry.'

Alex's stomach dropped. 'Well, that's that then. I guess we'll have to think of another way of finding Samuel.'

It was beginning to get dark now and the light in the room was dim. Alex pulled the chair back into position and closed the wardrobe doors.

'Who the fuck are you?' The voice made them jump and they span round to find a man looming in the open doorway. He was almost as tall as the doorframe and skinny, a beanie hat pulled down tightly on his head so that Alex could hardly make out any features in the gloom. His clothes hung off him. Alex's heart thumped wildly.

'Sorry, I—' Alex faltered as her breath caught in her throat.

'We're just going,' Caitlin said, stepping towards him. But rather than moving out of her way he stayed where he was, blocking her path. She stopped a few paces before she reached him.

'Excuse me, please.' Caitlin's voice was loud and clear but Alex knew her well enough to hear the wobble in it.

'Only if you tell me who you are and what the fuck you're doing in my room.' He took a step towards Caitlin and she flinched but didn't move back. Instinctively Alex moved to stand beside her and tried to ignore the terror pulsing through her veins. She wished Antun had come up with them now.

'We're friends of Antun,' Alex said, her voice quiet. She cleared her throat. 'We were looking for something and he said it might be in here.'

The man didn't reply but studied them both for a few seconds, peering at them through his overgrown eyebrows. There wasn't much light left in the room now and Alex could only just make out his face, but from what she could see his face looked as if it had folded in on itself, the creases around his eyes and mouth deep and dark. A face that had seen too much, she suspected. A vein pulsed in her temple as she waited for him to speak.

'Has this got something to do with Posh Boy?' The last two words were filled with contempt.

'Samuel, yes,' Alex said, heart thumping with hope.

'He's gone.'

'Yes, I know. I... I don't suppose you know where he might have gone, do you?'

He looked from Alex to Caitlin and back again as if trying to decide whether to tell them anything. A thought occurred to her then and she scrabbled inside her bag for the trophy. It felt heavy on her shoulder, like rocks were weighing her down.

'Have you ever seen this before?' Alex held the trophy out with shaking hands. He snatched it from her and peered at the front, his brow grooves deepening even further. Then his eyes flicked back to Alex and he held it back out again.

'Nope.'

'Oh.' She took it from him and dropped it back in her bag. Disappointment flooded through her.

'Are you absolutely sure you don't know where Samuel might have gone?' Caitlin said. 'I can't believe he didn't tell anyone.'

He lifted his chin up. 'You calling me a liar?'

'No!' Alex said before Caitlin could reply. 'We just really need to find him. Sorry.' She held her hand out but he ignored it.

'Get out of my room.' He stood to one side, and

before Caitlin could argue Alex pushed her towards him and they squeezed out and back into the corridor. As Alex passed him he grabbed her arm and she cried out.

'Don't come into my room and snoop about again.'

She nodded. 'Understood.'

Then he let her go and they practically ran out of the house, yanking open the stiff front door and slamming it shut behind them. They got into Caitlin's car as quickly as they could, and her heart didn't start to return to normal until they were well out of sight of the house.

'Fuck it,' Caitlin said, slamming her palm against the steering wheel.

'It doesn't matter,' Alex said, her voice quivering. Caitlin glanced across.

'Course it matters. It was our only lead.' She looked back at the road just as a car pulled out in front and she had to slam on the brakes. 'Arsehole!' she screamed, jabbing the horn with her hand. The man in the other car flicked them the Vs and drove off with a squeal. They sat for a moment in silence until a car behind them beeped its horn impatiently, and Caitlin pulled off again, more slowly this time.

'I'm sorry for dragging you here.'

'Don't be. I'm pretty sure it was my idea.'

Alex shook her head. 'I just feel so guilty for getting you caught up in all this.' She sat in silence for a moment. 'I hate the thought of Samuel living somewhere like that, with... with people like that.'

'I know. But Antun was all right. I'm sure they're not all terrifying.'

'Maybe not. But—' She stopped. 'You were right, what you said before about me not knowing Samuel at all. I was a complete idiot to welcome him into my home. I put us all at risk, didn't I?'

Caitlin didn't reply straight away and they both stared at the brake lights on the car in front. Finally, she said 'You weren't an idiot, Alex. I get it. I really do.' Caitlin glanced at her then back at the road. Her face was tinged orange from the streetlights and she looked serious. 'I should never have made you feel that way.'

'But you were right though, weren't you?'

'That's not the point. He's your son. Of course you wanted to help him.'

Alex turned to look at her properly. 'What's brought on this change of heart?'

Caitlin shrugged. 'I just thought about how I'd feel if it was Archie. It made me realise I was being out of order.' Her lips twitched. 'So that's why I wanted to help you today. To say sorry.'

Alex reached her hand out and laid it on Caitlin's arm. 'You don't have to be sorry.'

They drove in silence for the next few minutes. As they pulled up at some traffic lights about a five-minute drive from the office Caitlin spoke again.

'So if it wasn't Samuel, where *did* the trophy come from?'

Alex looked at her. 'What do you mean?'

'Well, we've pretty much established that it's un-likely to have been hidden at the squat. There's still the possibility that Samuel's mum kept it for him, but given she seems barely able to look at him, it doesn't seem likely. So if it *wasn't* Samuel that brought it into your house, who was it?'

32

Back in the office, Caitlin laid a notepad on the desk in front of them and grabbed a pen.

'We need to establish a timeline.'

'There's no point,' Alex said. 'The only other people who live in the house are Milo and Patrick and, even if I thought for one second it could have been either of them, which I don't, they didn't even know Scott or Samuel before the trial.'

Caitlin nodded. 'Exactly. Which means we need to work out who else might have been in your house in the meantime.'

She rubbed her hand over her face. It seemed impossible that someone else had murdered Scott then hidden the weapon in their house. How would they even know to do that? Unless...

'What if someone was trying to frame Samuel?'

Caitlin looked up at her. 'Go on.'

Alex sat down heavily, trying to get her brain to work out the details. 'If the murderer – whoever they are – had hit Scott with this trophy, then panicked and taken it away from the murder scene—' her words were coming out quickly now '—then they somehow discovered that Samuel, who had already been on trial for killing his father, had been found not guilty and come to live with me...' She trailed off, unable to work out who that could possibly be.

'This is good,' Caitlin said, scribbling down some notes.

'Is it?'

Caitlin nodded. 'We might not know who that person is yet, but if we really rack our brains and try to work out exactly who has been at your house in the last few weeks, then we might be able to work out who it is.'

Something occurred to Alex then. 'Don't you think we should go to the police with this now? If the murderer really has been here, we could be in danger.'

Caitlin looked up. 'Not yet.' She closed her eyes briefly, then opened them and gave Alex a dark look.

'What if it turns out to be someone we don't want to implicate?'

'Like who?'

She hesitated a moment. 'I don't know, Alex. But that's exactly what we're going to find out.'

* * *

It was amazing how much you could remember when you put your mind to it. An hour later they had two sides of paper filled with times and dates and names, and rough ideas of who was in Alex's house and when, including Caitlin herself, and Janie and Pete.

'There is one other person,' Alex said, uncertainly. She wasn't sure how Caitlin was going to take the news.

'Go on.' Her pen hovered above the paper, but when Alex didn't reply straight away she looked up, her brow knitted in confusion.

'Alex?'

Alex threaded her fingers together and shifted in her chair. Caitlin crossed her arms and waited.

'Archie was here the other day.'

Caitlin watched her but she didn't dare catch her eye. 'I know you said you didn't want him hanging out with Milo but he caught me by surprise and I didn't know what to say. He said they were doing homework so I let them...' She trailed off.

Caitlin licked her lips, then carefully wrote Archie's name on the list.

'I'll add my name as well, better not leave any stone unturned,' she said.

'Is that all you're going to say?'

Caitlin shrugged. 'Well, unless you think my son has anything to do with Scott's murder then I think we have bigger fish to fry, don't you?'

Alex didn't reply and Caitlin peered at her. 'You *don't* think Archie has something to do with this, do you?' Her voice was too high, and Alex shook her head.

'Of course not!' There was no point in confessing that it had crossed her mind on more than one occasion. They'd only just got things back on an even keel. Not to mention that Archie would have had no reason at all to leave the trophy at her house if it had been him.

The trouble was, none of this had brought them any closer to working out who might have planted the trophy at Alex's house, because none of them could realistically be suspects, and neither was there any reason for them to have gone near the garage apart from the tumble dryer repair man who'd been round one late November afternoon.

'Now what?' Alex said, throwing her pen down in frustration.

But when she looked over at Caitlin, she had a strange expression on her face.

'Cait? What is it?'

She looked up and Alex's stomach flipped over when she saw the look in her eyes, like a haunted woman. 'What's happening, Caitlin? What have you worked out?'

She hesitated a moment longer, 'When did Milo start having real problems at school?'

'Milo?' Alex frowned. 'Why?'

Caitlin pointed at the first page of our notes, right at the beginning of the timeline. 'It was about then, wasn't it? Last January, or around then?'

'I– I'm not sure. I think so.'

She didn't reply, and it slowly began to dawn on Alex what she was getting at.

'You can't possibly think this has got anything to do with Milo? That's absurd.'

Caitlin continued to stare into space, and Alex felt fury rise in her. 'Caitlin!'

Caitlin whipped her head up. 'Sorry. I was thinking.'

'About Milo being a murderer?'

'I don't know, Alex!' Caitlin stood suddenly and strode across the room, then swivelled and came back again. Alex watched as she paced several times, then came to a stop and placed her palms on the desk. Alex waited for her friend to explain herself.

'Of course I can't imagine it being Milo. But the truth is, right now we don't have anything else.'

'But you *know* Milo. He's fifteen! There's no way he would have done something like this. No way.'

Caitlin looked down at her hands. 'I know, Alex. But I don't think we should rule anything out right now, however unlikely.' She swallowed. 'Besides, if it wasn't him, maybe he knows who *did* do it. Maybe he's known all along. It would at least explain why he started behaving the way he did.'

Alex ignored the jibe, not in the mood to talk about Milo's misdemeanours. 'You seem to have forgotten that Milo and Patrick didn't even know anything about Samuel until *after* the trial, so there's no way either of them could have anything to do with this.' *Unlike Archie*, she thought but didn't say. *And you.* A shiver ran down her spine.

'You're right.' Caitlin rubbed the back of her neck. 'I'm sorry, you're right, I don't know what I was thinking.' She sat down on the chair again, defeated. Tears filled Alex's eyes and she swiped them away.

'I don't know what else to do,' Alex said, her voice small.

'Me neither. Unless...' Caitlin looked up at Alex. 'You have a Ring doorbell, don't you?'

'Yes.'

'How long does it keep videos of people coming to the front door?'

Alex shrugged. 'I've got no idea. It's Patrick's toy.' She frowned. 'Why?'

'I thought it might help us. Maybe there's someone else who came to the house that you've forgotten about.'

'Or someone who wasn't meant to be there.'

'Exactly.'

Alex grabbed her bag and the notebook and stood. 'Come on. Let's go and see if we can work out how to use this thing.'

* * *

It was a non-starter in the end, of course – at least, it was that night. Footage of the comings and goings at their front door went straight to Patrick's laptop, which meant there was no way they could access it.

'Do you think you can sneak a look when he's not here?' Caitlin said.

'I don't know. I rarely go into his office, and he's in there most of the time anyway. Besides, I wouldn't have a clue what his password is.'

'He must go out sometimes though? I'll come over next time he does and help you work it out.'

Caitlin left shortly after that. Alone in the house, Alex felt a creeping sense of unease. Was it fear of what she might discover? Or was it something else – a fear of the people she was meant to love most in the whole world?

Patrick was still upstairs working, and Milo was in his room. She needed something to distract her, to keep her mind away from the dark places it was trying to wander.

She scrubbed kitchen cupboards that didn't need cleaning, she mopped floors, dusted, and wiped skirting boards. As she cleaned she thought about everything they'd found over the last few days. She felt like there was something she'd missed, something nagging at her that she couldn't quite catch.

She thought about what Caitlin had suggested about Milo knowing who had killed Scott. She felt bile rise in the back of her throat. No. She couldn't go there. She considered the list Caitlin and she had made, of all the people who had been in the house over the last few weeks. Months, even. It felt impossible that she was ever going to get to the bottom of this.

But with the only other possibility currently Patrick or Archie, she needed to try.

Of course, they'd always known that a member of Scott's family could have killed him. There was a chance one of them could have done it and let Samuel take the rap. Maybe even planted the trophy later, when they realised he was living there, to frame him. Alex thought about the people she'd seen at the trial. She wouldn't put it past some of them. But it was also pretty far-fetched as theories went.

Then there were all the other people Scott had had dealings with – the drug dealers, the lowlifes. It could have been any one of them. Or one of the people he'd ripped off – whose money he'd taken on the promise of carrying out building work.

She cast her mind back to a year or so ago, and Caitlin's anger that she'd been left high and dry, with no money to get the half-arsed job her builder had started finished.

'People like him are utter lowlifes,' she'd said, full of fury. Alex had agreed, of course. But what if Scott had messed with the wrong person, someone who'd decided to take matters into their own hands?

'What on earth are you doing down there?'

She dropped her cloth and turned to find Patrick in the doorway. She stood shakily, stretched her back out. 'Just cleaning,' she said, not daring to meet his eye. He knew her frantic cleaning sessions meant she was stressed, and she didn't want him to ask too many questions. She hadn't told him about the visit to the squat, or about the discovery of the football trophy in the garage, and she wasn't ready to tell him yet, not until she'd worked out a few things in her mind first.

He closed the gap between them and she tried not to flinch as his hand moved towards her face. This was *Patrick* for goodness' sake. She was going insane. He pushed the strands of hair that had escaped her ponytail back from her damp face and held his fingers against her cheek.

'Is this about Milo?' he said.

She lowered her eyes and let relief wash over her. Of *course* she'd still be worried about Milo's suspension. She *was* worried about it, only it had become buried beneath everything else. She lifted her head and gazed into the familiar face that she'd loved for so many years. 'Yes.'

'Oh, love,' he said and wrapped his arms around

her. As he held her, swaddled in the cocoon of his arms, she allowed some of the tension to seep from her body. Patrick always knew how to make her feel safe. It was one of the things she first loved about him. How could she ever have doubted him, even for a second? It showed how much the events of the last few weeks were messing with her mind.

She closed her eyes and let her body mould to the shape of him. Finally, he pulled away.

'Fancy going out for dinner, just me and you?'

'What about Milo?'

'He'll be okay here for a couple of hours, won't he?'

Patrick must have noticed her hesitation. 'You have to start trusting him again at some point,' he said. 'I reckon this is a good way of showing him that we do, don't you?'

She smiled. 'You're right. We can't keep him under lock and key forever. I'll go and tell him.'

Patrick shook his head. 'You jump in the shower, I'll tell him.'

Alex hurried upstairs and got the shower going. As the water heated up she caught a glimpse of herself in the mirror and almost recoiled. The woman staring back at her was not the Alex she was used to seeing. This Alex looked slightly manic: dark circles under her eyes, hair frizzy and wild around her head, blotches of red on her otherwise stone-grey cheeks, which were hollow, the cheekbones sharp. She looked, quite frankly, dreadful.

She stepped into the shower and let the hot water run over her, trying to empty her mind and not let the thoughts of what had happened over the last few hours to seep in. But of course she couldn't keep them out forever, and they began to crowd in, coming to her in flashes... The squat... The football trophy... Samuel... The idea that Caitlin or Archie could have been involved... Milo...

Her legs felt weak and she crouched down, letting the hot water pummel her head, her back, her shoulders.

She didn't know how long she was there but she was brought back into the present by a gentle tapping on the door.

'Alex, are you nearly ready?' She stood up too quickly, all the blood draining from her head. She steadied herself against the wall and let the dizziness pass.

'Just getting out,' she said, turning the water off. The cold air hit her skin and she shivered, reaching for the towel. She dried quickly and hurried along the hallway towards her bedroom. Outside Milo's room she hesitated. Should she go in? She hovered, unsure, the chilly air rapidly cooling her shower-warmed skin until her teeth began to chatter.

Deciding against it she continued on to her bedroom. Patrick was nowhere to be seen and she assumed he was downstairs waiting for her, so she quickly threw some clothes on, roughly dried her hair and slicked on some mascara and lipstick. A quick glance in the mirror revealed a slight improvement on earlier, but the person looking back at her was still haggard-looking, a mad look in her eyes.

She turned away and headed back to the hallway. This time, fully dressed, she decided to look in on Milo. She tapped gently on his door and when there was no answer she pushed it open. He was hunched on his bed, Xbox controller in hand, the blue of the screen lighting up his face. He didn't look round, just carried on staring at the screen, furiously tapping buttons, his face screwed up in concentration.

'We're just going out for a couple of hours.'

Nothing.

'Milo, love?'

'What?'

'Me and your dad are popping out for a bit, will you be okay?'

'Yep, Dad already said.'

'Okay, good.' She stayed where she was for a moment. Then, 'Love you, sweetheart.'

His eyes flicked across to her and then immediately away again, and she sighed. 'See you soon, be good.' As she closed his door she caught an eyeroll and smiled. He was just a teenager, that was all. There was nothing sinister about his behaviour, nothing to worry about. Absolutely nothing at all.

* * *

Despite everything going on in Alex's mind, spending some proper time with Patrick was just what she needed. As they talked she was reminded of the man she'd always loved, of the man who adored her and who loved Milo; who would do whatever he could to protect his family from harm.

They chatted about work, about Milo, and about the upcoming summer holidays. Patrick didn't mention Samuel so Alex didn't bring him up either. As far as Patrick was concerned he was out of their lives for good and Alex didn't want to threaten the fragile truce they'd called.

She didn't mention her and Caitlin's visit to the squat, or the discovery of the football trophy in the garage, even though he was the person she would normally talk to about these things. Tonight was about Alex and Patrick, so she smothered her worries, squashing them down for a couple of hours until she was almost able to pretend they weren't there, and that everything was still normal.

The restaurant was emptying and Patrick had drunk most of a bottle of wine by the time the subject of Caitlin was brought up.

'How are things between you and Caitlin? Have you sorted it out?' His words were becoming slurred.

Alex paused with her glass of sparkling water suspended in mid-air. 'Yeah, they're fine thanks.'

'Good. I was worried for a while there. You know what she's like when she's pissed off.'

Alex frowned. 'What do you mean?'

The edge of Patrick's lip curled and he took another sip of wine. A red smile was left behind on his face, giving him a leering look. 'You know, what happened with her and Mick.'

Mick was Caitlin's ex, Archie's father, who her friend rarely spoke about. 'Patrick, I have absolutely no idea what you're talking about. What happened with her and Mick?'

He put his wine glass down and covered his mouth with his hand. 'Oops, I forgot she told me not to tell you.'

Alex leaned forward, her heart in her throat. 'Not to tell me what?'

He shook his head. 'I shouldn't say. I promised.' He mimed zipping his mouth shut and she was overcome with a sudden urge to punch him.

She leaned even closer. 'I don't want to make a scene but you need to tell me what you mean and you need to tell me right now.' Her voice was a hiss.

Patrick waved his hand dismissively. 'Oh, it was nothing really. Just – you know. She told me once when she was pissed that she put Mick in hospital.'

Alex felt like she'd been winded. Why was Patrick saying this? The Caitlin she knew was endlessly patient, would never just lash out. And why would she have told Patrick about it and not her? It made no sense. Besides, they didn't have secrets from each other.

Except they did, didn't they? At least, she did.

'When did she tell you this?' She tried to keep her voice calm, measured.

'Oh, it was years ago now. Back when Archie was being a little shit.'

'And you never thought to mention it to me at the time, or since?'

'She begged me not to. Said she hadn't meant to say anything and she didn't want you to know.' He shrugged. 'I agreed. I just assumed it was a one-off and he must have driven her to it.'

Alex's mind was buzzing. If what Patrick was saying was true, and Caitlin *had* lost it when Mick had pushed her too hard, was there a chance she could have lost it with Scott too? That she'd snapped and lashed out in the heat of the moment?

She shook her head, tried to dislodge the image.

Of course not!

But Alex could feel a tension building in her head, like an elastic band being tightened round her temple. She rubbed it furiously.

'But I've never even seen Caitlin lose her temper,' she said, her voice almost a whisper.

'And that's why I didn't tell you, love. It didn't seem relevant.'

'Except it might have been. When Milo was small and she was looking after him, it might have been very relevant. You should have told me.'

Patrick tipped the rest of his wine down his throat and picked up the bottle, squinted at it, and put it back down. 'Nah, come on, Ally, this is Caitlin we're talking about. You know she'd never harm anyone.'

Except she had.

'What if it happened again?'

Patrick looked at her, trying to focus. God, how

drunk was he? 'What are you getting at, Ally?' The last two words ran into each other.

'Nothing. It doesn't matter.'

This wasn't the time to talk to Patrick about this, not when he'd had this much to drink. But he was interested now.

So she told him everything. About the money Scott had taken from Caitlin, about Archie finding out that they could lose the house and getting into trouble at school, bringing Milo down with him. When she finished she looked up at him and he was staring at her, his mouth slightly open. His lips were a deep purple and his front teeth were blue.

'Fuck, Ally. Are you saying you think Caitlin might have killed Scott?'

Was she? It sounded absurd, even thinking about it.

And yet wasn't that exactly what she was worried about?

'I don't know. But I need to find out.'

'No!' Patrick spat the word out and Alex recoiled. He looked wild-eyed as he leaned over the table. The whites of his eyes were bloodshot.

'Patrick? What are you doing?'

'You can't tell Caitlin I told you about this.'

'But—'

'You can't.' A bit of spittle flew from the side of his mouth. 'Please. I promised her I wouldn't say anything. There's no way she had anything to do with Scott's murder, you know that really. So there's really no need to go and stir things up, is there?'

'I—' She didn't know what to say. But she didn't want to anger Patrick any more so she just nodded and said, 'Okay. My lips are sealed.'

* * *

Alex felt as though her world had been tipped up and shaken like a snow globe, all the things she thought she knew now in complete chaos. She needed time to think, to let things settle. When she got home she went straight to bed, claiming a headache. Patrick was too drunk to notice and she left him stretched out on the sofa with a beer watching the darts. Milo's light was off so she didn't say goodnight.

She cleaned her teeth and moisturised her face on autopilot, then climbed between the sheets and lay staring into the dark room.

There were so many loose threads in this story and she didn't know how to join them – or who she could trust.

First, there was Samuel. She'd trusted him, believed him when he said he hadn't killed Scott. But then the discovery of the trophy had thrown all doubt on his innocence.

Then there was Archie, who had been angry and scared about losing the only home he'd ever known.

Caitlin had been the one person Alex thought she could trust in all of this, but now it turned out even she was keeping secrets about her past which painted her in a totally different light.

Then there was Milo. She'd been trying hard to put her suspicions about Milo out of her mind, but no matter what she did she couldn't seem to eliminate the seed of doubt that nagged away at her. She'd assumed he couldn't have been involved in Scott's death because he hadn't known about him. But Archie had. What if Milo had been caught up in some sort of revenge plot? She never would have believed it before, but now she wasn't so sure.

Staring into the darkness, her mind rewound time, back to when she was a young girl, when she would lie in bed with her head buried under her pillow to muffle the sound of her parents fighting. It always started with raised voices, and she'd feel a familiar twist in her gut, and her muscles would tense. Then the voices became shouts; later, screams. It always ended with a bang, or a thump, followed by a terrible, deadly silence. Sometimes she'd lay there for a few minutes before creeping downstairs to see if her mother was all right. One night she found her, slumped against the radiator in the hallway, her head tipped back, her eye swollen and black. Her wrist was twisted at a funny angle and when she saw Alex she froze. Then she held her uninjured arm out and beckoned her forward and Alex had dropped to the floor and snuggled into her mum's body. They must have sat there for more than an hour and still Alex's father didn't come home, and they didn't talk about what her mother was doing on the floor. She knew Alex knew. Eventually, they'd stood, stiff-limbed, and made their way to bed. Mum had sat on the edge of Alex's bed while Alex had drifted off and told her everything would be okay. On other nights, Alex could hear her father was still in the house – he wasn't a quiet man, didn't believe in creeping around so she didn't wake up – and so she stayed where she was, in bed, hardly daring to breathe, feeling helpless that she couldn't do anything to help her mum.

Then there were the times when, reckless, her father would hit her mum when Alex was still awake, when he didn't care who saw. Those were the times Alex kept thinking about now, the rage in his face, like he'd lost all control.

Because she'd seen that look in Milo before. Not often, but there had been one or two occasions in the last few months when he'd been barely able to contain his anger, and had hit out at something, anything. He was only a teenager, but what would happen if he stopped being able to take his rage out on inanimate objects? Would his anger grow until it became as out of control as her father's?

She turned over, trying to empty her mind.

Because the only thing that was clear to her right now was that any one of them could be guilty. She just needed to work out who was lying to her.

33

Alex barely slept, and when she finally got up she felt like her limbs had been buried in concrete. It was starting to get light outside, a grey glow creeping round the edges of the curtains, and she listened for the sounds of people in the house.

Silence.

Stiff, she pulled her dressing gown on and made her way to the bedroom door. She stood for a moment, listening again. Milo's bedroom door was firmly shut, so she walked across the landing and tapped on it gently. Nothing at first, and she felt guilty when her main feeling was relief.

She tapped again. A rustling sound, like sheets, then Milo appeared. His hair was dishevelled, his face crumpled. Even though he was a couple of inches taller than Alex already, she saw the little boy he used to be in his still-sleepy features and longed to throw her arms around him. She knew it wouldn't be welcome.

'What?' he grunted.

'Aren't you going to school?'

'Yeah.'

'You'll be late, and you've only been back a couple of days.'

'It's fine.'

Alex said nothing more, just nodded and walked away as he closed the door behind her. Alex had learned there was no point nagging him, it only made him do the opposite. She walked down the stairs with heavy footsteps, and made tea and toast on autopilot, sitting at the table alone. Her brain was so deep in thought she almost screamed when Patrick appeared in the doorway.

'Morning.'

'Oh, hi.' She pulled her dressing gown round her more tightly, aware of how under-dressed she was for such a cold day. Since when had she felt nervous around Patrick?

It was then she noticed how he was dressed. A suit, in place of his usual jeans and T-shirt, his hair brushed neatly. He didn't look like a man who'd drunk the best part of two bottles of wine last night.

'Where are you going?'

'I've got a meeting in town.'

'Oh.' She felt a pang of sadness. There was a time when she knew Patrick's movements every day, and especially when he had a meeting, which was rare. 'Anything exciting?'

He shook his head and turned on the coffee machine. 'Just a client meeting.'

'Important one?'

He flicked her a look she couldn't read, and nodded. 'Fairly.'

Coffee poured, he stood sipping it at the counter. Alex studied him as she chewed her toast. He still looked the same as ever and it was hard to fathom the distance that had opened up between them. Had it really only started a few months before when she'd told him about Samuel?

Or had it been going on long before that, when Milo started playing up?

Alex wished she could properly open up to him, tell him about what she and Caitlin had found, about her suspicions about Samuel, about Caitlin, about Archie. But despite last night, she didn't think they were quite ready to move on to uncomfortable ground yet. They were still trying to rediscover their groove.

'Right, I'd better go, don't want to be late.' He almost threw his empty coffee cup into the sink and moved away.

'Will you be out all day?'

'Most of it.' He seemed to notice her state of undress for the first time. 'Are you not in the office today?'

'I'll go in later. I just want to make sure Milo gets off to school first.'

He looked as if he was about to say something more, but thought better of it and just gave a small nod. 'Okay, well, have a good day. See you later.' As he passed he leaned down and pressed his lips onto the top of Alex's head, his hand on her shoulder. It was the most contact they'd had in weeks and she lapped it up like a starving puppy.

* * *

Alex had forgotten she'd arranged for Caitlin to come and help her do some more digging today, so when she opened the door just after Milo had left for school to find her friend smiling at her she felt thrown.

'Oh, hi,' she said, moving aside as Caitlin stepped over the threshold.

'You look like you've seen a ghost,' Caitlin said, tugging off her scarf and looking at Alex intently. 'Did you forget I was coming?'

'Er, yeah.' Alex closed the door and led them through into the kitchen. Her heart thudded and she tried to work out what to say. 'Tea? Coffee?'

'Coffee, thanks.' Caitlin settled at the table and Alex could feel the burn of her stare as she pulled mugs from the cupboard. She was saved from having to make small talk by the buzz and whirr of the coffee machine warming up, and when she eventually turned to place a steaming mug in front of Caitlin, her friend was watching her with her dark eyebrows knitted together.

'What's going on?'

Alex sat down opposite her and interlaced her fingers round her cup. 'Nothing. Why?'

'You're... distant.'

'Am I?' Alex took a sip of her tea but it was too hot and her throat burned.

Caitlin rested her chin on her hand. 'Come on, Ally, out with it. Something's happened.'

Alex shook her head. 'No, really. I just—' She swallowed. 'I just feel guilty going through Patrick's stuff and was thinking I should probably do it on my own after all.'

The dishwasher beeped and Alex stood to open it. Steam billowed round her face, obscuring the flush that was creeping up her neck.

'Alex, I've taken the morning off work to help you today. You said you needed me.' She crossed her arms. 'Has Patrick said something?'

Alex looked up, her heart in her throat. 'Patrick?'

'You know, your husband?' Caitlin ran her fingers through her hair, exasperated. 'Honestly, Alex I don't know what's going on here but if you don't want my help I'm just going to go to the office.' She stood, her face a storm cloud, and started tugging on her jacket again. As she turned to leave Alex blurted out, 'Alex told me about Mick.'

Caitlin was halfway through the door and stopped dead, then turned slowly, round to face Alex. 'What?'

Alex's legs felt weak. 'Last night. Patrick got really pissed and he told me—' She broke off. God, was she really about to break Patrick's confidence already? But this was Caitlin, and she needed to know the truth. 'He said you told him you lost your temper with Mick once. That you put him in hospital.'

Caitlin went so white Alex thought she might be about to fall over. She stumbled to the nearest chair and sat down, and Alex followed suit. Thunder roared in Alex's ears and she waited to hear what her friend had to say.

'He said *what*?' Caitlin's voice was almost a growl.

'He said—' Alex cleared her throat. 'He said you told him when you were drunk one day that you'd lost your temper and...'

'Why the fuck would he say something like that?'

Alex's heart stopped. 'It's not true then?'

'No! Of course it's not true!'

'But then, why would Patrick say it?'

'I don't know, Ally.' Her voice was small. 'I guess he must have misunderstood.'

'So you did say something to him then? About a fight with Mick?'

Caitlin shrugged, stared at her nails. 'I can't remember. I mean, maybe I did. But I didn't tell him anything I've never told you.' She barked a laugh. 'Why would I? Besides, there's nothing to tell – just that one time Mick left me with a black eye, but you already knew about that.'

Alex leaned back and tried to digest the news. As what Caitlin was telling her sunk in, she felt nothing but relief. She hadn't been lying to her! And if she hadn't done this, then there was no chance at all that she'd lashed out at Scott Jones.

'I'm sorry I believed him,' Alex said. 'I'm shocked that he thought that's what you told him for all this time though.'

'Well, at least you know he's good at keeping secrets.' Caitlin gave a wonky smile, and rubbed the end of her nose. 'Although I can't believe he actually thought I was capable of something like that.'

'Don't worry, I'll make sure I put him right.'

'Whatever.' Caitlin picked up her mug and took a swig of her coffee. 'Patrick's out this morning then?'

'Yes, he said he had a meeting.'

'Well then, let's get on with it while he's not here.'

They stood and made their way up to the office where Patrick always kept his laptop. Alex hated sneaking around behind his back, but she still didn't feel ready to tell him about her suspicions, or about the trophy. Every time she thought about it being in her house she felt sick with dread.

She pushed open the door to Patrick's office. The sofa-bed where he was still sleeping every night had crumpled sheets on it and Alex noticed Caitlin glance over as she entered the room. It smelt of Patrick, and Alex's heart clenched with longing. God, she missed him. She hoped that once they'd got to the bottom of this things could start to get back to normal between them at last.

'Where's his laptop?'

Alex's belly dropped. 'Looks like he's taken it with him. He usually leaves it here.'

Caitlin marched round to the other side of the desk. Alex hovered in the doorway.

'Don't worry, most likely it downloads things onto the cloud,' Caitlin said, starting up the lumbering old desktop computer. 'Maybe we'll find it in here anyway.'

Alex made her way over to the desk and they waited while the computer whirred into life. 'He's still sleeping in here then?' Caitlin said, her voice laced with concern.

'Yes. I—' She stopped. 'For now.'

Caitlin didn't say anything else, and a few seconds later the monitor lit up as the computer woke from its sleep state. Luckily Patrick was still logged in and Alex peered over Caitlin's shoulder and watched while she clicked here and there and opened up some folders.

'Bingo,' she said, clicking on one final folder.

Alex squinted at the screen as the page loaded, and a list of dates appeared. She ran her eyes down them as Caitlin scrolled down. And then they stopped.

'Is that as far as it goes?' she said.

'It looks like it. Bugger.'

The doorbell entries only went back a month.

'Well, there might be something there,' Alex said, trying to stay hopeful. 'I mean, if it was planted here after Samuel moved in.'

'That's true.' Caitlin clicked on the earliest date, and they watched as a grainy picture of the street outside Alex's front door opened on the screen. Alex perched on the edge of the desk and waited to see what was going to happen, her heart thumping. Suddenly, there was a movement at the top of the screen by the pavement, then a body appeared and a face.

'It's just a delivery,' she said, disappointed.

'Don't worry, there are loads more.' Caitlin closed it and opened the next one. 'We're just going to have to be methodical about it.' She glanced up. 'How long did you say Patrick was out for?'

'Most of the day, I think. He said he's meeting a client.'

'Right, let's find out who's been to pay you a visit,' she said.

* * *

It was a fruitless search. Two boring hours later they'd been through most of the footage from the previous month and it hadn't revealed any new visitors that

Alex hadn't already known about, apart from the odd courier or cold caller.

'That's that, then,' Alex said.

Caitlin sat back in the chair, her fingers steepled under her chin. 'There's got to be some older footage somewhere,' she said. 'Surely they don't just delete everything more than a month old?'

'It looks like they do.' She stood. 'We've been in here ages, we'd better go.'

'Yeah, you're probably right.' Caitlin leaned forward and went to close down the computer.

'You'll make sure Patrick won't be able to tell we've been snooping on here, won't you?' Alex said. She felt a prickle of worry in the pit of her stomach.

'Course I will,' she said. 'Hang on, just one more thing before we get out of here.' Alex waited while Caitlin clicked a few more folders. Then she stopped, abruptly, and leaned closer to the screen, her face creased in a frown.

'What is it? What have you found?' Her pulse fluttered in her throat. 'Caitlin?'

She looked up at Alex slowly, her eyes like saucers.

'I—' She stopped, her mouth opening and closing a couple of times as if she was about to start speaking but had changed her mind. 'What was Samuel's address, before?'

'What, the squat? Belvedere something, wasn't it—'

'No,' she interrupted. 'Before that. His home address. With his mum and dad.'

'I don't know,' Alex said, a sense of unease creeping up the back of her neck. 'Why?'

'I'm not sure. Hang on.' She tapped on the keyboard a few more times and Alex watched as a page loaded. It was the news story about Samuel's trial, an in-depth piece rather than the short one she'd found that first day. Caitlin leaned closer to read it, then her face paled. 'Fuck.'

Alex's leg jiggled up and down. 'What?' She leaned in to the screen but still couldn't see what Caitlin was looking at. 'Tell me!'

'I think Patrick has been looking up Samuel's old address.'

Alex let her words process for a moment, but she still couldn't work out their significance. 'Why would he do that?'

She shook her head. 'I don't know. Unless...' She clicked the mouse a few more times, alternating between whatever had caught her eye in the first place and the newspaper story. 'I think he might have known about Samuel all along,' she said, her voice raspy.

All the air left Alex's lungs as Caitlin continued. 'I clicked on Patrick's internet search history, just quickly before I closed it all down,' she said. 'And look.' She followed her finger to where it was pointing at the screen. And there it was.

Samuel's address from the newspaper report.

Samuel's address in Patrick's search history.

And the search was dated two days before Scott's murder.

34

'Mum?' It was late afternoon when Milo got home and found Alex at the dining table.

Caitlin had left to pick Archie up an hour or so before and had begged Alex to go with her. 'You don't know what's going to happen if you confront him about this,' she'd said. 'You don't know what he's capable of.'

But Alex had refused. Partly because she was certain she *did* know what Patrick was capable of – after all, she'd loved him for more than twelve years – and it certainly wasn't murder, or anything even approaching it. That part of her was certain Patrick would have a reasonable explanation for what they had found, one that neither she nor Caitlin had thought of. The other part of her knew there couldn't possibly be one, and that she needed to have it out with him once and for all.

She looked up at Milo and saw fear in his eyes. She tried to speak, to reassure him, but it came out as a croak.

'Mum, what the fuck is going on?' She didn't have the strength to admonish him for his language.

'I'm not sure,' she said weakly.

'Do you want a drink? A cup of tea or something?'

'Yes. Thank you, love.'

Alex sat statue-still while her little boy made her a drink. Her mind turned over what she and Caitlin had discovered for the hundredth time, trying to make sense of it. These were the facts: Patrick must have known about Samuel's existence well before Alex told him about him – since before Scott was killed, yet he'd never told her; he'd looked up Samuel and Scott's address, just two days before Scott was killed; the football trophy that the police suspected Scott had been smashed round the head with was in their house.

She put her head in her hands. Was there any re-mote chance someone else could have used Patrick's computer? Milo? No. Caitlin? Possibly. She knew her way round technology better than Alex. But why wouldn't she just have looked it up from her own computer?

Every time she tried to work it out her head span, and she thought she might throw up.

Milo placed a steaming mug in front of her and she cupped her hands around it gratefully. He hovered for a moment, then sat down next to her.

'Mum, please talk to me. You're scaring me.'

She slid her gaze over to him, her lovely, confused boy, and felt a surge of love for him. Every piece of her wanted to protect him from what was going on – how could she tell him the truth about her suspicions, and shatter the trust he had in his father?

She shook her head. 'It's nothing. I'm just exhausted.'

He didn't reply for a while and Alex thought he'd accepted it. But then, 'Is this something to do with Dad?'

The world stood still. She looked up at Milo and tried to read his face. Did he *know* something?

'What—' She cleared her throat. 'What do you mean?'

He didn't say anything straight away, just stared at the table, head down. She wanted to shout at him, demand that he tell her what he knew. But she didn't want to frighten him into silence. She waited.

Finally, he looked up. The look on his face made her heart stop. He looked haunted.

'I need to tell you something.'

Her body stiffened. 'Go on, sweetheart, you can tell me anything.'

He shook his head. 'Not this.'

She took a long, slow breath in, trying to quell the terror. Her shoulders were hunched, her fingers fists, legs tense. She felt like she might explode at any minute. She reached out her hand and laid it on his arm. 'Please, Milo. Tell me what you know.'

His eyes were filled with fear and he was deathly white.

'Samuel rang here once and asked to speak to you. Ages ago.'

'What?' Alex realised she was gripping Milo's arm too tightly and released her fingers. He blinked once, twice, then opened his mouth. When he eventually started speaking the words came tumbling out like a torrent, as though they'd been dammed up forever, desperate to burst forth, and now he'd started, it was impossible to stop.

'Samuel rang the house. It was months ago, maybe a year. I didn't know it was Samuel back then, but I do now. I answered it, and a man asked for you. I told him you weren't here and was about to put the phone down but he asked if he could leave a message. I told him he could. He— His words were really slurry and I think he was drunk. Then he said he was your son and he wanted to talk to you.' He stopped and looked up at Alex. 'I didn't know what to say, so I just said *but I'm her son*. But then Dad appeared and took the phone off me and told me he'd handle it.'

He stopped and Alex stared at him for a minute.

'And then what happened, sweetheart?'

He sniffed and wiped his nose with his sleeve. Tears were forming in his eyes and he looked so distressed she wished she could pull him into her arms and end this conversation right now. But she needed to know the truth.

Milo rocked gently back and forth, hands beneath his thighs. 'I went upstairs, but I could still hear Dad speaking, and I heard him telling whoever it was never to ring here again. And then after, Dad came to find me and told me he'd sorted it and that it was nothing to worry about, just some stupid drunk man who'd got the wrong number. But he—' Again his voice broke. 'He told me not to tell you anything about it. That you were stressed enough with work and that you didn't need anything else upsetting you. So I didn't.'

Her blood ran cold as realisation dawned. 'So

you're saying that your dad knew about Samuel well before I told him?'

'Yeah.' He looked up at her, his eyes filled with worry. 'I wanted to tell you but I knew Dad was right and that you'd only worry. So I did what he said. But I hated it.' He hung his head.

'That's why I started behaving like an idiot. Because I felt so guilty about lying to you.'

Her heart cracked.

'Oh, love. You had nothing to feel guilty about. Your dad should never have put you in that position.' Her voice was trembling with fury as her mind spooled back. If Milo's timings were right – and she had no reason to doubt him – then this phone call had come a few days before Scott had been killed. That must have been around the same time that Milo had started getting into so much trouble. And it was all because he'd been made to keep a secret from her? Anger flared in her that he'd been put in such a terrible position by someone who was supposed to care for him.

But what she still couldn't work out was why Patrick had been so desperate to keep Samuel's phone call a secret from her – or why Samuel had never mentioned it to her in all the months since they'd known each other.

Milo shook his head miserably. 'I'm sorry, Mum. I've ruined everything.'

'Oh, darling, you haven't ruined anything.' She pulled him towards her and he leaned in for an awkward half-hug. It was the most contact they'd had for months and Alex savoured it for the few seconds while it lasted. But when he pulled away his face was drawn in fear.

'What's wrong?'

'Did—' He stopped, his words getting stuck in his throat. 'Do you think Dad killed Samuel's dad?'

Ice dripped down her spine. She wanted to reply, to laugh it off and tell him no, of *course* your dad didn't kill anyone. But her throat had closed up. How could they have come to this point, to be talking about the possibility of Patrick killing someone? It felt like a bad dream.

'I don't know, darling,' she rasped finally. 'I hope not.'

Milo's eyes widened like saucers. 'What if he's angry with me for telling you about Samuel? Do you think he'd hurt us?'

'Of course not.'

But the words sounded hollow even to her. Because as much as she would never have believed that Patrick would do anything to harm either of them, after everything she'd learned over the last couple of days, she couldn't be as certain of that as she should have been. Maybe he wasn't involved. Maybe he'd got Samuel's address but hadn't had a chance to go round there before this all happened.

She had to hope that was true. Because the alternative didn't bear thinking about.

35

Alex wanted Milo to go to Caitlin's while she waited for Patrick to come home, but he refused.

'I'm not leaving you here on your own,' he said.

She didn't argue. Quite apart from the fact there was no way she could manhandle him out of the house even if she wanted to – he'd been bigger and stronger than her for some time now – there was actually some comfort in having him here with her, on her side once more.

Besides, the more she thought about it, the more she was convinced that, once Patrick got home he'd have an explanation that made sense. One that would mean the worst he'd done was to keep a secret from her about Samuel trying to get in touch. It was hardly the crime of the century.

While they waited in the dimming light, Alex made dinner.

'Can't you sit down, Mum?' Milo said.

'I'm better being busy,' she said, furiously chopping onions.

Her phone buzzed a few times with messages from Caitlin checking she was okay. She tapped out a quick reply, telling her there was nothing to report.

Milo came and stood beside her. 'Let me help you.'

Tears pricked her eyes. It had been so long since Milo had wanted to even be in the same room as her, let alone want to help her prepare dinner. It felt like a reprieve from the relentless stress and worry of the last few months.

'Heat some oil in that pan and add these,' she said, handing him the chopping board.

They stood in silence while he stirred the onions and Alex chopped chicken. Her nerves about Patrick's imminent return diminished as they stood there, side by side.

'I'm sorry about all the shit I've caused you,' Milo said suddenly.

'Don't be.' She paused for a moment, knife hovering in mid-air as a thought occurred to her. 'But tell me something. Did you steal some money from me a while back?'

'What? No!' He continued to stir the onions and Alex realised this was the best way to have this conversation – not facing each other. It made it easier somehow to tell the truth – or in her case, to ask the difficult questions. 'Why?'

'I found some notes in your room. In an envelope.'

Milo didn't reply straight away, no doubt wondering whether to call her out for being in his room in the first place. 'Dad gave it to me,' he said eventually in a small voice.

'What? What do you mean?'

'He gave me some cash after I agreed not to tell you about the phone call. I didn't want you to know about it but I felt weird about spending it so I hid it. I thought I might buy you something with it, one day. To make up for everything.'

Alex stilled, while the implications sank in. But money had been taken from her purse since then – so who had taken that? Had it been Samuel after all? Or Archie? Before she could formulate a response, Milo spoke again. 'Dad really didn't want you to find out about Samuel being around again, did he?'

'It would appear that way.'

'Why though? Why would he be so desperate for me not to tell you about him? I mean, he's pretty cool most of the time.'

'I don't know, love. I guess he just didn't like the thought of someone else coming into the family, changing things. You know how protective he is of us.'

She thought about Patrick's parents and how obsessed they were with 'carrying on the family line'. How they'd made Patrick desperate to have a baby of his own, so he didn't let them down, didn't let the superior Harding genes wither and die. Then she imagined how they'd have reacted if they'd have known about Samuel. She could see why Patrick might have wanted to keep him away from the family.

And yet she knew Patrick. She loved him, had done for more than a decade. Surely she could put her hand on her heart and say for certain that he would never go as far as killing someone to stop his family from being torn apart?

The trouble was, right now she wasn't so sure she could.

The pair of them worked in silence for a while longer. Alex wasn't hungry and she doubted Milo was either, but they needed something to focus on other than the gnawing fear about what would happen when Patrick got home. Would he tell the truth, or would he try and lie his way out of it? Or would he be like a trapped tiger, and lash out?

They didn't have to wait long to find out.

36

Alex was so tense her hands were shaking when she heard his key in the lock. She put the knife down and held her breath as she waited for Patrick to come into the kitchen. Too late, she realised Milo shouldn't be here. She gestured for him to go into the back room, the room that had been Samuel's bedroom, but he just shook his head, turned off the hob, and pulled himself up an inch or two taller. Despite everything, she was overcome with pride.

Patrick whistled as he removed his shoes and coat, threw his keys onto the side. It felt unfathomable to Alex that Patrick didn't know how much had changed since he'd left the house that morning, that he still thought everything was the same as it had been only hours before. Her heart thumped wildly against her ribs.

'Alex, are you here?' he said, his voice growing louder as he approached. Alex stood stock-still, her body coiled, and waited for him without replying.

And then he was there, filling the doorway, a frown creasing his forehead.

'Alex? What's wrong?' He looked from Alex to Milo, and then back again. When he stepped into the room Alex felt her muscles clench even tighter. He paused about a metre away from her and smiled.

'Why do you both look so weird? Has something happened?' His smile wavered briefly, his eyes darting back and forth between them.

'I think you should sit down, Patrick,' Alex said, struggling to keep her voice steady.

'What do you mean, sit down? Why are you being so dramatic?'

She didn't answer, but she and Milo both took a seat at the table. It didn't take long for Patrick to do the same, sitting directly opposite Alex, then leaning back and crossing his arms.

'This looks ominous. Should I be worried?' His mouth was set in a grimace now, his smile long gone.

'Mum knows,' Milo said simply.

Patrick stared at him, his face blank. But Alex could see the panic behind his eyes.

'What on earth are you talking about?' he said.

Alex leaned forward and tried to still her shaking hands. 'I think you need to tell me everything, Patrick, don't you?' she said, struggling to keep her voice steady.

Patrick leaned forward, his face reddening. 'What *exactly* is it you think I need to tell you, Alex?' he spat, all pretence at joviality now gone. 'Are you going to tell me or would you like me to guess?'

A beat of silence. Alex glanced at Milo, who was staring at the table. She swallowed.

'I know that you knew about Samuel before I told you about him,' she said, lifting her chin in defiance.

'What the—' Patrick started, but Alex didn't give him the chance to say any more.

'I know that you found out where he lived. And I also know that you tried to pretend that all the things that went wrong after Samuel moved in with us – the missing money, the damaged car, the drugs – were his doing, when it was you all along.' This last accusation was a guess, but as soon as the words were out of her mouth Patrick's reaction told her she'd hit the nail on the head.

His eyes swivelled wildly from Alex to Milo. 'You

little fucker,' he hissed, his face turning puce. Milo recoiled.

'Don't you *dare* speak to him like that!' Alex slammed her hand on the table.

'Oh what, your precious little son, who can do no wrong?'

'Dad, stop it!' Milo shouted.

'Shut the fuck up, Milo. I told you to keep your mouth shut, but you just couldn't do it, could you?' His voice was a growl, so unlike him that it shocked Alex. She lay her palms flat against the table to stop them shaking, and steeled herself.

'I already knew, Patrick. Milo just confirmed it to me.' She swallowed. 'I know everything.'

She didn't, but she hoped he'd believe her.

'Oh, you know *everything*, do you?' he said with a smirk. 'What do you think this is, Alex, a fucking Agatha Christie novel?' He stood abruptly, the chair clattering to the floor behind him and Alex flinched. He leaned forward, his hands resting on the table, his face red. 'I don't know what it is you think you know, but I don't appreciate having accusations thrown at me left, right and centre in my own home.'

Alex stood too. Her legs shook but she held her nerve. 'Well then, why don't you explain to me why you asked Milo to keep quiet when Samuel rang the

house last year? Why did you think it was so important to keep *that* from me?'

Patrick's eyes widened and he barked out a laugh.
'Oh I see, you really have been enjoying a cosy little
chat haven't you?' He crossed his arms over his chest.

'Just tell me why you kept it from me, Patrick.'

He sighed as if she was merely an irritant. 'What
would have been the point? You were stretched thin
enough with Milo and me and the baby we'd been expecting. There was no way I was going to let a son you
hadn't given a shit about for more than twenty years
waltz into our lives and ruin the family we'd made
together.'

'But that was never your decision to make!'

'Of course it was my decision! *We're* your family,
Alex. Me, Milo, and our baby, not some loser who's out
to get everything he can from you.' His voice cracked.

'You mean you'd have been ashamed to have him
anywhere near your family, more like.'

Patrick shook his head. 'Do you really think that
little of me, Ally? It was never about that.' He fixed her
with a stare. 'I couldn't face losing you. Or Milo. You're
all I've got.'

For the first time since he realised he'd been
caught out, Patrick looked shame-faced and she felt a
prickle of pity. She knew family meant everything to

Patrick, it always had. Of course he'd want to do everything he could to protect it. And yet he'd lied to her, over and over again. She couldn't let herself be drawn into feeling sorry for him.

She folded her arms across her chest and drew herself up tall.

'I know you went to his house,' she said.

His eyes swivelled wildly. 'What? Whose house?'

'Samuel's. Scott's.'

Patrick froze for a moment, his whole body still. Then the blood drained from his face and Alex knew that, no matter what he said next, she was right about this.

'What?' There was a sheen of sweat on his skin. 'What are you talking about, why would I do that?'

'Oh come on, Patrick, there's no point in denying it. I *know*.'

Her words hovered in the air. She held her breath, her pulse thumped in her temple. And then, like air being expelled from a balloon, Patrick's whole body deflated, as if he'd lost the will to pretend any more.

'I didn't mean it to happen, I just wanted to warn him off,' he said, his voice a rasp. His eyes were wide and panicked. 'It was an accident, I swear...'

As the implication of his words sunk in, Alex's veins turned to ice.

37

'All I ever wanted to do was protect my family,' Patrick said, his voice weak, pleading as he slumped back down at the table, all fight gone.

'Protect us from what, though?' Alex sat down opposite him, her body shaking.

'Everything,' he said with a shrug. 'I was so scared that if Samuel came back into your life, you wouldn't want another baby. And I'd lose my chance of being a father.'

Oh, Patrick.

'But you are a father. To Milo. That's all we ever needed.'

He hung his head. 'I know.' He let out a puff of air and Alex watched him for a moment, trying to work out how she felt about him in the light of what she'd discovered.

'Why don't you tell me what happened?'

He looked up at her. His eyes were heavy.

'What do you want to know?'

'Everything. How about you start with how you knew who Samuel was in the first place?'

He looked back down at his hands which hung limply in his lap.

'I found your stuff. All your photos and things. On top of your wardrobe.' He gave a bitter laugh. 'It wasn't exactly well hidden. It was almost as though you wanted me to find it.'

'Why didn't you say anything? Ask me about it?'

'I wanted you to want to tell me about him, Alex. I didn't think we kept secrets.'

'This coming from you.'

He closed his eyes briefly. Acknowledged the truth. 'You wanted to know what happened that day.'

She waited. She wasn't sure she wanted to hear this. Because once she had, everything would be different. She held her breath and grasped for Milo's hand.

'You were right, about the phone call. Milo did answer, and when I realised who it was, I took the phone off him.' He rubbed his hand over his face, his stubble rough. He looked suddenly ten years older. 'I warned Samuel to stay away.'

'He never told me he rang.'

'I doubt he remembered. He was so off his face he could hardly string a sentence together.'

Alex nodded. 'So why did you need to go round there?'

'I was convinced he was going to try and get in touch again, and I thought that maybe next time he'd succeed. And that would have been a disaster.' He shook his head. 'I just couldn't let it happen.'

Alex squeezed Milo's hand and he squeezed back. 'So what did you do, Patrick?'

He looked up and met her gaze. 'You know me, Ally. I'm not a confrontational person.' He laughed. 'God, I'm even scared to go and talk to Mrs Kingston whenever Milo's in trouble.' He took a deep breath. 'So before I tell you what happened you've got to understand that all I ever wanted to do was warn him off. Tell him to leave us alone, leave *you* alone. I was going to give him money.'

'Bribe him?'

He gave a small nod. 'I'm not proud of it. But I couldn't think of any other way.' He rubbed his face and his skin was grey. 'I assumed that's what someone like him would respond to.'

In Alex's mind, the pieces slowly started slotting into place. 'So you looked up his address and went to find him?'

'Yes.'

She glanced at Milo. He looked broken, like he couldn't believe this of the man he'd always loved like a father. Who he'd trusted. *I feel the same,* she wanted to tell him. She turned back to Patrick.

'What happened when you got there?'

Patrick let out a long breath of air. When he looked up at her, the expression in his eyes made fear flare in her belly. Was this man she'd known for so many years really capable of killing someone in cold blood? She just couldn't believe it.

'When I got to his house, I knocked. But when the door opened, it was Scott.' He shook his head. 'It had never occurred to me he'd be there instead – stupid, I know. The guy lived there. I was about to leave, try again another day, but he kept asking who I was, what I wanted. He was so aggressive, got right up in my face, demanding to know over and over again who sent me. I didn't know what he meant and I just wanted to get away from there. From him. I knew no good was going to come of it if I stayed.' He paused and glanced up at her. 'But he grabbed my arm and stuck his face right here—' He held his hand up an inch in front of himself. 'I told him to get his hands off me but he went mad. Absolutely fucking ballistic.' He rubbed his eye. 'He pulled me into the house and pressed me up against the wall by the neck.' He let out a sob. 'I couldn't breathe, Ally. I honestly thought he was going to kill me.'

'But why? Who did he think you were?'

'I've no idea. But I was absolutely terrified. This guy was huge and I... I thought I was never going to see you again.'

She nodded. 'Go on.'

'I was about to pass out. Everything was spinning in front of my eyes. Then he... he let me go.'

'He let you go, just like that?'

'Yeah.'

'So what...' She couldn't finish the words. 'Why didn't you leave?'

'I was about to. But as he walked away he smirked and I... I just saw red. This man had threatened me, tried to choke me and he thought it was funny.' He was getting wound up now, a red flush creeping up his cheeks again.

'So you killed him.' Her voice was a whisper.

'I... I didn't mean to. It was only in self-defence—' Before he could finish his sentence there was a hammering at the door. Patrick's face drained of colour.

'Who's that?' Milo's voice sounded wobbly.

'I've no idea.' Alex stood, smoothed her hair. A sheen of sweat broke out on her neck. 'Wait here.'

She walked to the front door. The urgent thumping began again. Who was so desperate to speak to them?

She pulled the door open.

A police officer.

'Are you Mrs Harding?' he said.

'I am.' Her voice shook.

'And is your husband Patrick Harding here?'

'He... he is. Why—'

The police officer nodded. 'Do you mind if I just check that everything is all right? Are you safe?'

'Safe? Yes, of course.' She glanced at the road where the police car idled at the kerb, blue lights slowly turning. Then she stepped out outside and half-closed the door behind her. 'What's going on? Why are you here?'

'We've had a call from a friend concerned for your safety,' he said.

Caitlin.

Alex glanced behind her, suddenly nervous. 'I... We're fine... Thank you...' But before she could even finish her sentence, a figure dashed past them from the back of the house, and a car engine started.

'Patrick!' Alex yelled. He was already reversing out of the drive, wildly. 'Patrick!'

'Mum, Dad's gone!' Milo appeared behind her and stopped dead when he saw the police officer. He looked at Alex, fear in his eyes. 'Is Dad being arrested?'

'He wasn't, no,' the police officer said. 'Did he say where he was going?'

Milo shook his head. 'No, he just got up and ran out the back door.'

'Shit.' Instinctively, Alex stepped inside and swiped her keys from the side table. She couldn't let the police get to Patrick first. She had to go after him, talk to him, make him see sense.

'Sorry, I just need to...' she said, then she ran past the police officer and jumped in her car. Milo climbed in beside her. She stared at him. Shit, she'd lost her mind. She couldn't take Milo with her, this was insane.

'Come on!' he yelled. 'We'll lose him.'

She hesitated a split second then, before she could change her mind, she screeched off the drive, leaving the police officer on the doorstep looking bewildered.

'Where's he going?' Milo said, buckling up.

'No idea. Can you see him?' She squinted out of the windscreen, scanning left and right for the blue of Patrick's car.

'There!' Milo said, pointing to a car turning right at the end of the road. Alex put her foot down, praying nothing pulled out in front of her. By some miracle she reached the end of the road and spotted Patrick at the traffic lights to her right. She pulled up behind him. She flashed her lights at him and saw him glance into the rearview mirror. Their eyes met then, without warning, he screeched away from the still-red traffic lights and sped across the junction, narrowly missing a van which swerved, its horn blaring.

'What the hell's he doing?' Milo sounded terrified.

'I don't know.' Alex prayed it wasn't something stupid.

'Mum, don't let him get away!'

'I can't—'

'Go after him! Go!' Milo looked frantic. She hesitated a split second, then, when she was sure it was clear, she slammed her foot on the accelerator and raced after Patrick. They followed him for a few streets, then he pulled off onto a narrow side street.

'Where the hell are you going now?' Alex muttered, swinging the car round the corner to keep him in her sights. She sped up until she was right behind him again, almost bumper-to-bumper.

'Why won't he stop?' Milo said.

'I don't know, love.'

The roads became quieter and narrower until finally they were following Patrick along the country roads that twisted and turned around the fields surrounding the town. Many of them were only one lane wide. What would Patrick do if a car came in the other direction? Would it give her a chance to get out and beg him to stop?

'Dammit, Patrick, what are you doing?' she yelled, slamming her hand on the steering wheel.

'Will Dad go to prison?'

'What?' Milo's question took her by surprise as she navigated the tiny lanes, hedges brushing up against the window so it felt as though they were in a narrowing tunnel. Her heart was in her throat. Beside her, Milo twisted round to face her.

'If we stop him now, will you tell the police what he did? To Samuel's dad?'

'I— Shit!' Patrick's brake lights flared, and Alex slammed her foot onto her own brake, feeling the press of the seat belt as it dug into her chest. 'Sorry.' Ahead of them, Patrick squeezed himself into a passing place, and she pulled in behind him, leaving an impossibly small gap for the oncoming car to get through. She held her breath as wing mirrors smacked against each other. Did she have time to get out and run to Patrick's door before he set off again? But she dismissed the thought immediately. There literally wasn't an inch of space to spare until this car had passed them.

The second it had, Patrick roared away again. Alex followed, closing the gap as quickly as she could.

'Mum? Will you tell them?'

She glanced over at Milo. His face looked pale and haunted.

'I don't know, love,' she said.

'You can't!' He sounded desperate. 'I know he's been stupid, but he loves us. We love him. He's my dad...'

Ahead of Alex the gap between her and Patrick was growing. They were already doing 65 mph. If they went any faster they risked coming off the road completely and she wasn't prepared to put Milo or her unborn baby in any further danger. Her heart hammered in her temple, her whole body tense. She was gripping the steering wheel so tightly her knuckles had turned white.

'But he killed someone,' she gasped out between breaths. 'And he tried to let Samuel take the blame.'

'I know, but—'

'Patrick!' she screamed, as he reached a wider piece of road and raced off. The speedometer inched upwards, getting closer to 70 mph, then 75 mph.

'Mum,' Milo said, his voice a warning.

She took her foot off the pedal reflexively. To her relief, the brake lights of Patrick's car in front flared and the gap between them closed a little. Perhaps he'd decided to stop after all. She hoped so.

But the next second, horror struck her. Because Patrick was approaching a bend. A 90-degree bend in the road that surely required more braking than he would have time to do.

Alex tapped on her brakes and the tarmac beneath her tyres squealed as she skidded to the left. Righting herself, her pulse thumped, and her brain struggled to take in what was happening. Ahead of her, Patrick's brake lights were still red, he still seemed to be slowing down. Milliseconds stretched out into minutes, seconds into hours as she watched his car approach the bend in the road... getting closer and closer... Alex held her breath. Beside her, she could hear Milo, his breathing heavy, the whole world held in suspension, as they waited... waited... waited...

And then, as if in slow motion, Patrick's car veered off the road and into the adjoining field. They watched in horror as he headed straight towards a tree... closer and closer, his car bumping over the rough surface. There were only a couple of metres now between

Patrick and the tree, and he was surely going too fast to be able to stop...

Alex couldn't tear her eyes away, her breath caught in her throat, her hands frozen on the steering wheel... and then BANG! She was jolted back to reality as she hit a bump in the road and she lost control, skidding off in the same direction as Patrick had gone.

She hit the brakes.

A scream ripped through the air.

And then, there was blackness.

38

Alex peeled her left eye open.

'Milo!' she rasped. Her throat was so dry it felt like sand.

'Mum.' Alex turned her head. Milo was still beside her with his seat belt on.

'Are you okay?' she whispered.

'I think so.'

Thank God.

Her eyes burned with tears, and she turned her head slowly back to face the front. Where were they? What had just happened?

The sky was darkening now, a pale grey hanging heavy, but at least it was above their heads which meant they were the right way up. Beneath them, muddy fields, stretching to the horizon. She tugged her seat belt loose and popped it out of its catch. The relief was instant. She undid Milo's too. Then, in a daze, she opened the door and climbed out, slowly stretching herself to check for injuries. She looked down at her belly where her baby was growing, the bump small but taut now. There was no pain so she could only assume everything was all right. Her chest was bruised and she had what was possibly a whiplash injury, but everything else seemed to be in order.

The same couldn't be said for Patrick's car. Ahead of them, in the cluster of trees, his blue Honda lay upside down, one wheel spinning lazily. The air around it seemed utterly still, as though shocked into silence. Alex took a step closer, then another.

'Patrick?' she called. Her voice echoed, bounced back at her.

She felt her feet quicken beneath her as she approached the wreckage, trying to match the rapid gunfire of her heart. Her head was hot, and as she hurried round to the driver's side, bile rose in her throat. The whole driver's side of the car had taken the brunt of the impact, and was lying crumpled, like an old tin can, against the trunk of the oak tree.

'Patrick!' she screamed. She tugged desperately at

the door but the crushed metal resisted. She dropped to her knees and peered in through the smashed window, pressing her face close against the glass. It took her a moment to focus, but when she did, she recoiled in horror, her hand over her mouth.

There was blood everywhere, splattered across the windscreen, the upholstery, the dashboard. Patrick's face was ghostly white, his eyes closed.

'Mum?' Milo's voice was small, terrified. Alex glanced round and took in his pale face. 'What's happened to Dad?'

She opened her mouth but nothing came out. She swallowed, tried again, but by the time she'd managed to form a sound, Milo was crouching down beside her, his hands up against the window. Then, a piercing scream that she wasn't sure was coming from her or her son.

Alex didn't know how long they sat there on the cold, sticky ground, but by the time she realised what was going on, her trousers were soaked through with mud and sirens were filling the air.

* * *

Patrick wasn't dead.

He wasn't dead.

Alex kept having to repeat it to herself to believe it. She'd been so sure.

The impact of the crash had knocked him unconscious, and once the fire brigade had cut him out of the car, the paramedics had taken him straight to hospital.

That was where they were heading, Alex and Milo, in the back of another ambulance. They'd both been checked over for injuries – her baby was fine and Milo had miraculously got away with just a few scratches and bruises too – and now Alex felt numb with shock as she huddled in the chair, a polystyrene cup of too-strong tea in her hands.

Milo was opposite her, on the edge of the bed.

'He will be all right, won't he, Mum?' His voice was high, childlike, and her heart cracked. She dipped her head, but the paramedic – Lynne, that was her name, and she was so kind – saved her from having to answer.

'He's getting the best care possible,' she said, her Welsh lilt making the words sound melodic, soothing. Milo wrapped his arms round his knees and pulled himself into a ball.

Neither of them seemed to know what to say, so they sat and listened to the rumble of the tyres along the road, the sirens blaring and diminishing just ahead of them – Patrick's ambulance, much more urgent than theirs – and tried to process what had happened over the last couple of hours.

Patrick's unfinished confession lay heavy on Alex. He hadn't quite got to the end, to telling her what he had actually done that day, in Scott Jones's house. But she understood enough.

Given time, she felt she could understand what had led to him to push Scott. Even to flee the scene.

But what she didn't think she'd ever be able to forgive was the fact that he'd been happy to let Samuel take the blame.

39

The steady beep from the monitor was hypnotic, and Alex felt her eyes closing. Patrick was in recovery after emergency surgery to relieve the pressure on his brain. Doctors had explained how serious his injuries were, but that they were hopeful he'd recover.

The question was, would he want to?

'Mum?' Alex's eyes flicked open.

'Hey, love.' Milo came and sat beside her in the creaky plastic chair. He looked pale. 'Where did you get to?'

'Just went for a drink.' He held up two cans of Coke and a Twirl. She took the drink gratefully.

'Thanks, love.' She put her arm around him and he didn't pull away. 'You okay?'

She felt him shrug.

'Are you going to tell the police?'

There was the million-dollar question. The one Alex had been trying not to think about since Patrick had admitted what he'd done. It was such a momentous decision that she felt totally unequipped to make.

'I don't know,' she admitted.

Milo didn't move, and Alex waited. Then, 'Why did he do it, Mum?' His voice was low.

Good question, Milo. Why did *Patrick do it?* Her mind spooled back over all the things Patrick had told her, trying to work out where everything had gone wrong. How far back would you have to go to change the outcome, to make it so that this had never happened in the first place? To Patrick getting in the car? To Alex confronting him about the football trophy? Or further, to when she'd made the decision to go and visit Samuel in prison, or when she'd read about him in the paper and decided to get in touch? Or how about before that, back when Samuel had rung the house to speak to her, and Patrick had set in motion his treadmill of lies... or way back before that even, when Alex had chosen not to tell her husband about the baby she'd given away, or when she'd left home and got herself pregnant in the first place with a baby she couldn't look after... In the end it all came down to a series of events and bad decisions that had culminated in this moment right here, in this hospital, with her husband a killer – and his life hanging in the balance.

'I don't know that either, love. But I wish I did.'

* * *

The police came, as Alex had known they would. They wanted to know what had made Patrick run away. What he was hiding.

And until that moment she'd had no idea whether she was going to tell them the truth or keep Patrick's secret forever.

Except there was no real choice, in the end.

On the same day that Patrick regained consciousness, he was arrested on suspicion of murder.

Murder. It was such a horrific crime. Something nobody thinks will ever touch their family, their lives. Yet here it was, in terrible, full-blown high definition, smack bang in the middle of Alex's. Again.

'You did the right thing,' Caitlin said, as police questioned Patrick.

'I know. It's just a shame it doesn't feel like it at the moment.'

Alex's face was buried into Caitlin's chest so she couldn't see her face. But Alex knew what Caitlin was going to say next anyway. 'I can't believe it. Patrick.'

'I know.'

Alex pulled away and when she looked up Caitlin's dark eyes were watching her. 'Did you ever suspect me?'

'What?'

'I just wondered if you ever thought, even for a minute, that I might have had something to do with it, because of the money thing?'

'I—' Alex had been about to lie, to tell her of course the thought had never crossed her mind even for a second. But she owed her the truth.

'I thought about it. Only briefly.'

Caitlin raised her eyebrows and Alex realised she hadn't actually expected her to admit it.

'But I knew you never would.'

'You thought that about Patrick too,' she said.

'I know. I'm sorry.'

Caitlin shrugged. 'It's okay. I think I would have suspected me too, in your shoes. And to be fair, I can't say I was sorry that Scott got his comeuppance, in the end.'

'Thank you, Cait.'

'What for?'

Alex looked up and met her gaze. 'For helping me. For everything.'

Caitlin pressed her palm against Alex's cheek. 'Always.'

40

SEVEN MONTHS LATER

Alex gazed up at the intimidating brick and glass edifice of St Albans Crown Court, then closed her eyes. Here she was again.

Today was Patrick's sentencing. Alex hadn't been able to face coming to see the rest of the trial. Couldn't watch the faces of the jurors as they heard the details of what Patrick did that day. She'd had long enough to think about it over the last few months, and she'd reached her own conclusions.

She believed Patrick had acted in self-defence.

She believed he'd simply seen red when he thought, firstly, that his family was at risk, and, later, when he thought his life was in danger.

She believed that he panicked.

And she believed that he was sorry.

Because she knew her husband. She knew him. But these twelve people didn't. And she couldn't listen to the things being said about him, watch them judging him.

He said he understood her absence, and she hoped he was telling the truth.

Yet today was different. Today she'd had to come. To find out his fate.

She took a deep breath.

'Mum, I think she needs a change.' Alex snapped her eyes open to find Milo holding out his baby sister. She smiled at him.

'Thank you, love.'

'Do you want the pram?'

'No, I'll just take the bag. Meet you inside, okay?'

'Sure.'

Alex headed in and made her way to the toilets. Annabel had been born three months ago, and her arrival had been bittersweet.

After the worry about her boys, finding out she was having a girl had felt like a small miracle to Alex. But as her belly had grown, Milo had more than rallied round. He seemed to sense her distress about the prospect of bringing another child into the world without a father, and he closed ranks around her. Despite losing Patrick, Milo's behaviour improved almost instantly, and he became a model student. He went for counselling sessions organised by the school, and his grades picked up.

Samuel had been another story. Alex hadn't even been sure whether he'd want to see her again after everything that had happened. After all, she'd basically accused him of being a killer. Hadn't believed him when he swore he'd never do something like that.

And all the time, it had been Patrick's fault his life had fallen apart.

Why would he ever want to forgive her?

In the end, it had been Milo who'd brought them back together. He'd got in touch with his half-brother and told him he needed him. That Alex needed him.

And to her utter relief, Samuel had come.

They'd built bridges over the last few months, and Samuel had even moved back in with Alex and Milo. Turned out, Milo could be very persuasive when he wanted to be.

So although Alex had lost her husband – because even if he was found not guilty of murder today, they both knew there was no coming back from this – she felt protected. Safe.

And it was all thanks to the boys she'd spent so many months doubting.

Now Annabel was here, and it felt like the chance for a new beginning.

But first, they had to get today out of the way.

* * *

Annabel was asleep by the time they filed into the public gallery, and Alex hoped she'd stay that way.

'Want me to wait outside with her?' Samuel said. Alex took him in, so smart in his brand-new suit – a suit he'd paid for with his own money which he'd earned since he'd officially started working for Caitlin and Alex a few months before.

'I think it's about time I made it up to him as well, don't you?' Caitlin had said, when Alex asked her if she was sure. To his credit, he'd worked hard, getting all of their admin done, and keeping their accounts in better shape than they'd ever been before. He'd proven himself so invaluable that he'd even covered for Alex for the few weeks of maternity leave she could afford to take.

Now, she smiled at Samuel in thanks. 'No, it's fine. I'll take her in with me. But thank you.'

'Come on then.' Samuel took the pram and squeezed it through the door. 'Let's get this over and done with.'

Alex settled onto the bench, almost identical to the one in the other courtroom where she'd watched Samuel's trial, and felt her stomach roll over.

She stared at Patrick's face and willed him to look at her. She wanted him to know that she was here. That his stepson was here. That his daughter was here.

Alex had taken Annabel in to visit Patrick every week since she was born. She hadn't wanted him or Annabel to miss out. It was too important.

And the truth was, even though she could never bring herself to forgive him for what he'd put their family through, she still loved him.

Look at me, Patrick, she willed now. But he remained still, staring ahead.

Beside her, a hand crept into hers, linked fingers. Milo. She squeezed his hand gently and blinked back tears.

As they waited, Alex thought back over the days and weeks immediately following Patrick's revelation and the crash.

She'd heard the rest of Patrick's confession when she visited him in prison.

How the fight with Scott had progressed. How Patrick had panicked when Scott had pinned his arm behind his back, truly believed he was going to overpower him; how, when Scott had smirked at him he'd seen red, and so he'd reached for the closest thing – the football trophy – and smacked it down on Scott's head.

'I never meant to kill him, Alex. You know I wouldn't. I just needed him to get away from me.'

'But you left him there. You left him bleeding and walked away.'

'He was already dead. It was too late. I didn't know what else to do.' His voice was a whisper.

Alex believed him.

Patrick told Alex he'd come home, afterwards, after Patrick was killed, and hidden the trophy in the garage, planning to get rid of it one day.

Then Samuel had been arrested, and the police didn't seem to be looking for anyone else. Patrick thought he'd got away with it.

'I was so relieved,' he said, his voice cracking. 'I thought everything could go back to the way it was.'

'You thought you could stitch Samuel up,' she said. It wasn't a question, but it was something Alex would never be able to forgive and forget: the fact that Patrick had been willing to sacrifice someone else – her son – to save himself.

'I didn't plan it that way, I swear to you. But I couldn't lose you, Alex, and the police thought he'd done it anyway...' Patrick had sounded so weak, so pathetic, in that moment, Alex found herself feeling disappointed.

'Then Samuel was found not guilty,' Alex said.

Patrick nodded. 'And that's when everything started to go wrong.'

He told Alex how desperate he'd been when she'd invited Samuel to come and stay. 'Everything that happened after Samuel moved in – the missing money, the drugs, the car, the intruder. That was all you, wasn't it?'

Patrick nodded miserably. 'I just needed you to believe it was Samuel, and see that you were making a terrible mistake,' he said. 'I couldn't lose you.'

In the end, it had come down to this: Patrick had told Alex that he'd been so desperate for Samuel not to ruin the life they'd built together that he'd risked everything to protect it – even stooping to lie about Caitlin in a desperate last-ditch attempt to blame someone else.

But his gamble hadn't paid off.

Alex's thoughts were interrupted by a murmuring across the court. The judge entered, followed by the jury. Her heart was in her throat. She squeezed Milo's hand again, her pulse thumping in her head. She was dizzy and her mouth was completely dry.

She leaned forward. Beside her, Annabel murmured, and she held her breath. Prayed she wouldn't cry.

Silence.

A hush fell across the court. The sun slipped in through the high window, lit up part of the wall. Alex's eyes watered.

A hand on her forearm. Samuel's. Letting her know he was there too.

It felt as though the whole world was holding its breath.

The foreman of the jury stood. Cleared his throat.

'Have you reached a unanimous decision?' the judge said.

'We have.'

His face gave no clues. Alex glanced at Patrick, who was looking down at his lap.

'And how do you find the defendant on the charge of murder?'

Alex held her breath. A pin-drop silence. A heartbeat.

And then, an exhalation.

'Guilty.'

ACKNOWLEDGEMENTS

With every book I write, I have a whole load of other people to thank for helping and supporting me along the way. This is my very first psychological thriller – and I think there are even more people to thank than usual!

I started writing this book two years ago on a writing retreat in South West France with the lovely Janie and Mickey Wilson. Back then, it was just an idea I was playing round with, around the idea of nature vs nurture. But I couldn't seem to get it quite right. I was all set to put it to one side and come back to it another time when a chance chat with fellow writer Angela Clarke got me thinking – why not turn it into a thriller? And so, unbeknown to me, a whole new writing persona was born!

So I need to thank Ange first and foremost, because she put the germ of the idea in my mind, and helped me to come up with some possible scenarios, some of which made it into the book.

Authors are a supportive bunch, and it was on yet another writing retreat (I do work on these retreats, I promise!) a few months later that another author, Tracy Buchanan, listened to the plot of the thriller I had, by then, written half of, and said she'd be really happy to read it and give some feedback once it was finished. I didn't let her forget that promise, and I was thrilled when she gave me some quite detailed feedback on my very first draft. It was so helpful and helped me to shape *No Son of Mine* into what it is now. So thank you, both, for helping me to try something different, and also helping me to (hopefully) get it right.

But that wasn't the end of it. Because then I had a book written in a genre that I wasn't contracted to write. I was still, of course, writing my women's fiction, and loving it. But I wasn't sure where a psychological thriller would sit alongside that. So I tentatively asked my editor if she would be interested in reading it. She said yes – but made no promises. Fast forward three months and she said YES PLEASE – and promptly signed me up for three thrillers! And that's when I realised I'd taken on rather a lot – but I wouldn't have it any other way! So thank you, Sarah, for believing in me, taking a chance on me being capable of writing thrillers as well as women's fiction, and for pushing me to make this book the best it can be.

I also have to thank fellow authors Claire Allan, Ross Greenwood and Caroline Green, as well as the always excellent Graham Bartlett for checking court, prison and sentencing details for me. Any mistakes or inconsistencies are my own, whether deliberate to fit the plot or otherwise.

As always, my friend Serena was a huge champion of mine, as well as my mum, dad, brother, and my boys, Tom, Jack and Harry. I couldn't do this without any of you, so thank you for being there for me, for loving me, and for encouraging me when I doubt myself. I love you all.

ABOUT THE AUTHOR

C.L. Swatman is the author of seven women's fiction novels, which have been translated into over 20 languages. She has been a journalist for over twenty years, writing for Bella and Woman & Home amongst many other magazines. She lives in Hertfordshire.

Sign up to C.L. Swatman's mailing list here for news, competitions and updates on future books.

Visit C.L. Swatman's website: www.clareswatmanauthor.com

Follow C.L. Swatman on social media:

facebook.com/clareswatmanauthor
x.com/clareswatman
instagram.com/clareswatmanauthor

ALSO BY C.L. SWATMAN

No Son of Mine

C.L. Swatman writing as Clare Swatman

Before We Grow Old

The Night We First Met

The Mother's Secret

Before You Go

A Love to Last a Lifetime

The World Outside My Window

The Lost Letters of Evelyn Wright

Last Christmas

THE *Murder* LIST

THE MURDER LIST IS A NEWSLETTER DEDICATED TO SPINE-CHILLING FICTION AND GRIPPING PAGE-TURNERS!

SIGN UP TO MAKE SURE YOU'RE ON OUR HIT LIST FOR EXCLUSIVE DEALS, AUTHOR CONTENT, AND COMPETITIONS.

SIGN UP TO OUR NEWSLETTER

BIT.LY/THEMURDERLISTNEWS

Boldwood

Boldwood Books is an award-winning fiction publishing company seeking out the best stories from around the world.

Find out more at www.boldwoodbooks.com

Join our reader community for brilliant books, competitions and offers!

Follow us
@BoldwoodBooks
@TheBoldBookClub

Sign up to our weekly deals newsletter

https://bit.ly/BoldwoodBNewsletter

www.ingramcontent.com/pod-product-compliance
Lightning Source LLC
Chambersburg PA
CBHW010658100726
47900CB00010B/2712